ALONG THE SHORE OF DREAMS

ALONG THE SHORE OF DREAMS

Mercedes Salisachs

Translated by Gretta K. Siebentritt

Jorge Pinto Books Inc.
New York

PART ONE

LITTLE PUP

I

A labyrinth of cars has accompanied his arrival. Muted, droning sounds swallow up people, suitcases, even thoughts. Jacob Santillana has halted suddenly and his grandmother Katherine is motioning for him to keep moving and not just stand there like a lamppost.

"We're running late," she says.

No sooner had he gotten out of the car, than he realized his grandmother had tricked him. Nothing here matches what she had told him. So Jacob is looking at everything as if through a fogged mirror.

"Did you hear me, Jacob?"

He is about to call her on it: *Those things are not birds. They're airplanes.* What does the insolent old thing take him for anyway? There really was no reason for so many preambles just to end up here: "The belly of a big bird is going to open up, you know that, Jacob? They'll connect a staircase to the opening and you'll climb up it, and then the bird is going to carry you all the way to Spain."

Jacob remembers his grandmother's explanation very well. As she spoke, she was packing his suitcase with obvious difficulty, because her leg was in a cast and it was hard for her to move around. And instead of arranging his things, she was practically stuffing them in, as if she were making sausages. "By myself?" he had asked. "All by yourself, Pigeon. But don't worry: a good fairy will be waiting for you, and she will take good care of you until your uncle Eduardo gets there."

The truth was, she had been telling the big bird story for days now and he had even told his friend Pierre, "Guess what? I'm going to fly to Spain in the belly a huge bird." "You mean a plane," corrected Pierre. But Jacob had insisted. "No, grandmother Katherine swore it was a bird . . ." And Pierre had given him a mocking look, as if he were about to tell him to stop being so gullible.

Now, Jacob is sorry he had not listened. Once again, he has fallen into the trap of lies. Grown-ups always did that. They lied and twisted things around to make children look ridiculous. And he tells himself he will not believe anything they tell him ever again.

"There's the good fairy . . ."

3

All the talk about a "good fairy" also sounds fishy to him. Jacob has always had his own definite image of fairies. Specifically the ones in fairy tales: light beings in flowing, gauzy outfits with puffy sleeves. A twinkling star wielding a magic wand, a silver cone crowning her head. But the fairy grandmother Katherine is pointing to is not like that at all. She is wearing a little cap that barely covers her brown hair. Her skirt is short and her hands, sheathed in little white gloves, carry no magic wand. Worse yet: she does not even move right, with the weightless, swaying motion fairies are supposed to have.

Speaking with a heavy Spanish accent, the fairy is trying to communicate with Grandmother in French. She says yes, not to worry. She will take care of Jacob. And grandmother Katherine is smiling, thanking her and offering her own explanations.

"I would have preferred to have accompanied him myself, but as you can see . . ." She points to the cast as if it were a coffin.

Grandmother Katherine's French is not perfect either. She is English and, although she has lived in Paris for many years, she does not quite manage to nail down the 't's or get her 'r's to come out right.

Turning towards Jacob, the alleged fairy addresses him in Spanish. "What's your name?"

His grandmother answers for him: "Jacob Santillana Vivier." And seeing the woman's eyes widen in surprise, she hastens to add, "Yes. Like the painter. My son-in-law is Spanish. Eduardo Santillana is the boy's uncle."

While they are chatting, Jacob drifts off again. He usually finds grown-up conversations pretty boring. When you take a good look at them, those enormous mechanical beasts could belong to a strange and unusual species. Perhaps they are some kind of extra-large featherless flying creature.

Most of them have—as his grandmother had explained—a hole in their belly with a stairway attached to it, so you can go inside.

"I see. Yes, I understand completely," repeats the fairy lady, still smiling.

And grandmother is going into all sorts of detail about her accident. "It really was stupid. I was hit by a car in . . . leg was broken . . . needless to say . . ."

He could easily have broken his own leg the day he had climbed the apple tree in Roger's yard. And not so much from scurrying up the tree—that was something he had learned practically from the

4

moment he could crawl, which is why everybody said he was part monkey—but because he had taken it into his head to pretend he was Peter Pan and boy, had he hit the ground hard. "You little devil. Who do you think you are? Get it into your head once and for all, Jacob Santillana: you are not Peter Pan . . ." And to make sure he remembered that he could never be Peter Pan, his mother gave him a sharp cuff on the neck: "That's the only way you'll learn . . ."

The worst part was that when he hit the ground, his glasses had flown right off his face and everything looked all blurry and confusing without them. He had felt around for them, hoping his mother would calm down. He hated to see her so upset, so full of "It's your father's fault for putting all sorts of fantasies into the head of an irresponsible boy."

She had not softened up one bit, even when Jacob burst into tears. "And a coward to boot," she said. Furious, she had patted him all over to see whether he was still in one piece. But Jacob was not crying because he was a coward. It was the sheer disappointment of learning he would never be able to fly like Peter Pan.

And there was his grandmother again: "And most of all, Jacob, you have to promise me you won't leave her sight until you are with your uncle Eduardo."

His grandmother tended to speak in English when she was in a very serious mood. It was her way of making sure he was paying attention.

"Yes, Grandmother."

But he says it distractedly, as if he were talking to the wall. He is absorbed in the memory of the apple tree and his aborted flight. The worst part was his disappointment, the rude awakening. The impotence any normal child would feel. And his mother's insistence: "What if you'd fallen flat on your face with your glasses on? How would you have liked being blind for the rest of your life?"

Fortunately, his eyes were safe. And even though they were practically useless without his glasses—he could barely pick out shapes and people—, when he put them on, he had the eyesight of a hawk.

"Behave yourself, Pigeon."

In contrast, his grandmother had broken her leg without even climbing up an apple tree. She had been hit by a car or, as the driver of the car claimed, she had thrown herself at the car to hit *him*. But no one contradicted her, even though the accident could not have come at a worse time. It had happened just a few days after Jacob's parents had sent him to stay with her, had practically begged her to take charge of the boy. And it was all because of the wicked witch Hindrance.

It had been embarrassing to see grandmother Katherine came home with her leg all stiff and her hair messed up. It was going to be hard for Jacob to live with a grandmother who was all beat up. But his mother had insisted he had to spend the summer with her. Who else was there? "Your father and I have to deal with some serious matters and we don't need any hindrances . . ." And to Jacob, the word "hindrance" sounded just like a witch's name.

But the time spent in his grandmother's care had been short-lived. Less than a week later came the broken leg and "dear God, that's all I needed," and the idea to send him to Spain to spend the summer with his uncle Eduardo.

Jacob only knew his uncle Eduardo from a photograph, and a blurry one to boot. It had been clipped from a newspaper. "This is your uncle, did you know that, Jacob? He's a very eccentric fellow. A lot of fun."

Grandmother, on the other hand, was boring. She could not help it. She was one of those sour people who never do anything but whine and complain. And ever since his parents had started fighting with the wicked witch Hindrance, she had been as sour as a lemon. She would start in without warning, whenever she took it into her head, spitting out the words between her teeth, highlighting her bad luck, her homesickness. She would repeat the same old diatribes against the driver of the car, against the doctors, and especially against the younger generation. She was always saying that young people no longer have any sense of responsibility. A woman her age ought to have the right to be free. Ought not be put into a position of having to deal with five-year-olds after having suffered the terrible shock of a broken leg.

". . . and obey her . . . It is very important that you do just as this young lady tells you, Jacob."

Jacob regards the fairy uncertainly and she hastens to explain: "I'm the stewardess."

Stewardess sounds like duchess or countess. And Jacob would like to ask her whether she is also a fairy, but he does not dare. He is mortally afraid his grandmother will repeat what she said about his parents being totally mad and how she should have gone home long before her daughter approached her to look after the child. So Jacob bites his tongue and does not ask.

6

Despite the situation, he likes the stewardess lady. The way she moves and smiles reminds him of his mother a little.

"You're a good boy, aren't you Jacob?"

The thought of his mother gets all tangled up in the question and that is why he does not answer. He just stands there staring up at her.

A long time ago, his mother used to talk to him in that tone of voice, cover him with kisses and assure him that she could never live without her beloved Jacob . . . She was gentle, and she smelled like perfume, and she had a soft chest that made a perfect pillow when he had nightmares. "I saw the monster, Mommy. Just like I'm seeing you now . . ." And to chase the fear away, she would bring him into bed and hug him close to her.

Then his father would tell him not to be afraid and to go to sleep, because he was going to buy him a wooden horse just like Clavileño the Swift in Don Quixote.

"Why is that big bird making so much noise?" Jacob asks.

As he watches, the air starts to whirl around and the ground beneath the tail is swept up into hazy dunes.

"I warned you," is his grandmother's response. "He's always asking questions and his head is filled with fantasies. You know what I mean, don't you, Miss? He dreams something up and then he believes it's real."

Jacob turns towards his grandmother. He has never quite gotten used to the way grown-ups are always contradicting themselves. Wasn't she the one who had told him those big machines were birds? So why was she trying to make him look stupid? He should have had it out with her as soon as they arrived. Should have told her once and for all that he, Jacob, already knew that those birds were really airplanes. If he had not done so, well, it was out of respect. He had gone along with the whole thing just to humor her. Now she was probably going to tell the stewardess all about the apple tree and Peter Pan. Grown ups never seemed to get tired of repeating the same story over and over. And then came the smiles, and the exclamations, and the "Well, you know, when children are around you can't let your guard down even for a second . . ."

The stewardess smiles again. She says that Jacob is funny. And once again her voice reminds him of his mother's, back when it was caressing and mesmerizing. When listening to her was like listening to a creek flowing through a dry, shaded wood.

But one sad day, his mother had stopped using the gentle voice that gave Jacob such a warm feeling inside. And when she heard his urgent, obsessive cries over the night monster who roused him from sleep without warning, she no longer went to his side to calm him down and take him to her bed like she used to.

His father had changed too. He went from being understanding and calm to being grouchy and short-tempered and of course, he never mentioned Clavileño any more.

Clavileño, in fact, had suddenly turned into a bad horse. A taboo name that could only be uttered in disapproval. A character the family frowned upon, just like Peter Pan and the wicked witch Hindrance.

He had discovered the change when his mother said, "Your father's to blame for such nonsense, getting you all worked up with his Don Quixote tales: what else would you expect from a Spaniard . . . ?" And she was not just kidding because they both had those dark, ugly wrinkles between their eyebrows.

That was the first time Jacob had the feeling his life was going to change. And then came the yelling, the anger, the door slamming and the insults. And nothing was as before. The air filled with remarks that cut like a whip. With shouting matches full of "Go to hell," and "I don't ever want to see you again," and other, even worse, things that Jacob did not understand, especially when his father said them. And there were huge empty spaces too. Yawning chasms of nothingness. Long dreary days without presences or voices. And everything smelled just like the edges of poor neighborhoods after a heavy rain.

And that was the beginning of Jacob's disorientation. It was constant and wearing and very cold and, subconsciously, he turned to the only superior being he knew with his entreaties: his guardian angel. "Please make them stop yelling so much. Can you hear me, Angel? Make them stop yelling those things." But even when the yelling did stop, frowns were everywhere. Especially on the forehead of their Spanish housekeeper, Rosario: "Come, child. Why don't you watch a little TV?"

It was her way of keeping him entertained. "I can't play with you now. I'm too busy." Except whenever grandmother Katherine showed up, Rosario, frown and all, immediately disappeared with her behind closed doors to fill her in on every detail. She sure had enough time for that, the tricky old thing.

It bothered Jacob a great deal that no one ever told him anything. He had to guess every single thing. And then they would tell him he was too imaginative and that he believed everything he dreamed up was real.

At his age, though, it was not easy to figure everything out through intuition. So one day, he crept up to the door to listen to Rosario and grandmother Katherine as they talked. The bad part was when they caught him red-handed. "How could you stoop so low, Jacob? Eavesdropping behind the door! What a terrible thing to do."

He was mortified at having been caught. For a moment, he wished he would get the disease of the child with the enormous head—the one he had spied one day on a balcony in the village where they spent their summer vacation—so he could just die.

The fact was, pray as he might, his parents did not stop yelling. Soon enough, it was not just loud words being tossed back and forth, but terrible verbal lashings that left everything exposed and raw. One day, Jacob ventured to ask the guardian angel to make it so his parents did not see each other any more so they would stop saying such mean things. That time the guardian angel apparently heard his prayer, because his mother began to spend days on end away from home.

It was as if the whole world had stopped. As if everybody had died. And Jacob was sorry he had asked the angel to keep his parents from seeing each other. So then he prayed for the yelling to start again, because he felt as if he were to blame for the silence.

The child's anxiety grew. He was all tied up in knots inside and once he even threw up. When it happened, though, he had managed to cover it up. He had said nothing to the grown-ups. No, he had handled it like a real man and even Rosario had had no idea of the mishap.

The days went by as if on the knife edge of a calm that was almost irritating. A calm permeated by cold and shadows and dense fog, even though spring was already giving way to summer.

Until one day, his mother came back and the house was again full of rebukes, anxiety and frowning faces.

And fear—a diffuse sensation that he could not pin down to any one thing but somehow encompassed all the fears in the whole world—began to take hold of Jacob as virulently as the monster with the enormous head had taken hold of his dreams. While still very vague, it was caused by something taking shape on the margins of his being that was making him feel ashamed. It was as if he were left constantly red-faced by the mere fact of his existence. As if he were the fifth wheel. As if his presence were the main obstacle to his parents' happiness.

There was no telling what was behind all the upheaval. Probably, the wicked witch Hindrance had given them a poisonous brew like in Snow White. So whenever his parents were both home at the same time he, Jacob, kept his distance. He dared not face them or talk to them, much less try to explain the difference between a toad and a frog, or share some of the jokes his friend Pierre had told him, or brag about his good grades in school. He was afraid that if he inconvenienced his parents with such things, they would throw in his face—they had done it before—his very right to cough or take a deep breath.

"So to you, they're birds," says the stewardess lightly.

Jacob defends himself. He can no longer tolerate such double talk. "I didn't make it up," he says, turning to face his grandmother. "You told me that. You said I was going to fly to Spain inside a big bird."

His grandmother remembers, reacts, rectifies: "You're right, Pigeon. I did say that. But I was only kidding."

That is how grown-ups got out of everything: by saying it was a joke. Jacob wants to protest. He wants to tell his grandmother that she is thoughtless and inconsistent, but he does not know how to translate what he is feeling. He does not have the words. He is too young. He lacks the mental agility. That is why he used to burst into tears for no apparent reason. Because a translation of tears is the only language he has to express the feelings compressed inside him. Crying is a form of talking too. So when his parents fought, he would sometimes let them know that he, Jacob, was there—listening, breathing and suffering—by means of uncontrollable sobs.

Of course, the rebukes were not long in coming. Mainly from his mother: "Spoiled little devil. We're getting fed up with all the sobbing and histrionics." And she would leave the room—as she said—so she would not have to look at him with his glasses all fogged up.

His father was more practical: "Don't wear yourself out, Jacob. Damp or dry, they're not going to soften up your mother."

Now Jacob's glasses do not fog up, because he does not cry anymore. He just regards his grandmother with a neutral expression. "Well just say it then. Say I'm going to fly in an airplane."

"Just like everybody else."

No, not everybody else. Peter Pan could fly without wings because

Tinker Bell sprinkled magic dust on him. And Nils Holgersson flew all over Sweden on the back of a wild goose.

But explain that to grandmother Katherine and she would not hesitate to cut him right down to size. She would probably bring up the episode in the Paris café when Jacob, in a momentary lapse, had drunk from a glass filled with somebody else's saliva. That had definitely been humiliating, so it would not be a good idea to stir things up and get her in attack mode. He is so cowed at the moment he does not even dare to ask when he will be returning to Paris.

But his grandmother seems to read his mind. "The months will fly by, Pigeon. You'll be back in France in time to start school."

"And then will I see Mom?"

His grandmother clears her throat, coughs, moves a hand to her leg and grimaces. "Of course, Pigeon. Of course you will."

It is a timid yes, stunted, more like a no. And Jacob remembers his father telling him that his mother was not coming back. "Not even in two months?" "Not even then."

So he had been surprised the day he had seen her in the house again. It was as if she were a ghost. He had spied her swathed in the sunlight pouring in through the living room windows.

At first, he had thought she really was a ghost and he had felt a stab of fear. Backlit, surrounded by the hazy, wounding sunlight, it was as if she were a surreal and weightless being. He had not dared to approach her, much less touch her. He was afraid the apparition would evaporate. He had moved forward only slightly, cautiously, arms straight down at his side hoping, from that distance, to glimpse some clue that would tell him his mother really was there, a warm, living being. But she did not move a muscle. Even the rain streaks drying on the windowpane under the burning sun moved more than she did.

Suddenly, her voice registered. She was saying she had come to get some of her things and, hearing her, Jacob had stopped thinking and rushed headlong into her arms.

He had remained like that for a moment, bursting with happiness, retrieving lost memories. He yearned to feel protected, to be completely and totally safe. He even thought he felt his mother swell with a sob that was never released.

Then he heard her saying all sorts of strange things. Things that made no sense but kept him from surrendering completely to the comfort of the embrace. Her calm, reasonable tone of voice had brooked no argument: "Life isn't at all what you think it is, Jacob.

Life is struggle . . . From now on, you're going to have to fight and fend for yourself, without all the whims and fantasies . . . The wonder years are over Jacob . . . You're going to have to keep your feet firmly on the ground, understand, Son?"

A new language. One that was difficult to grasp. It was as if his mother was somebody else and a hex had been placed on his glasses, making him see things that were not really there.

"You're going to be six years old soon, Jacob," continued his mother who was not his mother, "and you're going to have to let go of the apron strings. You're a little man now. It isn't normal for you to continue clinging to my skirts. You'll end up soft, like a girl, right Jacob . . . ?"

Not right. All he wanted was his mother, no matter what, at any price, even if she never let him crawl into her bed to calm his night terrors when the monster with the enormous head appeared in his dreams. But apparently this was not possible. "You'll be staying with your father for a few days and then you will go live with your grandmother Katherine until everything is worked out." But she did not say what things had to be worked out. And she had said nothing about herself either. Her leaving was simply a fact. Then, Jacob had lost his composure. Once again, he had thrown himself into her arms and all he could say was "no, no, no . . ." until his mother had to push him away. "We'll be together again later. I promise."

She had been in a hurry. He had felt it in her quivering arms and in the instability of her legs. "Goodbye, Son." She had kissed him hurriedly on the forehead. A brief, incidental, elusive kiss, as if Jacob's skin might burn her. An insipid kiss that hardly left a mark. Then she had crossed the threshold of the front door and vanished.

His father had returned home later, nervous, somber and brooding. He had begun to hound Jacob with questions that would have been totally out of character before. "Did you wash your face and brush your teeth? Did you wash your hands . . . ?" As if his face, hands and teeth had anything at all to do with the terrible disorientation he was feeling. ". . . You have to wash up, Jacob. Hygiene is important."

It was weird the way his father was assuming his mother's role. Maybe for that reason—because it really was ridiculous—he had quickly passed the baton to Rosario, the Spanish maid. "Take care of the boy. You know what to do. Make sure he behaves."

Rosario, acquiescent and stiff, had simply blinked without of-fering a yes or a no.

But no sooner had his father left the room, than she began to grumble her protests: "I'm up to here with this state of affairs . . . Fed up with self-centered couples . . ." And Jacob had watched her, unsure whether Rosario was serious or maybe just joking. . . . "Sure, it's easy to have children. Bring them into this stinking world, feed them so that they can live and breathe . . . teach them to love . . . And then—that's that. The game's up and their little play toy can just get over it."

Rosario tended to mumble, but he got the gist of what she was saying. No doubt about it. You just had to look at the way her hands squeezed her apron to understand. It was as if the words were ooz-ing out of the grooves between her clenched fingers.

Sometimes Rosario's hands seemed like claws, but sometimes they became gentle and could almost replace his mother's: "Come child, I'll turn on the TV for you . . ." The TV was Rosario's lifeline. Ensconced before the moving screen, Jacob would forget everything else around him.

"Will I see Rosario again?" he asks now.

Grandmother Katherine quickly reassures him. "As soon as sum-mer vacation is over." And she leans towards the boy to embrace him. "Take off your glasses and give me a kiss."

Jacob complies. He stands on his tiptoes, stretches out his neck and lets his grandmother hug him, all teary and sighing.

"Maybe I've been a little brusque with you, Pigeon . . . Sometimes life imposes its own designs on us. You'll understand when you're older. Don't think I'm just trying to get rid of you Jacob, or wash my hands of you. We're sending you to Spain because of this stupid accident. I can hardly manage with these bones."

Jacob feels as if he should console her, but he does not know where to begin. It is disconcerting to see her so contrite, but he is cheered by the thought that she will not be in the picture any more.

"Don't think ill of me, Pigeon. By the time you return to Paris, I'll have recovered and everything will be different."

"Goodbye, Grandmother."

The stewardess immediately takes the child by the hand. "Let's go Jacob."

And his grandmother stays behind, sniffling and dabbing at her tears.

2

Viewed from a distance, what especially stands out is the contrast between the measured, maternal steps of the stewardess and the child's hurried strides.

His grandmother had dressed him in cowboy pants and a white shirt Roger had brought back from Florida, with Mickey Mouse on the front and a hard to miss "Jacob Santillana" emblazoned across the back. "So you won't get lost, Pigeon. Everyone will know exactly who you are."

The featherless bird is now, very obviously, an airplane, with its stairway, its large, oblique lettering and the dull sheen produced by an aggressive sun partially veiled by a thin coating of mist.

Jacob marches steadily up the steps holding fast to the stewardess' hand. The silvery rungs are far apart and dotted with cleats. His father sometimes wore boots with cleats. He said they helped him walk in the snow. "When you're older we'll take you to Gstaadt and you'll be able to ski down the hill . . ." But it was a promise made long ago, before all the crumbling and yelling and frowns. Then, grandmother Katherine had hardly figured in Jacob's world. He had only ever seen her when he was sick or when his parents decided to go off on a ski trip together.

In those days, his grandmother was not sad nor did she expel worlds of bitterness with every sigh. She would greet her grandson with open arms and plant noisy, sticky kisses on his cheeks, which Jacob accepted as a necessary ritual. "Come here, Pigeon . . ."

Grandmother always asked a lot of questions. She liked to know things about her grandson. So he, always a chatterbox, would tell her all about frogs and share Pierre's latest jokes with her. And Grandmother would be gratified. She would assure him that he was a lot like her. Even though he was half Spanish and half French, he still had some English in him, especially when it came to reasoning.

Now, his grandmother—with her peculiar accent and her British obsessions—was just another speck on his radar screen. A vague figure, hardly distinguishable in the vast and incomprehensible world of grown-ups. She had remained behind once and for all, along with his parents, and Rosario, and his teachers at school.

"When you fly, you have to keep your seat belt tightly fastened," the stewardess is explaining as she helps him settle into a window seat. She pulls the strap until he can barely move. Jacob does not protest: he has gotten used to silence, to letting people do things, to being good: *Here I am. Do whatever you want.*

"You're not much of a talker, are you, little fellow?

Slightly embarrassed, he shakes his head vigorously, allowing his blond hair to fall over his glasses. It is a trick he uses to hide the strange blushes that always seem to happen without warning.

The stewardess has removed her cap. She looks younger that way. She is no longer wearing her gloves either, but her hands are not anything like Rosario's. Those hands—when they were going to send Jacob off to Spain—had seemed to cry as they clutched her apron: "They're sending you into the lion's den, Jacob, my boy . . . This uncle of yours is a very dangerous fellow. Very dangerous . . ."

But there was no way of knowing why Rosario would say such a thing. Clearly, he shouldn't pay too much attention to her. Rosario tended to be suspicious and often made remarks without any explanation. But one thing was for sure: she had stuck to her guns, saying over and over again that no one had the right to send children off into orbit, off into such corrupt environments, as if they were nothing more than a package. And when Jacob shot back that Eduardo Santillana was his uncle and uncles are never bad, Rosario's counterattack was immediate and to the point: "That's no uncle," she said. "The man is a public menace. Through some divine oversight, he was born without a guardian angel."

Jacob found the part about the guardian angel very disturbing. If Rosario said it, there must be something to it. After all, it was she who had introduced him to the whole notion of the guardian angel in the first place. Nobody else had ever mentioned such a being to him before: not his parents, or his grandmother, or his teachers at school. Nobody.

"If you feel like you're going to throw up, let me know right away," the stewardess is telling him. "You can use this bag."

"Okay."

Soft music is playing in the background and a certain lethargy is taking over the cabin, but Jacob is very much awake. He is a little bewildered, perhaps, but razor sharp at the same time. His grandmother had given him something to eat before they left the house and his stomach is not growling with hunger like it sometimes does. Only the engines are growling in a harsh, gravelly monotone.

The stewardess leans in towards him. "You're going to fly, Jacob. Are you excited?"

He is not sure. Flying in an airplane is not like flying on the back of a bird like Nils Holgerssen did. It is not that he is afraid, but he does feel a little on edge. It is a faint, niggling sensation that he dares not show. Instinctively, he reaches out his hand to the stewardess.

"Don't worry. I won't leave you alone."

They take off like that, their hands clasped, while Jacob stares at the headrest of the seat in front of him and holds his breath.

His body sinks into the seat and the stewardess' hand is sweaty. *This is no way to fly*, he thinks. If it were a real bird, it would not fly with its wings so stiff or vibrate like that, and he would not be tied down to the seat.

"Pierre was right."

"Who is Pierre?"

"My friend."

"And what was he right about?"

"Nothing."

The stewardess does not press him. She merely asks whether he enjoys flying.

Jacob shrugs. He is still not sure. Everything seems strange to him: the soft puffs of cotton surrounding the plane. So many different shapes. The sweaty drops they leave on the wing.

"And the sea? Do you like the sea?"

"I've never seen it before."

Pierre, on the other hand, was an expert when it came to the sea. His parents took the family to the French Riviera every single year. And back at school, Pierre would be full of stories for Jacob: "The sand is very fine, you can make huge castles out of it . . . and there are shells and interesting rocks . . . and grasshoppers . . ." The grasshopper game was fun. Pierre would catch them and remove their legs and then insert the bodies into little cracks in the tightly packed, damp sand.

"I don't see any birds."

"They can't fly this high. There isn't enough oxygen."

"But we have enough."

It is not easy to explain to a child that one can also use a ventilation system to breathe, but the stewardess tries. She smiles as she speaks and once again she reminds Jacob of his mother.

As soon as the plane levels off, she rises from her seat. "Don't move. I'll be right back."

And Jacob is alone in a sea of passengers. A world of indistinct faces and amorphous forms which, just as soon as the stewardess has left, automatically accentuate his loneliness. They are unknown beings. People he will never know, but who take up space, move, cough and laugh, so that he can see them and convince himself that he is in the company of others.

The stewardess quickly returns with a tray. "Are you hungry?" And she places the tray on the fold-out table.

It was the same question, but in a different location. That time, he was in a large room full of tables, chairs and people. As soon as Jacob sat down, he had seen a half-filled glass right in front of him. It smelled like café-au-lait and the urge had hit him all at once, like a nasty thought. He could not resist. He had thought, naively, that someone had put the glass there just for him. And the reproaches had rained down in no time: "What have you done, you little devil? Can't you see that isn't your glass? God only knows who has been drinking out of it."

And while his mother was swabbing out his mouth and making him spit, his father had raised his hands to his head: "You little idiot. You've swallowed some stranger's saliva . . ."

And the thing was, he could feel the sickness in his body: "So I'm going to die?" he had asked. But the grown-ups did not answer. They just kept saying, "Spit it out. Spit it out . . ."

It is a serious infraction to drink from unknown, used glasses. He was going to have to be careful to avoid making such a disgusting mistake in the future. "You have to wait for the waiter, Jacob. You have to order your drink and then wait for him to bring it to you. There's a proper way to do everything."

"Come on, Jacob. You can eat something if you'd like to."

"But the waiter hasn't come yet."

"What waiter?"

"That one." And he points to a uniformed man pouring liquid into the passengers' cups.

"Oh, he'll be here soon. Shall I butter your roll?"

The stewardess seems very certain about it all. But Jacob is still not totally convinced. He is still paralyzed by the memory of "putting his foot in it."

He does not want to mess up again, or fall into a trap, or hear them say "Spit it out. Spit it out." The blunder was too costly and, even though it happened a long time ago, it is still his biggest scar. Day in and day out, his parents had repeated the story of the café-au-lait to every friend, every visitor, who came to the house. First, they would say how Jacob was very clever. "Come on, Jacob, make your fat face." And he would obediently puff out his cheeks. "Now do your skinny face." And he would suck them in. "He's very quick," they would all say. "If he keeps it up . . ." But as soon as the praise had reached a certain level, the humiliations would begin: "Come on Jacob. Tell them about the café-au-lait . . ." And since he refused to tell it, his father would, with all of the details: ". . . and just like that, he had the glass to his mouth. It was just awful. There was no time to stop him, was there, Jacob?" Burning with shame, Jacob paid for his crime a thousand and one times, lowering his head so his hair would drop over his flaming cheeks.

Then they would tell the story about the match head and the one about flying like Peter Pan. So it really was preferable not to be called into the living room to perform the fat and skinny number.

There is the stewardess again. "You really should eat something, Jacob. You have a long trip ahead of you and people usually eat dinner very late in Spain."

Fortunately, Pierre was not aware of the café-au-lait episode. He certainly would not have approved of it. Pierre was way too sharp to do something that dumb. Drinking from somebody else's glass . . . Sipping somebody else's saliva . . .

"There's your 'waiter'."

Jacob looks up. The waiter is the key. He is the green light. The chance to devour the food sitting right in front of him.

"With sugar?" inquires the smiling waiter, filling his cup.

But when he takes a sip, he burns his tongue. *You have to wait.* Pierre always says you have to take a deep breath before starting any new adventure. Pierre is two years older than Jacob. He has already lost three teeth and he gives himself a lot of airs, all because of those three holes in his mouth. "It means you're grown up, know what I mean, Jacob? Look at your grandmother. She must have false teeth." But when he had asked her, she had thrown a fit and threatened to spank him. "Say that again and you'll get what's coming to you."

"Okay, Jacob. It's cooled off now."

Cautiously, he takes another sip from the cup the stewardess is holding out to him.

"That's the way. You're a very handsome young man."

That is what everybody said, but Jacob would rather be ugly, like

Pierre. It would save him from a lot of unpleasantness, especially at school. Everybody said he looked like a girl—so blond, so delicate. They would take off his glasses to peer into his blue eyes.

Fortunately, he has Pierre to stand up for him. Pierre is a strong kid, determined and brave, and most of all, dead ugly.

"I don't like being handsome."

"Why not?"

Jacob shrugs again. It is a habit. It saves him on words and avoids pointless exertions.

The kids at school always said mean things: "You look just like a girl—a know-it-all, disgusting girl . . ." "Maybe if you stopped wearing those stupid glasses . . ." Until one day, Pierre jumped all over the kid who was teasing him and after that, no one dared to tell him he looked like a girl again.

Pierre was a good friend. Whenever he had the chance, he gave Jacob precious objects to add to the treasures he kept hidden in the shoebox. He had begun the collection right before starting school and now the box was a veritable arsenal of riches: erasers, miniature notepads, rocks from the French Riviera, desiccated leaves, screws, scraps of cloth. Pierre sure knows how to choose. That is why Jacob never parts from the box. When his grandmother proposed he leave it in Paris, he had clutched it fiercely to his chest and told her in a very serious voice: "Put it in the suitcase or I'll jump off the balcony."

It had definitely been a good move, because his grandmother had reacted immediately: "Okay, we'll put it in the suitcase . . ." She was probably remembering his aborted takeoff from the branch of the apple tree.

His passion for climbing had also helped him to shut up the classmates who teased him for being a "girl." "Since when does a 'girl' know how to climb like that?" Pierre would ask whenever his friend clambered up a trunk as well as any monkey. Once they had even shaken the tree to make him fall, but shake as they might, Jacob had clung fast to the branches.

"We'll be able to glimpse the sea soon."

Jacob turns towards the window. No, he cannot see any water yet. Just land crisscrossed with long, winding strips, and white lumps that look like houses, and blocks like jigsaw puzzles carefully superimposed on smooth surfaces.

"It's blue, just like your eyes," continues the stewardess.

"I know. Pierre told me."

"I would like to meet Pierre. He must be a nice boy."

The flattery warms Jacob's heart. It is nice when an adult recognizes your friend's good qualities. Maybe that is why Jacob suddenly feels chatty.

"Do you know the difference between a frog and a toad?"

"Yes," replies the stewardess. "The frog is an enchanted princess and the toad is an enchanted prince."

Jacob regards her with awe. "How did you know that?"

I read it in the Grimm's fairy tales, or maybe it was Perrault or Anderson—I don't remember which."

Jacob's admiration grows. He takes a deep breath. He is almost giddy with excitement and, behind his glasses, his eyes are sparkling as if they were filled with phosphorus.

"Are you missing any teeth?"

"Why do you say that? Do I look old?"

"No."

"So?"

Jacob is beginning to get it. The stewardess is not a grown up after all and that is why she knows about children's stories.

"Pierre is missing three."

"You'll soon be losing yours too."

"Do you think so?"

"Well, you're already growing up. Only very grown up children get to fly by themselves."

This stewardess is definitely a nice person. She could be a fairy. Even without the cone hat and flowing robes and magic wand, she could well be a fairy.

3

As they disembark, the afternoon warmth mingles with a clear, soothing sunlight that contracts the retina. The Barcelona airport is nothing like the one in Paris. There, everything was enormous and formal and permeated by muted sounds, but here everything is more direct and less refined, and the loudspeakers sound more metallic.

The stewardess has put her cap and gloves back on. "Let's go, Jacob."

The other passengers are smiling. They are giddy tourists who have come to Spain to soak up the sun. As soon as their feet hit the asphalt, they stretch and hop as if the pavement was burning their feet and their exclamations swell and multiply: "This is heat . . ." "We'll finally have a real summer . . ." But the Spanish summer still clings to some of the breezes left over from spring and the heat is not oppressive.

Once again, Jacob quickens his step to keep up with the stewardess. "You won't have to go through Customs."

Jacob has no idea what she is talking about and he does not ask either. He no longer asks questions unless it is absolutely necessary.

"You're in Spain now. This is your country."

Jacob nods. He looks around him. It is nice to know that the clear sky reflected in his glasses is *his* sky. He does not mind that he has to blink. The tears well up in his eyes a little, but real crying is definitely a thing of the past.

"Let's hope your uncle is on time."

He is alarmed by the remark. Is it possible his uncle could have forgotten him? He suddenly recalls Rosario's words and is overcome with terror: . . . *God-forsaken . . . an adventurer . . .*

It was just like Hop o' My Thumb, whose parents left him in the woods to get rid of him. Except Jacob has not taken any precautions. He had not even thought to throw little white pebbles from the plane window so he could find his way back to France.

He breaks out in a cold sweat at his own lack of foresight. It is as if a bleak wind were blowing inside him. That is why he clings to the stewardess' hand so she will not lose hold of him. So she will stay by his side until uncle Eduardo takes over.

The time they showed him his uncle's photograph they had said, "See that man? He is your uncle." But the truth is, uncle Eduardo looked more like a bear in the picture, with his wavy hair and thick beard, and fierce eyes like a tiger. They also said he was famous and that his paintings were in demand all over the world. At the time, no one was considering leaving Jacob in his care, and even his parents had remarked that he was not a very savory character.

At school, too, there seemed to be some doubts about him: "The famous nutcase with your same last name—is he some kind of relative of yours?" And Jacob would always deny it. He was horrified at the thought that his classmates—the same ones who dared to call him a "girl" and only shut up when they saw the way he could climb a tree—might discover the unfortunate truth about it: the famous nutcase was his father's brother.

But one day, his father had abruptly changed his mind. "You'll be better off with your uncle than with your grandmother Katherine. At least my brother is no traitor."

The word "traitor" took Jacob's breath away. His father had pronounced judgment in no uncertain terms. There could be no doubt that his grandmother was a traitor. He and his father had been walking together along the Champs-Élysées. They were not touching. Their steps were heavy and each was lost in his own thoughts. Every once in a while they would pause to rest before a shop window. And it was during one of these pauses that his father had called his grandmother a traitor.

There was a lot of movement in the street. People were hurrying along, stepping possessively on their own shadows. The traffic police blew piercing notes on their whistles and occasionally resorted to brusque gestures to keep people moving in a vague effort to relieve some traffic snarl or another, while the cars formed an uninterrupted barrier that made it impossible to cross the street. They were surrounded by frowns. Lots of frowns, and complaints, and irritation.

"And Mommy? Is she a traitor too?"

His father had not replied, but he did something strange. He bit his lips as if he were trying to cut off whatever words were about to come out. He had simply sidestepped the question in the age-old way grown-ups have of disorienting children and had begun to rail against a complicated civilization that created such awkward situations as this one: ". . . I'm fed up with all the hassles people get into . . . fed up with pollution . . . fed up with so much egocentricity . . ."

Seeing him so worked up reminded Jacob of the evil witch Hindrance and for a moment he feared his father might be a warlock. He quickly looked down to check whether his father had a shadow like everyone else, just to make sure.

But just as soon as he saw it there, shrunken and stuck to his father's feet, he wished his father would lose his shadow. That way, his mother would have the chance to sew it back on to his shoes, just as Wendy had done for Peter Pan when he lost his shadow. Maybe then his father and mother would be friends again and stay together forever just like in the stories.

"Do you like Spain, Jacob?"

The stewardess also has a shadow, which Jacob definitely finds reassuring. Everybody knows that only witches do not have one. The stewardess' shadow is long and narrow—as if reflected in one of those trick mirrors—but it leaves no doubt as to its owner. It would probably be easier to detach than his father's—which would have been impossible, especially that day in the Champs-Élysées. His was so solid it seemed to be encrusted into his pants leg. It was so faithful to its nature as a shadow that Jacob would never have had the strength to yank it off, even if his mother had begged him to so she could sew it back on just like Wendy did for Peter Pan.

As soon as they reach the waiting area at the gate, the shadows vanish and accented voices whirl around him.

"Come this way." The stewardess' steps echo in the wide corridor flanked by plate glass windows. She walks quickly, as if disconnected from the boy.

"Please," cries Jacob, grabbing onto her skirt.

"What's wrong?"

"Nothing."

But it is not true. Suddenly he is afraid again. He thinks it is possible that what is happening to him is not real. Or maybe it is the other way around: maybe *he* does not exist and everything around him does.

Anxiously, Jacob searches all the men's faces, looking for his uncle's. There are a lot of beards, chestnut, blond, brown and gray, but none of them belongs to Eduardo Santillana. Maybe the hopeless illusion that he is merely a child looking for his uncle will evaporate and the stewardess—who could have been a fairy but wasn't, and is now pretending to ask a uniformed security guard something the child cannot hear—will end up abandoning him just like Hop o' My Thumb's parents did with their children.

"What are you afraid of?"

He will not tell her. He will not say what he is thinking. Will not give her the satisfaction. This woman—who up to now was a stewardess and is now smiling with the evil delight of a goblin—has suddenly become just that: a tricky goblin disguised as a stewardess, who is about to vanish just as his parents and his grandmother Katherine had. Or else maybe she has brought him to Barcelona as a ploy to put an end to him: first she will torture and torment him with all sorts of miseries and losses like the ones he is feeling now, and then, with the slightest puff of air, she will blow him away like the ashes on a cigarette tip or a pile of bread crumbs.

And for a few seconds he feels terribly alone, much more so than when he was on the airplane. It is as if they had tossed him head first into a pit of new experiences he would never be able to understand or assimilate.

"Come, Jacob. There is your uncle."

Jacob picks him out right away. He is standing very erect, legs spread apart, a walking stick—more like a riding crop—in one hand, and an auburn beard covering half of his tanned face.

"Good afternoon, Mr. Santillana."

His uncle returns the greeting somewhat offhandedly. He apologizes for being late, adding that the highway was a mess. And as he speaks, Jacob gazes at the short, wavy hair framing his severe face dappled with coppery light.

"So you are my nephew."

The stewardess is speaking, explaining, handing him a letter, telling him what a well behaved boy Jacob has been.

And Jacob's fear begins to recede as he realizes that his uncle is real and so is everyone else around them.

What he likes most is looking at his uncle's outfit. He is wearing light blue pants and his shirt is open all the way down to his stomach. His chest is tanned too. Jacob can tell, despite the profusion of chest hairs sticking out from the shirt's opening.

"What is your name?"

The stewardess answers for him. "Jacob. His name is Jacob."

No. The stewardess could not possibly be a goblin about to tear him to pieces. She is a nice person who speaks for him and smoothes his path. And suddenly he thinks again that maybe he does not exist and only those around him are real. The apparition before him is so imposing, it is hard to believe it is all really happening.

He suddenly recalls his terrible dream about grandmother Katherine: *Run Jacob. Escape. Get away* . . . He has it frequently, just like the one about the hydrocephalous boy. Just when he least expects it, there is grandmother Katherine, her face contorted, screaming that fire is going to fall from the sky: *Run, Jacob, and make sure you don't look behind you!*

He had first had the dream after hearing the story of Lot at school. The episode was engraved in his mind: *Then the Lord rained brimstone and fire on Sodom and Gomorrah. . . .* And there is his grandmother, terrified and insistent: *Flee, Jacob, or you'll be turned into a pillar of salt, just like Lot's wife.*

It must be horrible to be changed into a salty creature and feel the itchy white crystals seeping into your skin. And be exposed to other people who might take a pinch of you to season their food. . . .

"I'm delighted to make your acquaintance," says his uncle, brushing Jacob's shoulder with the walking stick. "To be perfectly honest, I had forgotten I had a nephew."

Eduardo Santillana is smiling as he says it. It is a broad, furrowed smile, yet he looks young—younger than his father—and his green, oval eyes are just like a tiger's.

"What about you? Did you know you had an uncle?"

Jacob does not venture a reply. It is as if his uncle's deep, grave voice has caused his own to become paralyzed. He recalls futilely his grandmother Katherine's parting recommendation: "When you see your uncle, try to be very polite to him. First impressions are very important, Pigeon. Don't miss your chance." And when Jacob asked her what he should do to not miss it, she had responded that he should give him a hug.

But it is simply not possible to follow her recommendations. Jacob is finding that he cannot make his body move forward and he knows he has been turned into a pillar of salt. Even his saliva is pooling in his mouth and he cannot get rid of it. It is just like what happened on that other morning, by Roger's pool, when he thought he had swallowed the match head . . .

Once again, the stewardess bails him out. "You'll have to pardon his silence, Mr. Santillana. Jacob is a little bewildered. It has been a long trip for him."

Then she bends down to say goodbye to him. "So long, Jacob. I'm leaving you in good hands."

The stewardess no longer resembles his mother, not even when she kisses him goodbye. Suddenly she is just one more body among all the others pulsating around him.

"I hope I see you when you fly back to Paris," she adds in a lilting voice. And she is gone from view, leaving Jacob with his mind in a fog and his eyes fixed on the pools of sunlight reflecting off the pavement.

"We have to wait for your luggage," says his uncle, impatiently brandishing the stick against his leg.

The stewardess has taken care of everything and the suitcase arrives quickly. It is squat, medium-sized bag, very full, and firmly strapped to keep it from bursting apart.

"Is that it?"

Jacob is not totally sure, but he says yes.

"Let's go then." He extends the walking stick for Jacob to grab on to. Then uncle and nephew head for the parking lot, joined by the two ends of the stick. Once again, Jacob is trotting to keep up. His uncle's strides are long—even longer than the stewardess'—and though he does not seem to be hurrying, he outpaces the child by far.

People seem to regard them with some amusement as they pass by in that manner. Some are smiling and others are pointing out that the auburn-haired man is the famous painter. "Did you see him?" "Where do you think he is going with the little boy?"

Jacob is panting. The sun, round and imposing, is shining implacably on the sea of automobiles fanning out from the building. The heat rising up from the pavement has become irritating and damp, and it pricks at the soles of Jacob's feet as if his shoes were full of pins.

They soon reach a white convertible. Uncle Eduardo deposits the suitcase in the front passenger seat and points his nephew towards the back seat. "Children are not allowed to sit in front. It's against the law in Spain."

Jacob obeys. The important thing is to sit, it does not matter where. He is breathing hard and his heart is thumping as if it might jump right out of his chest.

"What's wrong? Are you tired?"

"No. I'm okay."

"Well, well. I finally get to hear your voice."

Sweating and shaky, Jacob wriggles into his place behind the driver's seat. The summer has completely invaded his body. He can feel it searing the skin under his Florida t-shirt, which sticks to his pores when he leans forward, especially where his name is appliquéd on the back so he will not get lost.

"You can take a nap if you want to. It will take us three hours to get there. It's a long trip for a kid your age."

And he tells himself again that uncle Eduardo's voice is unlike any other he has ever heard in his life. It is low-pitched, almost to the point of being hoarse, but there is a musical cadence to it.

"I'm not sleepy."

"Okay. Suit yourself, young man. Far be it from me to tell you what to do."

He starts the engine. It is powerful. It sounds like an expensive car—the kind of car that only rich people have. Jacob has sometimes seen them on those TV mystery series.

"What's its name?"

"Who?"

"The car."

"You mean the make."

"That's right."

He catches his uncle's amused look in the rearview mirror.

"Well then, the car's name is Mercedes."

"Like a woman's name?"

"One and the same." And he quickly explains: "Fortunately for it, it's not a woman. It's still a car, even though it's called Mercedes."

In the rearview mirror, his uncle's head is ringed by moving streaks of light that lend him a boyish look. But he talks like a man.

"Do you like it?"

Jacob says yes, but when Uncle Eduardo hits the gas, he braces his arms nervously against the back of the driver's seat to steady himself.

"Are you scared?"

"No."

Even if he were, he would deny it. He cannot act like a coward in front of uncle Eduardo. He has to uphold his image as the very grown up boy the stewardess has made him out to be.

"That's what I like to see. We Santillanas have always been a brave lot."

Jacob shyly brushes his fingers back and forth across the nape of uncle Eduardo's neck. It smells good: a powerful aroma of salt-water, tanned skin and cologne. It is a wonderful scent, one that

Jacob has never noticed on his father, and suddenly he is no longer ashamed that the painter is his uncle or shares his name. He is feeling almost proud to be a Santillana.

"How do you like the countryside?"

He has hardly looked at the view, distracted as he was by the back of his uncle's neck.

"It's nice."

"Wait until we get to the village—you've never seen anything more spectacular."

And he begins to describe it. The tamarind trees lining the esplanade, the black rocks ringing the bay, creamy dawns from the vantage point of Can Boig and azure afternoons on pebbled beaches.

"Tomorrow we will tour the coast in my boat," he promises. The sea is truly spectacular, especially when you are seeing it for the first time. Sometimes it is angry, you know what I mean? And other times it is gentle and confiding and you would never know it had been so irritable before."

Then he explains how the cicadas tune up their orchestra on starlit nights and how flocks of seagulls populate the tiny, barren islands. And though Jacob does not understand all the words, he grasps his uncle's meaning perfectly well.

"Some day, you'll see a storm unleash its fury on the water. You can't even imagine how much beauty there is in a storm. It's like brushing up against the world of the gods."

And for the first time ever, Jacob hears the names of the winds that only uncle Eduardo seems to know: the northerly wind called "tramontana," and "levanter" from the east . . .

He describes the patterns made by errant leaves blown along dusty streets and the way the lizards in the stone walls jerk and leap when discovered by a curious human happening by. He assures Jacob that the pulse of life beats more intensely in the villages than in the cities, which is why he had decided to take refuge there fifteen years before.

And listening to him is like listening to a lullaby that is somehow, strangely, in color. That is what uncle Eduardo's voice is like: colored music.

"I have been informed that you will soon be turning six," says his uncle, interrupting his own musings. "We'll have to celebrate."

He had celebrated his last birthday in a restaurant in the Bois de Boulogne, during a heat wave. The place was air conditioned, with a bucolic view of trees swaying good-naturedly in a breeze that was not called tramontana or levanter. It was just a breeze.

The waiter had brought a tart with five little candles. "Go on, Jacob, blow them out all by yourself." And then his parents had applauded as if he had just done something very special and grown up. Everything had evolved according to plan that day. His mother had given him a collection of Indians, complete with tepees and totem poles, and his father's gift had been a box of paints so he could become a famous painter just like his uncle Eduardo.

But his favorite present of all had been Pierre's. He had given it to him before leaving for the French Riviera and it was wrapped in lots of extra paper to increase the anticipation. It was a set of pictures depicting the flora and fauna of the Bermuda Islands. "I've been collecting them for you." They were one-of-a-kind pictures. Pictures worthy of the shoe box.

That was the day Rosario had made him a saber out of newspaper. And as she was rolling up the ends to form the shaft, she had assured Jacob that he would never lose a battle with such a weapon. "I, Rosario, am telling you here and now that this is an enchanted saber." She had shaped the curved blade and attached the handle with string, leaving a space so Jacob could grip and brandish it easily. Assuring him that he would also be needing a hat, she had quickly fashioned one, also out of folded newspapers. She had even inserted a large feather in the top so he would look exactly like a brigadier general.

It had been a glorious day for Jacob. *The only thing missing is Clavileño the Swift,* he had thought. But the wooden horse so often promised by his father never materialized. The wicked witch Hindrance got in the way and Jacob had a feeling he should not count on getting it—ever.

"If you feel carsick, tell me right away. I don't want you to ruin the seats of my car."

Grown-ups always seemed to be worried about kids throwing up, but Jacob was never carsick. He was a born traveler. There was a time when his parents had taken him along whenever they went someplace.

He wonders now what sort of present his uncle Eduardo will give him for his birthday, but he dares not ask.

"Do you like to swim?"

"Yes."

"Where did you learn how?"

"In Roger's pool."

Uncle Eduardo does not seem to like the name Roger, because his expression changes completely the moment he hears it. After a brief silence, the painter asks another question: "So what do you think of this Roger?"

Jacob shrugs. It is a recently acquired habit. Before, when he used to talk a lot, he almost never did it. But when you got right down to it, shrugging has saved him a lot of trouble.

The truth is, he finds it difficult to describe Roger. For a long time, Roger was just one more blurry form among the many that surrounded his parents. A rather gruff man who sometimes gave him presents and other times regarded him with something akin to resentment, as if he had not, just a short while before, said, "Go ahead and open it, you little climber. It's for you."

His milder side—as Jacob had finally figured out—only came out when his mother was around. Then he was affectionate towards the boy and even ventured some familiar caresses, as if he had some right to do so.

"Do you like him?"

"I don't know."

There is something about Roger he just does not get—something that slips from his grasp just when he thinks he has it figured out. One minute, he thinks he likes him, and the next, he is telling himself that Roger is the most hateful person he knows. For some reason he does not understand, Roger has a way of putting him on alert, of triggering a signal, which could be positive or negative.

It is probably all related to the long ago morning at the pool when he thought he had swallowed a match head and, petrified, had screamed that he was going to die.

"No question about it. Kids have a sixth sense."

And even though he is not exactly sure what uncle Eduardo means, Jacob can tell that he is not a big fan of Roger's.

"Do you know him?"

Uncle Eduardo says he does not. And Jacob thinks maybe his parents have talked about him, and his grandmother must have told him in her letter that Jacob does not go swimming in his pool any more.

Grown-ups seem capable of developing violent dislikes from one day to the next, and children sometimes have a hard time keeping up. There must have been a lot of bad things going on between all of them, because suddenly the mere mention of Roger's name was enough to cause a terrible outburst. That is how grown-ups were: contradictory beings, full of agitation and silences and pretenses and hurtful words hurled into the air with sharp gestures and sour expressions.

For an instant, the expressions of the child and his uncle merge in the rearview mirror. It is an abrupt fusion that is gone in an instant. Prickly fluids film their pupils and silence rises up between them like a wall.

But the uncle quickly knocks it back down. He changes the subject. He describes the sea. Not the vast, deceptive ocean you can see from the airplane, but the other one—the one that continually brushes the shoreline and bathes the rocks, rendering them fertile and slippery.

"Sometimes the surface is incredibly smooth, you know that, Jacob? But suddenly, for no reason at all, it bucks up like a rutting stallion or, depending on its mood, knots itself up into a grumpy face, just like yours is now."

Jacob smiles. He likes the images of the rutting stallion and the grumpy face. And taking advantage of the opening, his uncle tells him that Can Boig has its own private beach where no one will dare to disturb them.

"And trees? Does it have lots of trees?"

"Some. Why?"

"Roger had an apple tree and I liked to climb it."

"So you like to climb."

"I do it better than anyone."

"Well, then, we will have to climb."

Jacob falls silent again. He really has had difficulty with words ever since his mother told him that he was not a child any more and he was going to have to take care of himself. He also had plenty of time to get used to, "Be quiet, Pigeon. You're talking too much." Little by little, he had simply lost interest in talking.

"Your eyes are closing."

Slowly he lets go of the driver's seatback and lies down on the back seat, drawing up his knees.

"It's okay, little guy. Just rest."

And as the Mercedes speeds along the Gerona highway, Jacob Santillana falls fast asleep.

4

Gradually emerging from sleep, Jacob is not sure what is happening. He is being shaken. It is a pesky sensation, but one he cannot quite identify in his drowsy state. For a split second, he thinks he is still in Paris and his bed has suddenly begun to vibrate. This gives him the impression of emerging from one dream only to sink into another. But as soon as he spies the back of his uncle's neck, he snaps back to awareness.

Still feeling rather numb, he struggles to pull himself together. The countryside has changed. Two arid mountains, dark and immense, flank a badly paved road that winds upward. He guesses they have left the highway behind and are nearing the village.

"Good day, young man. That was a pretty good nap you had."

Jacob takes off his glasses to rub his eyes. He is hot. Sleep has left behind a light coating of sweat that sticks to his hair and makes his eyes itch.

"Where are we?" he asks.

"Very close to the village."

The sun is still shining and the sharp light makes him squint.

"As soon as we reach the top," explains his uncle, "we will drive downhill to the sea."

"Did I sleep for a long time?"

"Over two hours."

It is embarrassing to have slept so long. He is afraid his uncle will think he is a little kid who still needs a nap. Appearances notwithstanding, the fact is, Jacob put an end to the humiliating habit of taking a nap long ago. Pierre told him napping was for babies. "By the time you're five, nobody goes to bed while the sun is still out."

"I dreamed I was in Paris in my grandmother's house."

"Do you miss her?"

"No. She's old and she broke her leg."

His uncle's laugh strums the air and, once again, it seems to Jacob as if the painter's laugh were just as breathable.

"Sometimes I dream about the monster."

"What kind of monster?"

"The one with the big head."

His uncle frowns, his expression slightly contorted, and meets the child's eyes in the rearview mirror.

"Okay, Jacob. Tell me about this monster."

"It's a small boy with a huge head like this—It's so big his mother has to hold it up for him, because otherwise his neck would break and his head would fall on the floor. It's a horrible monster."

"But it's only in your dreams. You don't have to believe those dreams."

The bad part is that Jacob has actually seen him. That is why he cannot forget him. He spied him one day while out walking with Rosario along the main street of the village where they spent their summer vacations. Jacob had looked up and there he was, on the balcony, sitting on his mother's lap. It upset him terribly. He had instinctively closed his eyes, hoping the image would be gone when he opened them back up. But when he opened his eyes, the monster was still there and, if it had not been for Rosario, Jacob would have fallen down from the shock. "Don't even think about looking up there," the maid had said. "The little boy is very sick." But all he could say was: "His head, his head."

Rosario had tried to explain that there were children like that. Their heads were filled with water and since there was no way to get it out, their heads kept swelling as they grew up. "Can you drink the water?" With a look of revulsion, Rosario had said, "No, that's filthy—how could someone drink water so disgusting and full of microbes?"

"Maybe he's an extraterrestrial," says uncle Eduardo now.

"That's what I thought, but Rosario said he wasn't. He was just a kid like anybody else."

According to Rosario—and she knew a lot about this kind of thing—extraterrestrials are tall and strong and even if their heads are covered, they are normally proportioned. And that child's body was wasted away because his head consumed everything. "It's a terrible disease, Jacob. When a child has hydrocephalus, the head grows and grows and then, one fine day, it just bursts open." Then Jacob had asked whether it was contagious. And even though Rosario assured him that it was not, whenever Jacob came upon the monster he touched his own head to make sure it had not grown.

"You shouldn't let something like that scare you, Jacob."

After that encounter, Jacob began to have terrible nightmares. The hydrocephalus monster would appear without warning—his forehead bulging, his small, sterile eyes staring vacantly, while the woman holding up his head would beckon to Jacob to come closer. Terrified, he would call out to his mother to come get him and let him come to her bed.

"There are extraterrestrials with big heads and little bodies. Didn't you know that?"

"Have you seen them?"

Uncle Eduardo's expression has become very serious. He bites his lip and says yes, he speaks with them all the time.

"Aren't you afraid?"

"I told you before: we Santillanas have never been cowards."

He says it so seriously that Jacob has no choice but to believe him. Probably, uncle Eduardo is different from the others. He probably does not lie, because if he did, the extraterrestrials would punish him.

Whistling, he calmly guides the car up the mountain. Wherever the road levels off, the rain of the past several days has left standing puddles.

"Crickets like to breed in puddles. Did you know that, Jacob?"

Hearing that, Jacob would like his uncle to stop the car so he can see for himself, but the painter seems anxious to get to the village. The hillsides are covered with scraggly vines and carved by rock terraces, sloping downward. The road is nearly deserted. Every once in a while, a speeding car shoots by the Mercedes as it rounds a curve. A dog prowls alongside the ditch, furtive and frightened. A vague silhouette retreats cautiously as the car goes by.

"How well do you get along with dogs?"

"Good."

"So you'll definitely have company. There's a mastiff at the house. His name is Duke and he's about as tall as you are."

Jacob points to the vines. "What's that?"

"Those are grapevines. Soon they'll start producing grapes."

"No. That."

It looks like a man on a cross. A strange man who commands fear and respect.

"It's a scarecrow. It's there to protect the grapes."

He explains how the howling winds and the birds can wipe out the fruit. "You have to scare them off somehow."

"And the wind? Does it scare off the wind too?"

Eduardo Santillana lets out another guffaw. He has definitely taken a liking to the boy.

"No. It isn't easy to scare the wind. The wind scares you."

Jacob listens attentively as his uncle tells him about the terrors of the wind.

"It's a terrible enemy in this district. Especially when you're out in the boat."

"Well, that man does not scare me."

"It's not a man, it's a dummy."

He had also thought at first that the child with hydrocephalus was a dummy, or maybe a doll. But he had quickly realized it was not when Rosario said, "Don't look, Jacob."

In a way, the scarecrow has a lot in common with the big-headed monster. Were it not that the Santillanas had never been cowards, Jacob would have closed his eyes, just like he did the first time he saw the monster.

Now the precipices are huge. They are bigger every time you look. It's daunting to see the drop from the steep and narrow road. But uncle Eduardo does not seem in the least worried about driving his car in such risky circumstances. He must be used to it. Fifteen years is a long time, after all.

Beyond the grapevines, chunks of stark black mountains can be seen in the distance. They are titanic masses of burned earth, stones blackened by the smoke of an extinct fire, or perhaps the giant tongue of a dragon hiding among the caves visible through the gaps between the mountains.

"There's a village down below. Is that where you live?"

"No, mine is further on."

It is a village without sun, set in a river bed and flanked by two tall, arid mountains. It seems sad, this village without sun. But its roofs, with their yellow and pink tiles, could well pass for flying carpets. At least that's how they are colored in the stories. Some day, when he feels a little more at ease with his uncle, he, Jacob, will ask permission to see for himself whether those tiles really are carpets or just look like them.

If they really were carpets, all he would have to do would be to sit cross-legged on one of them, close his eyes and say the magic words—the ones his friend Pierre taught him—and it would take off.

Naturally, it would not be an artificial, mechanical flight. He would really be *flying*, with birds escorting him on all sides. And the carpet's rhythmic swaying would cause all of grandmother Katherine's hateful comments to unravel, one by one.

"We'll be heading down towards the village now."

But the daydream about the flying carpets momentarily subsumes his desire to reach Can Boig.

He remembers the time he had very nearly gotten to fly on one. It was the day he climbed onto Pierre's roof. If his friend had not talked him out of it—by telling him that witches sometimes blow on them and they lose their magic powers—Jacob probably would already know what it is like to fly without all of the artificial props of mechanical flights.

"Are there witches in the village, Uncle Eduardo?"

"Witches?" But he recovers himself quickly. "Of course there are. Every village has its very own witch, who is recognized, supported, and whose services are often in demand."

"What about warlocks?"

"No. There is only one witch."

He hastens to explain that women are much better suited to practice witchcraft than men.

"We're different. We lack their capacity for evil."

"How do they get to be witches?"

"By cheating, lying, doing bad things just for the fun of it . . . So along comes the devil and asks them if they would like to be witches and, if they say yes, he protects them."

"What's the village witch like?"

"Wicked. Very wicked. She dresses all in black and has a hooked nose and she doesn't have any teeth. Her name is Visitación Arana, but everyone calls her Visitarana for short."

"I want to see her."

"I'll point her out to you one day, but you'd best be very careful. She can cause you trouble."

"What has she done to you?"

Eduardo Santillana's eyes shift, he inhales deeply and tries to clear his throat. "It wasn't her. A different witch hurt me. Fortunately, I was able to defend myself."

"With a paper saber?"

His uncle hesitates a moment before replying, most likely trying to recall—"Yes, that's it. A paper saber, How did you know you're supposed to fight off witches with a paper saber?"

"Rosario told me so."

"Who is Rosario?"

"The Spanish maid. She's not a witch."

"How can you be so sure?"

36

"Because she has a shadow. Witches lose them right away."

His uncle regards him, incredulous. His nephew's definite notions about the matter leave him speechless.

"You're right. Witches lose their shadows."

Emboldened, Jacob tells him that Rosario has never been a witch, because her shadow has gotten stronger every day. He has to admit that she could sometimes get grouchy and she often smelled like rotten fish, but she also smiled like a guardian angel and usually played with him to keep him entertained.

"She's the one who taught me how to handle the sword."

She would take hold of the handle in her right hand, raise the left one with the index finger pointing straight up, flex her knees slightly and say, *En garde.* Then she would stab the sofa cushion and tell Jacob that, since he was half Spanish, he had to fight his adversary with grace and gallantry.

"My saber has magical powers, did you know that, Uncle?"

"I suppose you will let me borrow it."

"You might not like it."

"If it has magical powers, I'll like it."

There is no question that Uncle Eduardo is a reasonable and understanding grown-up. A man who knows how to take the measure of things. The proof is that he is not fazed by his nephew's audacity, like grandmother Katherine was, and he is not shocked by a saber with magical powers.

"Can you smell it?"

"What?"

"The sea. It's very close now. You'll see it as soon as we start down the mountain."

They see it almost right away. It's right there. Imposing. Purplish. Edging a village that could be a big sugar bowl set down in the middle of a rocky horseshoe.

It is an enormous pond, darkening slightly in the waning afternoon light, dotted with white caps off in the distance. An immense body of water that runs into itself, into its own horizon, spurred by a dark and irate northerly: the tramontana. At least this is what uncle Eduardo is telling him. And he adds that when the tramontana blows with all its might, you have to be ready. "It will deposit you in Majorca in a heartbeat."

The smell of the sea is becoming more and more tangible as they descend. The insistent aroma pervades Jacob's nostrils, awakening new sensations. And he is beginning to pick out sounds too.

Although still vague and intermingled, they are beginning to take on the cadences of a village.

Occasionally, the gravelly hum of a motorboat crossing the bay breaks through distinctly. Or there is the slow, mellow chop chop of the fishing boats rocking gently as they grumble their way out to sea.

And sometimes silences takes over. No one perceives them, perhaps, but they are there, in the vessels anchored in the bay or the boats tied at the pier, in the cars waiting single file or the people ringing the tables at the cafés and bars.

"We're nearly there."

They just had to drive into the village, turn right, go over the bridge, cross several beaches and climb the hill that leads to the lighthouse and Can Boig.

Viewed from the last overlook, this village also could be a hangar for flying carpets.

"Uncle, why are the tiles yellow?"

The painter explains that time, the humidity, and the vague wanderings of certain seeds have left the roofs covered with flowering mosses.

"They look like flying carpets."

"Maybe they are."

They reach the square. It is filled with tourists and automobiles. Clashing music issues anarchically from any number of radios behind any number of windows.

To the left is the esplanade, lined with tamarinds, and beyond them a string of bars, their decks extending out over the sea.

"There's the Garota Bar." It is a vibrant, eclectic place full of tables, exotic people and foreign accents. "Some day I'll bring you here to meet my friends," the painter tells him.

Jacob contemplates the esplanade. There is a constant back and forth of people. Sometimes, they look up into the trees at the nests of goldfinches, drawn by their ceaseless trilling. And Jacob thinks that some day, when his uncle gives him permission, he will climb to the very top of one of those trees to see whether the melodies trickling out from among their branches actually come from real live birds.

"What do you think about it all, Jacob?"

So that dense, blue, swaying mass is the sea. Rosario had told him: "It will seem very big to you." And she had opened her arms wide as if to encompass the whole sea. "It's not like Roger's pool,"

Rosario had emphasized. "You can go out so far you can't even see land any more."

"I didn't know it was this big," replied the child.

"It's even bigger than you think. And it's full of mysteries. It has caves and hideaways and a whole lot of secrets that only I know about . . . the Pirates' Cave, for instance."

"Is it very far from your house?"

"You can get there in about an hour, even taking your time. They say that it's very big and deep and dangerous, but very beautiful."

"There must be a hidden treasure."

"Naturally."

Pierre had discovered a treasure in the village where he spent the summer. It was stuck in a rock crevice, but when he tried to get it out he had to give up because it was too heavy for him. "So what did you do, Pierre?" He had not even mentioned it to his parents. He had gone back with a friend the very next day, but the treasure was gone.

"Pierre discovered a huge treasure by the sea in a French village."

"Pierre must be a very important fellow."

Soon they are driving along the beach and then they turn in between two river beds towards the lighthouse. When they reach the crossroads, they will have to head back downhill again.

"The road to the left leads to my house. The one to the right is only used by the keeper of the lighthouse."

Jacob asks him what Can Boig means.

"That's what it has been called ever since I bought it. "*Can* is Catalan for house and *Boig* means crazy. So it would be The Crazy Man's House."

"But you're not crazy."

"Who's to say where reason begins and ends . . ."

"Do you live alone?"

"I live with Dots and Quasimodo. Well, those aren't their real names. They're nicknames."

"What does that mean?"

"It means they were given different names at the baptismal font."

"Do you have a nickname too?"

"I have several. They call me the evil painter, the godless hermit, the enigma, the reprobate. . . ."

"Who calls you those things?"

"Gossips. Like the ones you just saw in the village."

"And Dots? Who is she?"

"Dots is a crazy old lady who cooks, cleans the house when she feels like it and bends the elbow whenever she has a mind to."

Jacob does not know what "bends the elbow" means, but he does not really care. What really concerns him is the old lady herself. "Does she have a shadow?"

"Relax, nephew of mine. She is not a witch," his uncle replies with a snort that sounds as if he is chuckling. "And she is a very good cook. Sometimes you'll hear her talking to herself, but don't be afraid. It's just how she is."

Rosario also liked to talk to herself when she was cooking. It must be a habit women have, because even his mother would mumble vague things that probably did not make sense even to her. And whenever his father chanced to overhear, he would make fun of her, saying it was a way of escaping from the real world.

"Will you take me to the Pirates' Cave?"

"If you'd like me to."

He is definitely lucky to have an uncle like Eduardo Santillana. It is not anything like they said about him being a nutcase painter, or how embarrassing it would be to have to live with a man like that, or how he was born without a guardian angel.

With a new confidence, Jacob can picture himself defending his uncle to his classmates at school. *Do you know who Eduardo Santillana is? He's my dad's brother. And whoever doesn't like it, too bad.* And if they did not back off, he would get out the saber Rosario made for him. That would make them see reason.

"Do you think we might find the treasure?"

"Who knows? Maybe we will."

They reach the crossroads and his uncle points out the lighthouse.

"When it gets dark you'll see the lights come on. It's there to warn boats at sea."

"About what?"

"Reefs, shallow water, how close they are to the village. That way the boats won't run aground at night and they can get their bearings in case they need help."

The car is heading downhill once more, on the road that will take them to the house. There in the distance, in the exact center of the horseshoe, they can spot the village. It is pyramid-like and at the highest point a white building rises up, which his uncle says is a church.

"What do you think?"

"I don't know."

"Take a good look, little fellow, because when we turn the corner, you won't be able to see it any more."

His uncle's house is situated by a creek that feeds into the sea. The garden is surrounded by a stone wall.

"This is Can Boig."

Suddenly the deep, excited barking of the mastiff is heard.

"And there you have Duke." He is a gigantic, happy dog, with stiff ears and bulging eyes. "Say hello, Jacob. Duke wants to welcome you."

5

Quasimodo is there in an instant: part monkey and part dwarf, he has a head like a weasel, a rabbit's smile, and bowed legs. He is middle aged, with a slight hunchback and only one good eye. The other slants off in such a way that it probably does not work. But Quasimodo is not repulsive, only strange.

As soon as the car has pulled into the driveway, Dots, Quasimodo's mother, appears at the front door. She is a thick, gray-haired woman and her eyes are ringed with small scabs, so that it looks as if she has been crying dry tears.

"You're finally here," she yells from the doorway, and she rushes forward to inspect Jacob.

"Get the suitcase, Quasimodo."

Dots shakes her head as she regards him. She probably does not like his looks.

"Dear Jesus, look how thin the child is."

Duke is more eloquent. He has jumped up on his master in a fit of delirium, whining and cavorting about on his hind legs. Then, tail wagging furiously, he licks the bearded face.

When he is tired of that, he turns to Jacob and sniffs him methodically all over.

"He likes you," his uncle assures him.

The narrow garden is full of flowers and edged with white tiles. The front of the house has been taken over completely by dense bougainvilleas, through which fragments of whitewashed walls can be glimpsed in the bright afternoon sun.

Inside, they pass through a large white foyer with bare walls. Beyond that lies the entrance to a beautiful living room with an adjoining terrace whose gigantic plate glass windows offer a panoramic view. A robust, flowering magnolia tree is growing right in the center and its sweet fragrance permeates the entire house.

And beyond it lies the sea. Sheltered by the hillock topped by the lighthouse, the waves lap the beach gently, slightly shadowed by the rocks and by the unruffled calm of innocuous afternoons.

"Do you like my house, Jacob?"

The boy nods, even though he is still trying to decide whether or not he likes it. To him, the living room is a slightly overwhelming mix of strange colors. It is spacious, but irregular in shape, with lots of nooks and crannies. A hodgepodge of different styles is apparent in the modern sofa sets vying for space with antique pieces. An endless array of knick-knacks covers every surface: shells, ceramic ashtrays, horns, statuettes.

"Come with me, Jacob. I'll show you your room."

And while Dots leads him towards the stairs, she tells him she will sleep in his room with him the whole time he is in Can Boig. "They told me you have nightmares, so don't worry, you won't be alone."

The worst thing about Dots is her smell, which is sort of damp and boggy. Rosario sometimes smelled like that, causing his mother to remark that Rosario was not on friendly terms with water.

Dots talks a lot. Her ideas come out all jumbled together. She is full of strange expressions and sometimes she yells for emphasis. But her hands are nothing like Rosario's, and this definitely makes it harder for Jacob to understand what she is trying to say.

Upstairs, they cross a gallery of portraits painted by his uncle. They are all of women. "If you take a good look, you'll see they're all the same woman. Was a time when the only thing he painted was her."

"Who is she?"

"Teresa."

"Who is Teresa?"

"Haven't they told you about her?"

Jacob shakes his head. And Dots explains, in her own fashion, that Teresa was the love of his uncle's life.

"But it would be better if you didn't mention her name to him."

"Why not?"

"He doesn't like it."

Maybe so, but he clearly likes to see copies of her all over the gallery walls. Teresa has been painted in every possible expression and position, in all shapes and sizes: clothed, nude, smiling, serious, thoughtful, distressed . . .

"If he doesn't like Teresa, why does he have her all over the place?"

"God only knows why. Your uncle is a little strange . . ."

"Strange?"

"You'll notice it as you go along. He's got a bit of a crazy streak, but he's good as gold." She goes on to say that his uncle sometimes gets the urge to dress up. He has a closet full of bizarre costumes and he likes to do pantomimes. And he plays the guitar and can sing like a professional. But his passion is painting. Especially seascapes and shells and other things Jacob would not understand . . .

"What things?"

Dots quickly clears her throat and quickens her step, steering them firmly towards the bedroom wing.

Then she tells him about the chamber of secrets—a hidden alcove where his uncle keeps all sorts of useless objects. "Tell your uncle to show it to you. You'll find all sorts of unexpected things. He's been collecting odd bits and pieces for years. Any old piece of junk is like a valuable treasure to him."

Teresa is behind them now, but Jacob can still feel her eyes boring into his neck.

"Where is she now?"

"Who?"

"Teresa."

"She's been gone for years. She left your uncle. Left him for another man before he became famous. You wouldn't understand such things, but there are women like that: opportunists. And even though she seemed nice enough, Teresa must have been one."

Jacob's room is just past the gallery. Dots opens the door and the first thing he sees is a balcony facing out to the lighthouse.

The room is large, with warm colors and somber furniture that call to mind the illustrations from a book his father had gotten for him during his last trip to Spain: "Look Jacob. This is what the houses look like in our country. It's like paradise compared to France."

But the wicked witch Hindrance must have already been working her spells, because his mother had shot his father a derogatory look and said he should not put inappropriate ideas in the boy's head. After all, he was as French as he was Spanish, and had some British in him to boot: "Mother counts for something too, doesn't she?"

And his father had replied in an irritated voice that when it came to appropriate manners, actions mattered more than ideas . . . and yours leave a lot to be desired, so you might want to see to it that the boy doesn't figure out what you're up to. . . ." It was exactly as if he'd said it to him straight out: "Don't trust your mother, Jacob." And that is why he was beginning to hate his father, even though he did give him the book.

Worst of all, his mother had made no attempt to defend herself and that had left Jacob with a tiny, niggling doubt, a lingering fear.

44

Left him with everything he did not understand and probably never would.

Dots is indicating the door adjacent to his room. That's Mr. Raimundo's room.

"Who is Mr. Raimundo?"

"The administrator. He's traveling outside the country right now. He's your uncle's right hand. Mr. Raimundo's orders must be carried out to the letter."

But Jacob is not worried about Mr. Raimundo. According to people who know about these things, women are more into witchcraft than men are.

"Uncle Eduardo says a lot of women are witches."

"He's not far off on that one."

"And he says you aren't one because you have a shadow. Can I see it?"

Dots agreeably moves to the balcony where a glimmer of sun is still filtering through the wrought iron bars.

"Convinced?" she asks him, pointing to her shadow on the ground.

He is beginning to like Dots, especially when she tells him that it is not good to be too trustful and that, unfortunately, his uncle was correct: most women are about to become witches, if they aren't one already.

"Even my mom?"

Dots frowns and utters an expletive, which she does not bother to explain.

"The things you get into your head, child!"

And to distract him, she begins to unpack his suitcase.

The clothes grandmother Katherine packed for him are piling up on the bed, a mass of wrinkles: sweaters, pants, shirts and an extra pair of glasses, in case his break.

Meanwhile, through the open balcony door comes the increasingly assertive slap of the waves against the rocks lining the cliffs.

"So who made you this nice saber?"

Jacob grabs it by the handle and brandishes it just as Rosario taught him. "It's my magic saber."

"I don't doubt it."

"And this is my general's helmet."

Dots looks impressed. "If it breaks, I'll make you a new one. I know how to make sabers and hats too . . ."

And Jacob likes this chunky woman who is beginning to resemble Rosario more and more.

"... except I use Spanish newspapers, which are a lot feistier than French ones." She says it proudly, as if Spanish newspapers were sturdier and tougher than any other newspaper in the world.

Jacob stares up at her, fascinated by the marks dotting her eyelids.

"What did they do to your eyes?"

"Nothing. That's just how they are. That's why everybody calls me Dots." She even seems proud of the whole thing, as if the blemishes made her a real person.

"What the devil are you hiding in here?" exclaims Dots, holding up the shoebox.

"Secrets."

"What kind of secrets?"

Jacob regards her doubtfully. He is still not totally sure he can trust her. It's better to be cautious and keep quiet to avoid what happened when his mother wanted to know what Jacob had in there.

"Okay, don't tell me if you don't want to. Probably trophies just like your uncle's. You're his blood."

And turning her back to him, she resumes her work.

On that other occasion, Jacob still did not have the photograph collection from Pierre or the little rock in the shape of a skull his friend brought him from The French Riviera. And his mother had said, "Take good care of those things, Son. They are valuable treasures."

But later that night, as his mother was telling grandmother Katherine about the box, she had said in a loud voice that her son Jacob was living in a fantasy world and if he kept it up, he would be a mess when he grew up. "... No one will ever be able to persuade him that those things are simply junk."

And always one to go with the flow, his grandmother had said, "You're going to have to educate him. You have to get his head out of the clouds."

So after listening for a while, his ear glued to the door, Jacob went to bed without saying goodnight to his mother. And when his mother came to his room to ask him why in God's name he had become so distant and anti-social, he had clung to silence, as stubborn as a mule.

But it hurt to go to bed without a kiss goodnight from his mother. It hurt so much that the first thing he did, was go find her to say he was sorry. "At least tell me what upset you," she had said. But he would not. In the first place, he did not want to embarrass his mother. Plus, he did not want to have to confess that he had been eavesdropping on the grown-ups' conversation.

"I guess you like to paint too," says Dots.

Jacob says yes, he does, but probably his uncle paints better than him. And hearing that, Dots lets out a hearty guffaw, the kind that always goes with such voluminous bosoms. But it is not an irritating guffaw, nor is it sarcastic like his grandmother's sharp little laugh.

"Sometimes he takes his portable easel to the beach, or he goes into the village to sketch. You'll be able to go with him, if you want to."

Jacob does not answer. He goes out onto the balcony. The view seems to change with every passing minute. To the right, cradled between the house and the lighthouse, is the long, narrow beach, edged by the terrace and the rocks. The terrace is wide and surrounded by geraniums.

"Sometimes," Dots says, "they have to drop the canvas awnings to keep out the dampness, but tonight there is a nice dry breeze, so the awnings are drawn up."

That is why the magnolia is visible there in the center. Its white flowers are slowly folding into themselves in the waning afternoon light and sending sweet fragrances wafting up to the balcony.

"Those stairs take you down to the beach," Dots tells him, indicating a barely perceptible opening on the southern exposure of the terrace.

And to the left is the sea. A sea demarcated by crags that cannot hide the horizon or the opposite extreme of the horseshoe. But just as his uncle has told him, the village is hidden, tucked away behind them. You know it is there—beyond the hill that protects the tile garden and the covering of bougainvilleas—only by the far-off murmur that is carried towards them on the wind. The lighthouse is directly in front of the balcony, set slightly higher than the house. It is still dark because the sun has not set.

Even so, occasional tenuous stars are beginning to flicker in the sky as Jacob watches in wonder. The silence is so vast that the hum of insects scraping the air seems noisy. The same is true of the brusque flapping of a bird tardily seeking shelter for the night.

"Ever seen anything more beautiful than that?"

Jacob remembers what his uncle has said about the beach being isolated and hard to reach, except by sea. "Visitors can only get down there by way of the house, so no one comes around to bother me." The surrounding hills are so steep, that it would be dangerous to attempt it from that direction.

"When will I get to go swimming?"

"Tomorrow. I don't see any reason why not."

She explains that his uncle had a boathouse built underneath the terrace and to make it even easier, there is a jetty. "You can't see it from here. Tomorrow . . ."

To Jacob, tomorrow is a shining promise. A joyful newness on its way to buffer the still nascent, ill-defined disorientation of "today."

"What's that?" he asks, pointing to the left.

Dots explains that it is an islet, with no vegetation or human life on it. Probably it was put there to further accentuate the sense of remoteness and isolation surrounding Can Boig.

All at once, the sound of guitar chords can be heard, accompanied by a whistled melody.

"That's your uncle," says Dots. "It's a good sign. When he plays, it means he's in a good mood."

Jacob says he wants to see him and can she please take him there. But Dots replies that he knows the way now. He just has to cross the gallery, go down the stairs and into the living room.

Feeling a little nervous about traversing the portrait gallery by himself, Jacob walks with his eyes tightly shut. He soon finds the stairway. The bad part is the prickly feeling at the back of his neck that must be coming from Teresa's gaze. "Don't mention her to your uncle," Dots had warned him. He won't. Why should he? Teresa is probably dead. Everybody who abandons somebody else ends up dying.

When he reaches the living room he can see his uncle on the terrace, with his back to the glass doors. He is sitting next to the magnolia, facing the sea.

He is singing in English. Jacob knows the song, because it had won the Eurovision song contest: *Save Your Kisses for Me.*

He remembers it well. In fact, his grandmother Katherine was the one who had taught him the words. "You know what, Pigeon? It was written for a three-year-old boy . . ." It seems to Jacob that his uncle is singing it for that very reason: because it was written for a boy.

He walks slowly towards the terrace, not daring to interrupt.

He is afraid that if his uncle Eduardo discovers him, he might stop strumming the guitar and then the enchantment of his voice, soft, low and caressing, will dissolve.

Duke is stretched out at the painter's feet. He appears to be sleeping, but as soon as Jacob enters the living room, his ears move, alert and expectant.

His uncle turns abruptly in his direction. "What are you doing there?"

"I heard you singing."

"Do you know the song?"

Jacob nods, cowed, as if he's done something wrong.

"Do you speak English?"

"My grandmother's English."

"I'd forgotten that."

Uncle Eduardo extends a hand to him. "Come on, young fellow. Come over here and sing with me."

He invites him to sit on a bench near his feet, next to Duke.

"Okay, here we go."

And he recreates the beat. The chords start out slow and plaintive, but quickly pick up, and uncle Eduardo's voice catches the rhythm. And it's not just the voice, it's his entire body, excited, dynamic, smiling. "Save your kisses for me—come on Jacob—. Save your kisses for me . . . You have to be happy, little one. You have to approach life like this. Singing . . . Save your . . ." And he trills and whistles and the guitar joins in the unusual duet of two diametrically opposed, but happy and confident, voices.

"You can carry a tune, Jacob. Let's begin again."

Duke is asleep, the afternoon is asleep, the sea is beginning to recede and soon real nightfall sets in, lighting up the sky with starry smiles, as it begins its journey towards the moon.

All at once, the lighthouse is illuminated.

"Look at it, Uncle. It's all lit up."

As the lighthouse traces its course, the lacquered surface of the black islet gleams where the moonlight touches it.

"It's pretty."

Suddenly, Uncle Eduardo takes his hand, drawing him in. He puts his arm around the boy's back and presses his head against his shoulder.

"We're going to get along just fine, aren't we, Little Pup?"

Uncle Eduardo smells good. And the touch of his skin makes Jacob feel warm.

"Give me a kiss."

He does not have to ask twice. Impulsively Jacob throws his arms around his uncle's neck, just as his grandmother Katherine had instructed him. It was an irrepressible act. A physical need he had probably been feeling ever since his parents started to fight with the wicked witch Hindrance. It is no matter that uncle Eduardo has a beard, or that his skin is a little scratchy, or that the hands supporting his head are not as soft as his mother's.

"That's what I like, Little Pup. I have a feeling you and I are going to be very good friends."

. . . Save your kisses for me. . . .

And the briny evening breeze loses itself in the guitar strings, and is transformed into a gentle cooing.

The hours fly by. They are taken by surprise when Quasimodo appears on the terrace to announce that dinner is ready.

6

During dinner, uncle Eduardo's voice has not stopped dissecting all sorts of ideas. Novel concepts that smack of intrigue, fantastic forays, mysteries . . . And every once in a while, he addresses himself to the servant: "Isn't that right, Quasimodo?"

"Right," he replies as he switches the plates and refills Jacob's water glass. And, although he cannot seem to suppress a teasing grin, he squeezes his good eye with a conviction that puts to rest any possible doubt.

Jacob's favorite part is the story of Princess Kilsa. According to his uncle, Princess Kilsa had a precious treasure that Malabrun the pirate wanted for himself.

"So what did he do?"

"He kidnapped her. He took her with him to a cave and, ever since then, it has been known as the 'Pirates' Cave.' The princess' father, King Kataplum, gave up the treasure to get his daughter back."

"And did they give her back?"

"Yes, but then something terrible happened. Most of the pirates, including Malabrun, were turned into stones. Princess Kilsa had magical powers, did you know that, Little Pup?"

"And what happened to Kilsa?"

"She rode back to her castle on a dolphin's back. But in her haste, she left the treasure behind."

He quickly explains that dolphins are cetaceans, very intelligent, and friends of mankind. And then he says that, even though Princess Kilsa seemed to be very good, she was really very wicked.

Astonished, Jacob just stares at him openmouthed. No one had ever told him such delectable stories.

"Slimy character that she was, fearing the dolphins might get hold of her treasure, she turned on them just as soon as she saw that she was safe."

"But why?"

"I already told you: she was a witch. And besides that, she wanted to be the empress of the sea."

Jacob is very taken by the story of Kilsa.

"Was she pretty?"

"Very."

"Did she have blond hair or brown hair?"

"Brown. And she had green eyes."

Kilsa's image is slowly beginning to emerge. She looks exactly like the woman in the gallery. At least that is the way the painter is describing her.

"Did she have a shadow?"

"She probably lost it. She made a pact with the devil."

"Who did she look like?"

Uncle Eduardo inhales deeply, makes a clucking noise with his tongue and shakes his head skeptically. "Like every other beautiful woman. That was the bad part about Kilsa: her incredible beauty."

"She died?"

"Who knows? Witches have a hard time dying. Maybe that's why no one has dared to explore the Pirates' Cave up to now. Everyone is afraid that Kilsa will suddenly appear and turn them into stones, just like she did to Malabrun and his cohorts."

"So the treasure's still there?"

"That's what they say."

A heavy silence descends on the dining room. Not even the clatter of plates can be heard.

"My saber has magical powers," says Jacob.

"Really." His uncle is jarred from his musings. He looks Jacob over from top to bottom.

"We could try it out."

"Why not?" And looking pointedly at Quasimodo, he adds, "I am sure we'll get lucky." He stresses the word "lucky" as if Quasimodo might have something to do with it.

After dinner, they move into the living room. A chilly dampness has pervaded the terrace. As soon as the moon had risen, the dry wind had dropped off and a film of humidity had impregnated the tables and lounge chairs.

"Are you sleepy?"

Jacob says no. Pierre had advised him to say no anytime grownups started talking about how kids must be sleepy: "It's babyish to have to go to bed right after dinner." Pierre, on the other hand, has nocturnal experience. His parents never make him go to bed when the other kids do. At least that is what he says: "You have to resist, Jacob. You have to stand up to them. Otherwise, you'll end up having to obey them your whole life."

And he explained how his parents often took him to the movies with them, or for a walk around the village where they spent their summers. That is why Jacob has claimed he is not sleepy. Perhaps his uncle will decide to take him out for a stroll.

"Do you know the wicked witch Hindrance?"

Eduardo Santillana does not seem surprised by the question. That's the good think about uncle Eduardo: His absolute and total acceptance of whatever comes.

"I think I recall someone mentioning her to me."

"She's worse than Princess Kilsa," Jacob says.

"So I do know her. I've probably seen her around somewhere."

It is the first time Jacob has discussed these matters with a grown-up. But his uncle's matter-of-fact tone encourages him to continue.

"She broke my grandmother's leg, and she gave my mom a potion, and she wouldn't let my dad give me a wooden horse."

"She really did all those things?"

"Yes, really."

"Then she is definitely the same witch I knew. And even so, she is not quite as bad as Kilsa."

But Jacob disagrees. Hindrance is the worst witch of all. "She knows a magic spell that puts people in a bad mood." And he adds that his parents were the main victims of her potions. From one day to the next, they had stopped visiting Roger's pool and, to top it all off, his father was always calling his mother a traitor.

Eduardo Santillana listens in silence, resting his forehead against the plate glass window of the terrace. He is gazing at the night sky, so clear it could be a mild afternoon.

And the child's confidences just keep tumbling out. Jacob Santillana is no longer a quiet child. He is reverting to his old self: a cascade of ideas gushing forth.

His uncle stops him abruptly. He strides over to him purposefully and contemplates the slight, tense figure: his glasses somewhat askew, his straight blond hair disheveled and pushed back off his face, blue eyes glittering behind the lenses.

"Tomorrow I will begin your portrait."

"You're going to paint a picture of me?"

"It will be an equestrian pose, okay Little Pup? I just happen to have the wooden horse you mentioned."

Jacob almost cannot believe his ears. It seems impossible that his uncle is going to give him what his father has withheld for so long.

"You're not tricking me, are you?"

"I never lie."

"Can I wear my general's helmet?"

"Why not?" And he adds that Jacob can also brandish the magic saber.

Jacob's excitement grows. Uncle Eduardo is definitely not at all as Rosario described him. Uncle Eduardo is a "different" sort of grown-up. A grown-up full of good sense and understanding. A reasonable person. Someone Jacob can trust.

And his joy is such that he is almost inclined to explain the scare he had when he thought he had swallowed the match head. And also his attempt to fly like Peter Pan. What he would never dare mention is his utter humiliation when he accidentally sipped a stranger's saliva.

"I paint too," he announces suddenly.

"You'll have inherited that from me." The painter searches the child's face, as if drawn in like a magnet by his glasses.

"Dots says you have a chamber of secrets . . ."

"Dots is right."

". . . and all you have in there is junk. But I didn't listen to her. Everybody says the things I keep in my shoebox are junk too."

"Dots is a little slow. She's a good person, but she is not really on the ball."

"That's exactly what I was thinking."

"Would you like me to show you the room?"

"Right now?"

"Let's go."

And once again, he extends the stick for the child to grab on to it. But Jacob is no longer bothered by running behind his uncle. Together, they bound up the stairs, panting and laughing at the same time.

"Hurry, Jacob."

The laughter fades when they reach the portrait gallery, but Teresa's stare seem less damaging with his uncle there to support him.

"You're going to see my sanctuary."

And their trot turns to a canter until they reach the door of the studio. The child's entire body is brimming with anticipation. Especially when his uncle tells him that almost nobody ever goes in there.

It is a spacious room. The picture windows to the north and east offer a view of the sea and a patch of sky, so that the first thing

Jacob notices when the door opens is a mass of twinkling lights reflected on a nearly black sea. The rest is a jumble of pictures, sofas, tables, brushes and tubes.

"Don't just stand there, Little Pup. The chamber of secrets lies straight ahead."

He strides across the room, still leading Jacob by the stick. At the far end, he raises a curtain to reveal a staircase. "This is it. Just go up the stairs and push on that door."

Jacob's excitement grows. Currents of anticipation are rushing through his body. It is a strangely visceral, vibrant sensation. It makes him feel as if he is riding above the situation.

He thinks again about Pierre and everything he will tell him when he gets back to Paris. Such extraordinary things that Pierre will probably think he is making them up.

"Go ahead, Little Pup," his uncle says now, turning on the light.

The chamber of secrets is right there, fascinatingly real and full of wonders that take Jacob's breath away.

"Like it?"

The child does not answer. He simply stares. He is drunk on the images before him. He wants to take it all in at once so that he will remember it when it is no longer there, when the summer ends and he has to return to France.

There are so many astonishing objects that each one seems to devour the other: masks, costumes, feathers, chests, bushes, stuffed birds, musical instruments, shells, elephant tusks, rhinoceros horns, and toys, thousands of toys, old and new, big and small.

"That's a 'hurdy-gurdy,' a barrel organ," and he shows him how to crank the handle to make it sound.

"And this is a pianola." It is a large instrument that looks like a piano but the keys move by themselves, as if it were being played by a ghost.

Jacob finds it impossible to grasp that his uncle can play the piano without even touching the keys. "How do you do it?"

And then he shows him the horse.

It is as tall as Jacob. One front hoof is raised and its mane is made of real horsehair.

"Clavileño."

He does not dare touch it. He is afraid it might not be made of wood after all. But his uncle tells him not to be afraid, to go ahead and stroke it.

"Look at the bridle." Its large muzzle reveals a full set of teeth and a bit, and it even has reins. The animal strikes Jacob as so real that he is surprised that he cannot hear whinnying or see streaks of saliva.

"Would you like to ride him?"

And before Jacob can respond, his uncle lifts him up off the floor and places him astride the horse.

"Try to keep your feet in the stirrups, because he is about to break into a trot."

His uncle drags the horse forward by a cord attached to the wheeled platform on which the horse stands.

"Here we go, Jacob."

It is as if he is dreaming, but with the certainty that he is still awake.

"Giddy up, boy."

Jacob enthusiastically repeats what he hears, holding fast to the reins and spurring the horse's flanks.

"Very good. That is how it's done."

He will never ever get tired of trotting on such a marvelous Clavileño. But his uncle tells him to dismount, because there is so much more to see.

At the far end of the room a large closet is awaiting Jacob's inspection: antique telephones, gramophones, guitars, flutes, drums, castanets, battery-powered automobiles, wooden boats, lead soldiers. . . .

"What are those?"

"Corals. I harvested them myself from the bottom of the sea." He quickly corrects himself: "Well, a friend helped me. She's a professional diver."

"What's her name?"

"Lori. You'll meet her soon." And he explains that corals are petrified plants.

"Like the pillar of salt?"

And his uncle lets out a guffaw before saying yes, something like that.

"So the plants looked back?"

"That's it. The plants looked back, just like Lot's wife did."

"And that thing? It looks like a car."

"It's a tram."

"What's a tram? What do they use it for?"

"It's like a bus. But they don't have them anymore."

Behind the tram, Jacob spies a jewelry box. It is a large case, filled with all sorts of jewelry and gems.

"Leave it there. They aren't real."

But Jacob gazes at it, hypnotized. Next to the case is a crown. His uncle assures him that the crown belonged to King Kataplum and came into his hands thanks to the collaboration of the dolphins. He also shows him the silver strands that Prince Kalem wore when he made Kilsa his wife.

"Were they happy together?"

"No way. No one can be happy with a witch."

Jacob regards the silver strands and tells his uncle that they look a lot like the ones his mother puts on the Christmas tree every year. But his uncle assures him that they might look the same, those are made of tin and these are real silver. Don't touch them.

"Not even fairies have so many things."

"From this day forward, all of this belongs to you."

"You're giving it to me?"

"Naturally."

"And the horse too? You're giving me the horse?"

"Of course."

"You mean I can take him with me when I go back to Paris?"

"You may take him with you to Paris."

Jacob shuts his eyes. It feels as if the room is spinning around him. Take the wooden horse with him! Tell his father: *I don't need you to bring me Clavileño from Spain any more.*

"Do you think it can fly?"

"Why not? All Clavileños can fly."

And they can fly in place. At least—according to his father—that is what Don Quixote had done. He had flown on a Clavileño that never moved from its place. The only bad thing is, sometimes his father lies. It was his mother who had clued Jacob in to his father's tendency to lie: "He's putting stupid ideas into your head, you know that, Son? Do you really think it's possible for someone to fly without flying?" And she had gotten very angry at her husband for saying such a thing.

But uncle Eduardo does not lie. He has just proven it. Every single thing he said about the chamber of secrets has been true.

"Trust me, Little Pup. You will fly."

And Jacob trusts him. No one has ever played with him the way uncle Eduardo does. No one, not even his parents. Especially when they played Savage Beasts. As soon as the game began, they would say, "Leave the room, Jacob. Your mother and I have to talk." But they did not talk, they played. More than once he had seen them playing through the keyhole. That is why he would get so upset with them. Because they would not let him play too.

Until one day, fed up with being left out all the time, he had decided to surprise them by climbing through their bedroom window. They had just come back from Roger's pool and Jacob was getting bored watching television.

He had planted himself at the foot of the bed and yelled to get their attention. That was when his father, furious, had wrapped himself in the sheet and asked what the hell he was doing there. "I want to play with you. I want to play with you." But his father had paid no attention to his entreaties. "Get out of here right now." And he had unceremoniously dragged him out by his ear.

Terribly wounded by this rudeness, Jacob ran to the living room to cry his eyes out.

His father soon came out to apologize. "You took us by surprise, Son. You gave us a colossal scare. For a few seconds there, we thought you really were a savage beast."

But the child knew it wasn't true. He was only saying it because they did not like to play savage beasts with him. To placate him, his father had taken him out to buy ice cream, but Jacob was not to be appeased.

"Tell me, Uncle Eduardo. Do you know how to play savage beasts?"

"Maybe if you explain the rules to me."

"It's easy, you just take off all your clothes, and you howl, and you attack the other person, and you roll around together on the bed or the floor."

"Don't tell me you've played it."

"I was going to, but they wouldn't let me. They were being selfish."

"Who?"

"My parents. They wanted to play all by themselves."

Uncle Eduardo bursts out laughing and Jacob cannot understand why. Sometimes uncle Eduardo has confusing reactions.

"When did this happen?"

"A long time ago, when I was little. After that the wicked witch Hindrance came along and then they didn't play any more, they just fought."

"I see."

He is no longer laughing. To the contrary, a tremendous sadness seems to have taken over his face. Then he pulls himself together. With a pat on the back, he tells Jacob to dance with him. His uncle is clicking two little plates between his index finger and his thumb. "Let's go, Jacob."

It's fun to watch how uncle Eduardo's body sways and rocks to the beat he is clacking out between his fingers.

"Let's go, Little Pup. Don't be shy."

With one long stride, he is standing before his nephew, hips in motion and holding his head as if it is disconnected from his body, he begins to dance the robot.

"How do you do that?"

"It's easy. Try it."

Jacob tries, but he can't get it.

"No, not like that. Watch carefully . . ."

And abruptly a crowing smile takes over. Jacob forgets all about his parents and how they excluded him from their games. And the dance continues. And the little instrument sounds the rhythm as their feet twist and slide along the floor like happy reptiles.

All of the sadness and adversity evaporates with the rhythm of the dance. His uncle is smiling. It's nice to see his perfect, white teeth. It is a special smile, as if he were telling Jacob, Don't worry Little Pup. From now on you won't be sad and you won't have to cry . . .

All at once, Jacob stops dancing. He looks his uncle straight in the eyes and yells, "I love you so much." And to make sure his uncle understands, he hugs him around the legs, anxiously, desperately. The little plates clatter to the floor with a noise that resounds throughout the room.

Eduardo Santillana bends down and lifts the child in his arms. This time, though, he is not doing it to sit him atop Clavileño, but rather to look at him, just look at him. His eyes are becoming red and shiny and he holds the child's face close to his beard so he won't see the tears.

"You're like a little elf, you know that, Jacob? An adorable little elf."

And they remain like that for a while, silent, sharing a kind of tenderness neither of them had ever experienced up until then.

7

Sleep gradually recedes as the sun's piercing rays filter in through the gap in the half-opened window. Jacob inhales deeply, taking the warm, salty air into his lungs. He suddenly recalls that he is not in Paris and that last night, uncle Eduardo had shown him the chamber of secrets and then took him to his room riding Clavileño, his wooden horse.

Clavileño is probably still there beside the bed, right where his uncle left him, with his tangled mane and his foreleg raised in a perpetual trot.

Motionless, eyes still closed, Jacob waits lethargically for somebody to come rouse him from bed. He feels good like that, half asleep, remembering, anticipating . . . The sound of hens clucking against a chorus of cicadas floats in the air, occasionally drowned out by Duke's barking. He cannot hear the sea. It is as if it had evaporated all at once. But he knows it is still there because occasionally he hears the slap of a body diving into the water.

Suddenly Quasimodo's voice can be heard, yelling for his mother. Dots' falsetto voice responds from the terrace, saying that Jacob is still sleeping and would he please not raise such a ruckus. He might wake the boy.

Jacob feels around the bedside table, finds his glasses, walks over to the balcony and opens the door. The sudden light assails his retinas but they quickly adjust. Quasimodo is out there squatting on a rock by the cliff, cleaning fish. He can see Duke down on the beach gnawing at a bone and there, at the water's edge, he notices his uncle Eduardo, clad in a swimsuit and sketching.

Jacob does not dare interrupt his work, but his uncle motions for him to come down.

Dots rushes out to meet him and leads him to the kitchen. "There's fresh milk and bread with tomato and olive oil."

Jacob has never tasted bread with tomato, but he eats it right off because Dots has assured him that it is the most exquisite delicacy. "Let's see if we can fatten you up a bit, little one."

She then leads him to the bathroom and hands him some trunks to wear down to the beach. Fortunately, she does not offer to help him brush his teeth or his hair, or take a shower.

"Habits for city folks, living in their glorified prisons. The ways of a few fancy shmancy people who think they're so refined," she exclaims, gazing at the assortment of toiletries he had distributed on the shelf the previous afternoon. "Now you just tell me what good all of that does you."

And Jacob gazes up at her admiringly, as if Dots and her scabs were the most important thing in the world.

"There's nothing more purifying than just being a kid, don't you think, Jacob?" And she suddenly confides that she is happy sleeping in his room. "You're like a corpse. You don't even snore."

"Do I breathe?"

"Dear God yes, you breathe, but you do it quietly."

Jacob wonders how a person can breathe without realizing he's breathing. "Probably I'll just forget one day and I'll suffocate myself."

Dots bursts out laughing. Then she reassures him. Tells him everybody forgets they are breathing when they are asleep and no one ever dies of that kind of forgetting.

"Hurry up, Jacob. Your uncle is going to take you to the cave."

Jacob recalls the promise of the night before. Once more, uncle Eduardo is making it clear he wants to make him happy. And even though they are brothers, Jacob has to admit his uncle doesn't resemble his father in the slightest.

His father has always used any sort of excuse to get out of a promise. As in, the way Jacob was behaving, he didn't deserve any rewards. Or, he should study more and play less. Or, he had talked back, or had not cleaned his plate, or any other bad thing . . .

But the truth of the matter was, his father couldn't be bothered to try to please his son. That's why he was always looking for excuses. "Next Sunday, Jacob. I swear I'll take you to the zoo next Sunday." But next Sunday would become the next one, and the next, until Jacob had despaired of ever seeing the zoo at all. There was nothing for it but to satisfy his curiosity with Pierre's descriptions of all the different animal species that came from around the world.

His uncle is not like that. His uncle does not make promises he cannot keep. His uncle is ready and willing to take him to the Pirates' Cave and look for the treasure together.

"Good morning, Pup." As soon as he reaches the terrace, his uncle comes over to greet him. It is strange to see him without his walking stick. It seems as if the stick and his uncle go together.

"Are you ready?" And he picks him up to carry him down to the beach.

"Look, Jacob. Look how I gut this fish," Quasimodo calls out to him from his perch on the rock.

It is interesting to watch Quasimodo work. First he scales the thing with his knife and cuts off the fins and the tail with a pair of scissors. After that, he opens up the stomach and guts the fish, and then shakes it in the water to rinse it off. "They taste better than if you clean them in the kitchen," he explains.

For a few seconds, the water around Quasimodo is stained red, but it soon fades to pink and then becomes blue again, just like before.

Jacob asks whether he is going with them to the cave.

Quasimodo laughs, unabashedly exposing his notched teeth, and says no, he was there earlier, while Jacob was still sleeping.

Suddenly serious, his uncle chides him. "Where did you come up with that story? Since when has anyone actually summoned up the courage to visit the Pirates' Cave?"

Ashamed, Quasimodo corrects himself, apologizes, stutters. He realizes he has dropped the ball and does not deserve to be on the team.

Probably Quasimodo is just like his dad, thinks the child. The type of people who say things just for the sake of hearing themselves talk. False heroes who make up daring feats just to prove how brave they are.

"Let's go, Little Pup. Hurry along."

The boat is there by the jetty, waiting for them. It is a white outboard with seats covered in a white material that does not get hot no matter how strong the sun is.

"Put on this cap and cover yourself with the towel. The sun can mess you up pretty badly."

His uncle, however, is practically naked and his bronzed skin is glistening. "Have you ever steered a boat?"

"Never."

"Not even in a river?"

"No. I only swam in Roger's pool and you can't fit boats or canoes or anything in there."

His uncle settles him in the bow. "You're the figurehead," he jokes. A figurehead with red and blue stripes, crowned by a white cap.

They set out against the current, in the direction of the islet. Soon they have crossed the bay. The village is there on the left, at the very center of the rocky horseshoe, flanked by a huge mountain. The houses are reflected peacefully on the water's surface. They are very white, as if they had fallen down from the heavens. There are several beaches but his uncle explains that they are not sandy, but pebbly, like the one at Can Boig. They were probably the first rocks ever created, crushed by time and by the pummeling of the waves.

The boat slowly nears the islet which—as Dots had already explained—had no vegetation or human life. It is frightening to observe such a black, bare hunk of rock. Fortunately, just a few meters beyond the islet is a neighborhood of houses and pine trees. "That's where Lori lives," his uncle remarks.

Lori. The diver. His uncle's friend. The one who helped him discover the marine plants that "looked back."

It is a happy house, situated on the far end of the horseshoe, directly opposite Can Boig. You could probably see it from the lighthouse and also from the painter's studio.

"What's Lori like?"

"Young, full of energy, nice. You'll like her." He says it distractedly, as if Lori were not even a person. "The truth is you can't take Lori very seriously, you know what I mean, Little Pup? She can be pretty foolish sometimes."

Jacob is cold. He has suddenly started to tremble.

"Come here, Jacob. Sit beside me. You're better off here in the stern."

Still wrapped in the towel, the cap pulled down over his glasses, Jacob attempts the move, trying to keep his balance. He finds it very strange to be floating in all that water without anything besides liquid to hold them up.

"It's nice to go out in the boat on days like this," his uncle says, draping his arm over his body. "You could even steer the boat yourself."

But Jacob does not dare touch the tiller. The thought of steering the boat is overwhelming. Even more than flying in an airplane was.

As they leave the bay behind, they see sheer cliffs and black forms rising out of the water, which his uncle says are enchanted rocks. "Look at that one, Jacob. They call it the Cat. You know why that is? Because before it was a rock, it was a real cat."

It is shaped like a cat. A cat crowned by a battalion of seagulls that fly off apprehensively as the boat passes by.

Then there is the Horse, the Bear, the Leaning Tower of Pisa. All of the rocks have a name. They are all pretending to be something.

But as the boat leaves them behind, they lose their unique forms and become just rocks again.

"I don't know why they call you 'the Reprobate'."

His uncle seems to find that amusing. "Maybe because nobody likes me."

"It isn't true," Jacob protests indignantly. "I love you, and Dots and Quasimodo and your friend Lori—I bet she loves you too." But he does not continue because he suddenly has the suspicion that his uncle does not like what he is saying.

The canoe approaches the cliffs, those deserted, stark, obsessively savage places. "Sometimes I think this is where the world ends," exclaims the painter.

And Jacob thinks he would not care if the world ended as long as his uncle Eduardo were with him.

A strange silence pervades the place. It is as if human life really did stop there. Besides the two of them, there is only the beating and flapping of the seagulls. Everything else is rigid, looming, and jagged. But seagulls do not speak, they only fly. Except his uncle has assured him that as they fly they emit a very clear language that Jacob will certainly be able to understand some day.

"So they talk with their wings?"

"That's right. With their wings."

Jacob finds it very strange that an animal could talk just with its wings, but if his uncle says so, it must be true. It is also strange to see them perched along the cliff peaks, silent and grave.

"I like birds that sing."

"Like the goldfinches in the tamarind trees?" And he quickly imitates their whistle to entertain the boy. It is just like being back along the esplanade in the village, with the finches fluttering among the branches.

"How do you do that?"

His uncle replies that he is not sure how he does it, but if Jacob would like him to, he will tell him why he does it. "I was born on an afternoon when the northerly was blowing, just like yesterday, next to a square lined with tamarind trees just like the one you saw. That's why my fairy godmother gave me the power to imitate their song."

"I don't have a fairy godmother."

"It doesn't matter. I'll tell mine to take care of you. She is very kind. You'll see. When we get to the Pirates' Cave, she'll do everything in her power to help us find the treasure."

64

"I should've brought my magic saber."

"For what? You won't need it with me at your side."

Suddenly his uncle points out a dark, high crag. A giant with its legs spread apart, its fists raised high in the air. "That's the Pirate Malabrun."

It's amazing to see him there, towering, fierce, defying the sea.

"We have to get ourselves wet, nephew. If we enter the cave dry, it could be dangerous."

And he quickly explains that the enchanted rocks can affect people, especially when they are dry. The best way to exorcise their powers is to jump into the water. "Damp bodies terrify petrified bodies. It scares them away."

The boat reaches a solitary beach. The shallow strip where they make land is flinty too, just like the others in the district and it is covered with tiny snails that blend into what little sand there is along the water's edge. "You couldn't build any sand castles here."

"But you can build houses and you can skip stones like flying saucers and play shoe store." He jumps out onto the beach to demonstrate. "Watch this, Little Pup." His uncle has taken a flat stone and thrown it onto the water, but instead of sinking it skips along, leaving little whorls in its wake.

"It's just like a flying saucer."

Jacob tries to imitate him, but all of his stones sink immediately.

"Throw it harder, Little Pup. And tilt your hand like this."

Maybe, when he tells Pierre about this, he will lie just a little. Maybe he will tell him that his uncle had tossed real flying saucers." Vehicles from other planets where the inhabitants are tiny, like ants.

"And shoe store? How do you play that?"

"We'll play that tomorrow."

Then his uncle instructs him to take off his cap and glasses and jump in the water with him. The water is cold. Much colder than Roger's swimming pool.

"Come on then. Show me how you can swim."

"Not so fast, Jacob," his father would tell him. "Remember Tarzan." And Jacob would try to imitate him because Tarzan was his idol when it came to climbing.

"That's perfect, Jacob. Perfect."

In contrast, his father always said he swam like a dog. And when he could see that Jacob was having difficulties, he'd leave him to his own devices in order to make a man out of him.

Then his mother would confront his father and say he was not human. It would serve him right if Jacob drowned, just to show him that you cannot ask so much of a little kid. And his father would retort that he would rather see him drown than turn into a pansy.

"Don't tire yourself out," his uncle warns.

But Jacob keeps on swimming so that his uncle does not think he might have turned into that thing his father was so worried about.

"That's enough now." He pulls him from the water, dries him off and places his glasses on his face.

The boat is still stuck in the sand and he suddenly notices the name *Teresa* emblazoned on the side of the boat. "Why did you name it that?"

"I once knew a woman by that name."

"The one in all the paintings in the gallery?" He suddenly recalls that he is not supposed to mention Teresa to his uncle, but he forges ahead anyway.

"Did you marry her?"

"No."

"But you loved her."

"Maybe."

"And she went away?"

His uncle does not reply. He rises and tells Jacob it is getting late.

"And it smells rotten too." It is inevitable. When the waters retreat at low tide, the limpets dry up and rot.

"We have to get to the cave before the seagulls discover it."

Jacob does not hear what he is saying. He is thinking about Teresa. In the paintings in the gallery. In the name his uncle has put on the boat.

"Your turn. You steer the boat now."

He places the boy's hands on the tiller and explains that to go left you have to turn it to the right and he should play close attention because a lot of things in life are like that: contradictory and absurd.

"Now you know, Little Pup. When you want something really badly, pretend you don't." He laughs, clears his throat, coughs, and then tells Jacob that he is going to begin his portrait just as soon as they return to Can Boig.

They are abruptly plunged into a silence devoid of images or memories. A kind of silence-truce in which uncle Eduardo frowns and forgets that Jacob is beside him, wrapped in the blue and red striped towel.

Distractedly, Jacob gazes into the water's depths as the boat passes among the rock formations. The seabed is clearly visible, with its sea urchins, algae and sea tomatoes.

"I'd like to grab one of those tomatoes."

"Watch out for them," his uncle warns. "They're not like regular tomatoes. They're poisonous."

Poisonous tomatoes. He would never have guessed that tomatoes could be poisonous.

"Now close your eyes and don't open them until I tell you to."

The motor stops and Jacob's damp skin perceives a new freshness, as if it were coming off the rocks around them. The sounds have changed too. There is a lot more echo.

"You can open them now."

It is a long cave, dimly lighted by the narrow opening through which the vessel has passed. Jacob gazes around him with growing amazement. He has never seen anything like it. Above, a vaulted ceiling flashes grayish-brown lights with marble overtones and below a school of silver fish glow like phosphorous in the water.

Frightened, he would like to take refuge with his uncle, but with one hop, Eduardo Santillana has moved towards the bow, legs apart, using an oar to feel the bottom and push the vessel farther into the cave.

"Is it very long?" asks the child.

And the echo repeats, "ong, ong, ong. . . ."

"I think so, o, o, o. . . ."

As he turns, his uncle's teeth seem even whiter than in full sunlight. Everything has changed color since they entered the cave. Everything has taken on a different hue.

"Are you afraid?" But he does not wait for the answer. The echo's response is sufficient. "In a minute we'll turn to the right and anchor on the beach."

It is a small, shady beach with white sand. His uncle says they must leave the boat and continue on foot.

"Barefoot?"

"If your feet hurt, I'll carry you."

Beyond the beach, between the ridges, shines a tenuous light that probably comes from the roof.

"Come on, Jacob."

Hand in hand, the two of them follow the path towards the light. It is a sinuous tunnel that requires navigating twists and turns and narrow passageways.

He does not even remember that he is barefoot. All he can think about is that, since Princess Kilsa's kidnapping, no one has ventured into this cave until now. The only thing that matters is to follow the trail of light and get to the room where the enchanted pirates guard the treasure.

"Incredible, isn't it, Little Pup?"

The earth under their feet is soft and feels more like dust than sand, sort of like a dried-up marsh.

The passageway widens as the mass of lime and salt residue hardens. Again the path below their feet becomes almost rocky and the cave is beginning to resemble an enchanted palace.

Uneven columns are suspended from the roof like enormous drops jutting downward to merge with those rising from the ground.

"Those are the petrified pirates," his uncle says.

The cave walls are also rutted and full of holes which, from a distance, look as if they could be wall vaults in a cemetery. They do not even need a flashlight. The light penetrating the vaulted ceiling is sufficient to take in every detail.

"The treasure must be in one of those holes."

The search begins. It is thrilling to explore such a mysterious cave, full of shafts, hidden corners and deep grooves. Jacob's heart is beating wildly. "Look at this."

Behind a bend half hidden by a stalactite, a white arrow is painted on the wall. "An arrow." Impulsively he touches it with his fingers and realizes it is wet. "Someone just painted it."

But his uncle hastens to clarify that though it was painted many years before, paint never dries completely in such shaded places. "Let's follow the arrow. The treasure cannot be far now."

A string of sensations right out of an epic poem are sifting through Jacob's mind in a hodgepodge of memories and plans. Something very powerful is growing inside him. The excitement of feeling his own importance, the conviction born of undertaking great feats that can never be refuted, and the self-assurance created by the sense of omnipotence so generously conferred on him by his uncle.

The arrow, in fact, leads to another. It has been placed at the entrance of a small dark space with a low overhang and uneven walls.

"Here."

His uncle's voice is firm, and there is no longer an echo. The narrow space quickly absorbs his words. "We'll need the flashlight here."

It is a granulated room covered with saline deposits. A corner that smells of an ancestral sea, long since evaporated. But the treasure does not appear to be there.

"Wait, Jacob. Hold the flashlight."

Cautiously Jacob moves towards the entrance to make sure the petrified pirates have not moved from their places. A mixture of fear, respect and premonition is challenging his equilibrium.

His uncle does not even register Jacob's state of mind. He probably intuits that the big moment has arrived and his age-old dream is about to be realized. Instinctively, he falls to his knees and begins to dig into the cave floor, while his nephew regards him in amazement.

"Help me, Jacob."

And Jacob helps him. Right then, the two of them bear a strong resemblance to Duke when he is digging for a bone. Panting, they claw at the whitish dust with their nails, synchronized, concentrating, their gestures and breathing imperceptibly becoming one.

"It's here, Jacob. I'm sure it's here."

And since his uncle is never wrong, Jacob works even harder, having given himself over completely to the rhythm of all of the discoverers in the history of the world. He is completely removed from his fear, exempt from all danger. He does not even remember that behind, in the large room, is an army of pirates bent on keeping their prisoner.

"Look at this, Jacob."

Jacob's fingers brush against a hard object—something solid and heavy is slowly coming into view.

"The treasure," exclaims his uncle, euphoric. We got it, Jacob. We got it."

And the mechanism of illusions ignites in the child's mind. It is like enjoying the impossible or dreaming the unimaginable.

"We got it," he echoes.

Uncle and nephew embrace wildly. "We did it, Little Pup. We did it."

The petrified pirates hardly count now. What does it matter that they are there, in the larger cave, watching the two from their enchanted state. The only thing that matters is that his uncle has uncovered the treasure and is handing it to him.

"It's all yours, Jacob. It belongs to you."

And Jacob's screeches crash against the cave walls producing interminable, uninhibited echoes, almost demented in their excitement.

8

It had been a big day for Jacob. Perhaps the most important one of his whole life. A day that was truly unforgettable.

In the chest were necklaces, rings, diadems, bracelets. It was so heavy they had to carry it between them back to the boat. "I'll give a present to Mommy and Grandmother and Rosario. . . ."

Then his uncle asked him whether he was going to set something aside for his father. He stalled and stuttered at first. Then he said he would just as soon toss the whole thing into the sea.

"And why is that, Little Pup?"

So Jacob, flushing, told his uncle that his father lied and didn't like his mother at all. He insulted her and said she was a traitor.

The trip back was short. The sea remained calm and his uncle cranked the engine to get them back as quickly as possible.

As soon as they glimpsed the beach at Can Boig, they could see Dots and Quasimodo waving handkerchiefs from the terrace. They were probably curious to know how the investigation had proceeded, because they both ran down to the jetty to meet them.

Jacob's excitement was such that he could barely eat, or sleep, or talk about anything that was not directly related to the Pirates' Cave.

One by one, he regaled Dots with tales of the dangers they had encountered and the fears they had had to overcome. "But we faced it all, you know that, Dots? And since we were all wet, the petrified pirates couldn't do anything against us."

Dots buried her face in her hands and although at first glance she might have appeared to be laughing, she was really crying from the emotion of it all. Jacob was able to confirm this when she lowered her hands, because damp tears were staining her eyelids, right on top of the dry ones she always had. "To think you could have been trapped in that cave forever," she repeated, shaking her head. "To think you could have ended up petrified, just like those pirates."

As soon as he went up to his room, he placed the chest in the closet right next to the shoebox.

His uncle began his portrait that very afternoon. According to him, it was going to be a very important painting—his most important work yet. It was going to revolutionize the thinking of the foremost art critics worldwide. An aristocratic and capitalist painting ..., his uncle would repeat. And every time he posed, Jacob felt as if he were nothing less than a king.

The sittings were long and pleasant. First, his uncle would place Clavileño by the window, along with a desiccated owl. Then, he would mount Jacob astride the horse, outfitted with his paper saber and the brigadier general's hat and tell him, "Close your eyes, Little Pup, because now you're going to fly."

An almost brutal wind slapped against the child and Jacob raised his sword to attack it. "You're approaching a star, Jacob. But don't even think about opening your eyes or you'll be sent back to earth straightaway."

That was what the trips on Clavileño were like. Brief, but delicious. His uncle would describe everything he came upon along the way: rivers flowing with a golden liquid, roads paved with silver, roses that smelled of jasmine and lilies that smelled of roses. And the equestrian portrait grew and took shape.

Other diversions followed. Fishing from the boat for serranos and eels. The painting sessions at the top of the lighthouse. "I want you to paint whatever you see, Little Pup. In your own style, of course. Then I'll tell you what works and what doesn't ..." Hunting butterflies in the fields on the hillsides. The trips to the village to sketch: "That's where Visitarana lives, there by the church, Remember, Little Pup? She's the village witch." The costumes in the big chest: fur capes and wigs, princely undergarments ... The matching pairs of stones to play shoe store: "I'm the customer and you're the salesman, okay?" The singing sessions on the terrace: "Save your kisses for me ..." And searching for the sun as it sank behind the mountain: "Let's go, Little Pup." They would sprint towards the lighthouse to catch it and, just as it disappeared behind the hump of the hillock, Jacob and his uncle would wave goodbye.

And his uncle also taught him to drive. He'd sit the child on his lap and place his hands on the wheel. "Let's go to the village, Jacob." Once there, they would plunge into the bustling cafés to gorge themselves on ice cream and listen to the song of the goldfinches as they fluttered among the branches of the tamarind trees.

Jacob liked the village a great deal. Especially in the evening. They almost always ended up at the Garota bar so his uncle's friends could play with him. That was where he first met Lori. She was blond, with grey eyes and her skin was so tanned it was almost black and she treated Jacob like a kid brother. "I also like to fly a lot, did you know that, Pup? But in a different way." And when she said things like that everybody would laugh, as if Lori were making up the part about flying.

Coco said she also flew frequently, except nobody paid any attention to her. She always seemed half-asleep and she said boring things.

Mr. Cusi was the owner and whenever he saw the painter come in with his young nephew, he would drop everything to hurry over and attend to him. "Come in, maestro. They are waiting for you, maestro . . ."

He was a lanky fellow with a thick mustache and two big wet patches under his armpits. He would immediately escort them to the best table: the one up on the platform overlooking the sea, set slightly apart from the rest.

A sea of the most varied looks seemed to follow them whenever they walked through the place. Eduardo Santillana must be very well known, because as soon as they saw him, people would whisper and strain their eyes for a better look. "Tomorrow I will dress up as an Indian," he had assured Jacob once, and that is just what he did. And when, upon reaching their table, his friends had given him a round of applause, Eduardo Santillana had executed a formal bow and remarked that if the crowd wanted a show, then they must have it, and that being an Indian was just as important as being a European.

Fabian, the sculptor also tended to show up in costume, except his was always the same: white tunics, necklaces, headbands to keep his hair in place. "I request the floor, maestro, I request the floor." It was as if you had to get authorization from his uncle if you wished to speak at the gathering. "Permission granted, darling girl." And Fabian would launch into a speech about the importance of aesthetics and a harmony of intellects as a factor in seduction. "Do you understand any of it, Jacob?" And he would say yes, but he really did not understand a thing. What mattered was being allowed to participate in the gathering and be part of the group.

Most of the tables were occupied by gray, taciturn, nostalgic people. People who, try as they might to seem friendly with his uncle, never quite succeeded. So Jacob regarded them with suspicion. Probably they were the ones who called his uncle the reprobate, or that damned painter, or the enigma. You could see their hostility in the way they glanced his way and talked among themselves about the idiosyncrasies of the secluded table.

They must be very unfriendly people. People who never laughed, or played shoe store with pairs of matching stones, or skipped rocks like flying saucers on the water's surface. They would not be the type to search for buried treasure in an ancestral cave. They would be serious people like grandmother Katherine, who probably had never watched in rapture as the sea turned to red in the misty sunsets or traipsed up a hill to build a bonfire big enough to frighten off the evil spirits after the northerly had abated. Probably they never woke up at dawn as his uncle did, to get a clear view of those strange creatures, half plant half animal, called jellyfish. And they would not have dogs like Duke around, always willing to run after rocks moistened with saliva when they played fetch.

Sometimes, Lori would let Jacob take a sip from her cup. "Do you like it, Little Pup?" Jacob would feel a pleasant tingling in his throat and eyes and, in about a minute, everything would begin to seem much more real and relevant. It made his uncle laugh to see Jacob so euphoric. "What the devil did you give him?" Fabian would roll his eyes and press his hands together just like a woman: "Oh to be a child again!" he would repeat.

"A child nothing," Paul would interject. "Being a child was a pain. The fun part was being a teenager." In any event, Paul's opinions did not matter very much either. He had a very soft voice and the words came out in a nasally tone.

Jacob was always struck by the contrast between the village women and the ones that surrounded his uncle. The former were always wearing black. Even their arms were always covered. But his uncle's friends tended to wear very clear, transparent clothing, as if the purpose of having a dress on was to seem even more naked than you would be without it.

There were usually a lot of people milling around the table at the Garota Bar and Jacob frequently had a hard time figuring out the sex of each one. Except for Lori and Coco, everyone else could have been genderless creatures. Hybrid people who chattered away in different languages and occasionally yawned or yelled, or stood up abruptly only to sit right back down again.

When they left, they did not even say goodbye. They ambled towards the exit, holding themselves very straight, daring people to stare at them, and causing the fetishes they wore around their necks to jangle.

The company remaining behind at the table would say strange things, such as whether so and so was "tanked," and whether he had been "cut off" and wouldn't be able to "jump," and one of these days he was going to put a bullet in his head to put an end to so much crap. That afternoon, Jacob had asked, "Why can't he jump, Uncle? And his uncle had replied that they'd cut off his legs just like Pierre's grasshoppers. It was horrible to imagine one of those friends ending up in a sandy cemetery like those Pierre built on the beach at The French Riviera.

And seeing him so low, Lori had begged him to teach her the magic words his uncle had pronounced at the cave's entrance: "Kans, Kins, Kuns, Kilsa, Katapum, Kalen. And then I answered Klipoff and the spell was broken . . ." Then Lori had asked, "Did it really happen like that?" And Eduardo Santillana had not skipped a beat: "Of course . . ."

Even though Lori was nice and tried hard to please his uncle, the painter often treated her in a condescending way. It was as if Lori was not really part of Eduardo Santillana's circle and, no matter how many petrified plants she might take from the sea, she would never reach his level.

Jacob would always be half asleep as they headed for home. "Did you have fun, Little Pup?" And he would just nod, because the words would get stuck and his eyelids would feel very heavy. And his uncle would drive along, whistling a tune. But as soon as Dots saw them coming, it was nothing but reproaches: "That's no way to care for a child . . . He's never going to grow at this rate . . . Children who drink end up as midgets . . ."

His uncle would pay no attention to her at all. "Just bring us some food and stop babbling. Leave all the sermonizing to the priest." He would finish by saying that people who lived in glass houses . . .

And Dots would shut up, because his uncle's arguments were final and brooked no argument.

"When winter comes, his boring grandmother will bring him right back into line. Isn't that right, Jacob?"

What Jacob liked most was that his uncle also thought his grandmother Katherine was boring. But it hurt to think that when winter came, Eduardo Santillana would no longer be there by his side.

The child was finding his path smoothed for him. His uncle was helping to assimilate the most far-flung or obscure things. "See Jacob. The cicadas are saying your name." And sure enough, if he listened very hard, he could to hear the name Jacob cavorting in the air among the crickets' chirping and gentle breezes.

He could even understand the seagulls. "You hear them, Jacob? Each flap of the wing is a syllable. Right now they are saying that Ruan remembers you and he is planning to pay you a visit."

According to his uncle, Ruan was an extraterrestrial and Jacob would be meeting him soon. Very soon. "... Because the gold-finches and the seagulls are friends of the Venusians—especially the goldfinches, Little Pup. Every goldfinch in the world has been to Venus, so when they announce that a Venusian is going to visit, well, they are never mistaken."

Jacob had learned so many unusual things since arriving in Can Boig. One day, it was the execution of the chickens carried out by Quasimodo. First he would hypnotize them: "That way, they don't suffer so much, know what I mean, Jacob?" Another day, it was the pebbled paths his uncle traced so as not to tread on the new grass. Or watering the magnolia, fist tightly closed around the hose, because the drought was becoming protracted and the flowers were withering.

He was also allowed to paint on the flaking walls at will, using his uncle's paintbrushes. "It looks like a Picasso, Little Pup. I swear it does." And he would always say if he kept up like that, he'd end up being a great abstract painter.

One evening he learned to project hand shadows on the white walls of the living room and his uncle would invent an action-packed story to go with the scene he was creating. Of course, it would be full of witches and warlocks—"... because shadows don't have shadows, get it?"

He also learned that, in times of drought, the winds stimulated the soul and enabled it to divine other people's thoughts and, depending on the forces that drove them, could turn the same view into a happy painting or a melancholy one. "... All of the views in the world are paintings. Get that into your head. And any corner, any little fragment of those paintings, could be a work of art."

One afternoon, his uncle took him to the mountain. The one where the sun hid just as the moon was coming out. "Breathe deeply, Little Pup," he had said, poking his stick at the boy's abdomen. "This is a privilege. That's what this is: a privilege." And he assured the child that few had the opportunity to breathe air so pure, so sweet.

Jacob would breathe very hard and then he would start to feel a little dizzy. "What does it smell like, Uncle?"

And he would say like salt and rosemary and thyme. Before long they would come upon the aromatic plants. His uncle would make him pluck some of the branches and then instructed him to smell his hands. Smell that perfume.

And that was how one day he came across a branch that walked and moved, and was even capable of holding very still as if it were about to dry up completely.

Eduardo Santillana quickly explained that the branch was really a mimetic insect that used camouflage to defend itself against predators. So the child asked what "mimetic" meant and his uncle told him something was mimetic if it imitated something or someone else.

So the next day, the child had decided to imitate his uncle. He asked Quasimodo to burn a cork and he rubbed it on his face. Then he grabbed a piece of firewood and paraded before his uncle mimicking the way he walked.

"Do I look like you?"

Moved, his uncle had gathered him up and kissed him. "We're like two peas in a pod. Don't ever doubt it, Little Pup. We're of the same mold you and I." Even Duke, yawning and whining, thought Jacob was his uncle. You could tell by the way he licked his feet and wagged his tail.

Jacob had never felt so happy. No one had ever planned such an intense and entertaining life for him. He did not even have nightmares. And naturally, he no longer dreamed about the big-headed monster or the pillar of salt.

His dreams were calm, a little confusing perhaps, but pleasant. They were harmless dreams, the kind that are immediately forgotten upon wakening, the way you forget a speck of dust, or a piece of pie you ate the day before.

9

The morning has dawned wan and homesick: there is no sun, or wind, or shadow. It is one of those days when the light is purplish and the apparent calm can be whipped into a storm from one minute to the next.

Uncle Eduardo likes these kinds of days very much. He says they are the best days to paint. Even the smells emanating from the drains and from the denuded rocks, dried and exposed, excite his imagination and make it easy for him to work.

"This kind of day stirs up memories." And as he says the words, it is as if he were preparing a speech. As if he were privately analyzing what he should say and what should remain unsaid.

In contrast, Jacob does not like days like this. He finds them insipid. Maybe it is because, as his uncle says, they dredge up memories: dull, boring things you'd rather forget.

"What are you thinking about?"

Right then, Jacob is thinking about Roger's swimming pool, the match episode and how the sky is just the same as it was that day.

"Stop frowning, Jacob."

And he brings the paintbrush to his eyes, as if he were tracing a horizontal line. Eduardo Santillana is totally transformed when he is painting. It is as if he were someone else. Sometimes Jacob feels a little frightened when he sees him so lost in his work. It is as if something fundamental changes inside him. Instead of being right there by Jacob's side, his uncle seems to have broken free of himself and escaped to far-flung regions where his nephew cannot follow.

"Are you tired?"

Eduardo Santillana often asks him if he is tired. He is probably afraid Jacob is going to say he has had enough. But Jacob can never be tired when he is riding Clavileño, occasionally thrusting with the saber made out of French newspapers and wearing his brigadier general's hat.

In the silence pervading the studio, however, he sometimes finds himself connecting shadowy dots in his mind. Niggling doubts that evaporate in an instant. Pinpricks of vague suspicion that seemed determined to crash headlong into irrefutable facts: the still damp arrows painted on the walls of the Pirates' Cave. The way Dots' sobs had sounded like laughter. The treasure chest so like the one his uncle kept in the chamber of secrets . . .

"I was thinking about Roger," he answers.

The name Roger always causes uncle Eduardo's expression to change. All Jacob has to do is mention it and his uncle will invariably clear his throat, cough or pretend to be looking for something. But this time it was different. He just stood there, the paintbrush suspended in midair like a baton, and asked, "Do you think a lot about Roger?"

"Sometimes."

There are times when it seems as if uncle Eduardo is fighting with his painting. He starts out wielding the palette knife furiously, as if he were stabbing the canvas instead of applying paint to it.

"Tell me the truth, Pup. You don't really like this Roger guy, do you?"

Jacob is not sure how to answer that. He always seems to run into problems when he tries to analyze his feelings towards Roger. Especially since the whole headless match episode.

"But you have to try to love him. Or at least pretend you do. That's my advice to you."

"Why?"

"Because you're going to have to put up with him more than you might have thought."

That morning at the pool he had thought he would never be able to stand him. *To heck with Roger.* After the way he had acted, Jacob was through with him.

But after a while, he was okay with Roger again, especially when his father seemed reluctant to reinstate the visits to the pool. "Besides, my dad doesn't like him."

But that other morning, his father had shown no sign of not liking Roger. To the contrary, Jacob recalls how effusively he sang his praises and patted him on the back the way you do when you want to flatter somebody.

"That doesn't really matter, Little Pup. What matters is that your mother likes him."

But that day, his mother had hardly spoken with Roger at all. She had just glanced over at him occasionally, as if there were some unspoken agreement between them, or else a problem that might explode all of the sudden.

It had been brutally hot that day. The sky had turned gray

without warning and the guests were grumbling about where the sun had gone. There were a lot of people milling around the pool, deck chairs filled with tanned figures, ice melting in glasses, and wet footprints on the deck and the lawn.

Trudi, the German girl, was playing with him. They had climbed the apple tree two or three times. "Where did you learn to climb like that, Jacob?" But Trudi's voice was drowned out by the din coming from the grown-ups. Roger was pouring martinis, serving hors d'oeuvres, and laughing a lot in the strident, brusque way he had, as if he were coughing or choking.

No. His laugh did not sound nice, but Jacob knew that thanks to that laugh, he and his parents had the chance to swim in a big, clean, and much coveted pool.

"Roger is really weird."

Uncle Eduardo smiles enigmatically, replaces the palette knife and grabs a brush.

"What do you mean?"

Jacob shrugs, looks at the ceiling and makes a disgusted face. "He was mean to me once."

His blood still runs cold whenever he thinks about it. It all started when he had absentmindedly put a little stick he found on the floor into his mouth. Trudi, the German girl, had jumped down out of the tree and yelled, "Since when do you suck on matches?"

Jacob immediately recalled Rosario's warnings: "Matches are poisonous. You should never put them in your mouth." He began to feel the effects of the poison at once. Everything around him started spinning. The pool looked blurry and the voices floating around it sounded as if they were coming from far away, like in a dream. "I'm going to die," he had screamed. "I'm dying, Trudi. I'm dying . . ."

Death was plastered on his face, as if he had donned a cold hard mask. There was no getting around it: life was flowing from his body. "Tell my mother. Tell her I'm dying." But Trudi had not moved an inch. She just stood there staring at him fearfully, as if she were responsible for Jacob's death. "Please, run and tell her. Tell her I swallowed a poison match." And seeing that Trudi did not react, he started yelling like a maniac: "I've been poisoned, Mommy, I've been poisoned . . ."

His mother had rushed over to him frightened. "What are you yelling about?"

"He swallowed a match head and he thinks he's going to die," explained Trudi. Jacob had just nodded wordlessly, unable to make a sound.

"Let's see it. Give me the match stick." She had examined it carefully, brought it to her nose and sniffed it and then tossed it carelessly on the ground. "You're out of your mind, Son. Since when do people die of something as ridiculous as that?"

Even so, Jacob still felt death taking over his body. "Help me, Mom. Help me." Suddenly he was surrounded by faces, their expressions ranging from skeptical to amused. They seemed to be making fun of him instead of helping him. "What is going on with the child?"

And his mother had responded, "Nothing. It's all nonsense."

Jacob was sweating. *This is probably how you sweat when you die*, he was thinking. It was a clammy sweat plastered to his forehead, and it made him notice how dry his mouth was. But no one seemed to care. Not even his mother.

"You're getting stranger every day, Jacob. You're much too old for these kinds of hysterics."

It struck him as cruel that his mother would say that, especially in front of all those people. Even though he wasn't exactly sure what the word "hysterics" meant, he knew very well that it was only used for people who acted out and tried to draw attention to themselves.

But the cruelest thing of all was her comment to Roger: "Where did I get such an hysterical child?" And Roger's reply, "You shouldn't coddle him so much—" followed by the weird laugh that was more like a cough . . .

"He made fun of me when I was dying."

Eduardo Santillana put down the paintbrush and crossed his arms across his chest.

"I can't believe it. Did he really do that?"

Jacob nods, his frown deepening.

"Were you sick?"

"I swallowed a match head."

But the grown-ups had all said no, the match head was long gone when Jacob had put the stick in his mouth. "Look, kid, can't you see it's an old match?"

Even his father made a joke of it. "He's just trying to get attention, that's all." But since his father always said things like that, Jacob did not pay much attention to it. In the end his father could say whatever he felt like. But Roger . . .

Jacob had continued to cling desperately to his mother's legs. "Save me, Mommy. I don't want to die. Not yet." It was a horrible death. It had started in his legs and risen up through his stomach and gotten stuck in his throat. But not a single one of the grown-ups made a move to rescue him. No one tried to bring him back to life. All they could say was, "Come on Jacob, that's enough sobbing for now."

And suddenly his father had repeated the very mean word he reserved for cowards: "You're just a faggot. A total faggot . . ."

Jacob had taken off running towards the apple tree to lean against its trunk and die alone. Meanwhile, Roger was doling out advice: "Just leave him. Better to let him cry it out. He'll soon realize that nothing really happened."

"Well I'm not positive, but I thought I was going to die."

"And what did your mother do?"

She had followed him to the apple tree and taken off his glasses to keep them from getting fogged up. "Don't be such a goose, Jacob." She had tried to hug him but Jacob—his humiliation at her indifference disguised as anger—had pushed her away. And that was when a furious Roger had taken him by the shoulders and shaken him, saying he'd had enough of his games and would he please do them all the favor of treating his mother with a little more consideration.

"She got there too late."

"What do you mean? You're still alive."

Jacob does not know how to explain why his mother was too late. He just knows that is how it was. And even though he did not die, he was acutely aware of the delay. The fact was, dead or alive, his mother had reacted too late, when Jacob no longer needed her. And to top it off, Roger had taken it upon himself to shake him.

It occurred to him then that, one day, Roger might end up becoming his enemy. The worst kind of enemy. Especially when he kept telling Jacob that he should stop being so spoiled, should think about others. After all, he wasn't the only child on earth and he certainly wasn't the only one who had feelings. And his mother, uncomfortable and anxious, kept shooting him looks as if to tell him to be quiet.

"So what if I'm alive. Mom got there too late." And he turns his gaze to the sea. It is like a tin sheet, dry and sterile.

"You must have your reasons for saying so."

"Roger didn't want her to take care of me and she obeyed him."

"And what did you do?"

"I don't know. I forget."

Eduardo Santillana lays the brushes on the table and tells Jacob to rest. Perhaps he has understood that the paper saber suddenly seems very heavy to Jacob, as if it were made of lead, and his legs have gone numb from galloping for so long on Clavileño's back.

"Do you want to see the painting?"

He prefers to look at the sea. A sea that looks as if it could be the inside of the lid of a cookie tin.

"You shouldn't be surprised that your mother did what Roger said."

"Why?"

Eduardo Santillana hesitates. He looks at the painting, then at the boy, and then at the owl, and he grabs his walking stick and begins to hit it against his leg.

"Well, I'm going tell you. You're going to find out sooner or later anyway."

Down below, a solitary boat is floating. Its oars are drawn in and an underwater fisherman is clinging to the bow.

"The truth is, I should have told you before, when you first came to Can Boig. But, the devil take it, it isn't easy."

Jacob does not ask. He waits. He leaves it to his uncle to explain. There are moments in life that seem to happen in slow motion: inevitable flashes of intuition that suddenly take off of their own volition.

"Your mother has married Roger."

Below them, the boat has receded into the distance and is lost from view. The fisherman is going to be hard pressed to track it down again.

"There," says his uncle. "I've told you."

But the statement strikes Jacob as hollow, like a lie or a whip cracked in the air. He does not feel it in his guts yet. Probably it is just something that was said for the heck of it and has nothing to do with reality. Still totally composed, he turns towards his uncle: "She can't," he replied. "She can't marry Roger, because she's already married to my dad."

His uncle takes a deep breath and sucks in his lips so forcefully that his beard and his mustache merge into one and his mouth seems to vanish.

"Their divorce came through a short time ago."

"Why didn't they tell me?"

He had the right to know. He had the right to an explanation. In the end, he was in this world because of them.

"They wanted me to tell you, Little Pup. They sent me a letter."

He is probably dreaming. Probably what is happening now is a nightmare, like the big-headed monster or the pillar of salt.

"They could have waited until I got back," Jacob stammered.

But even to him the words smacked of fantasy or blatant foolishness or shattered illusions.

"No," insisted his uncle. "They couldn't wait. Your mother is expecting a baby with Roger, so they had to get married quickly."

It is like a blow to the head, or as if he actually had swallowed the poison from a match head. In a daze, he turns back towards the picture window. His vision clouds over and the memory solidifies. So Roger is, in fact, the enemy. Jacob is not the only child on earth. There is the "other one." The other one that Jacob could not see that morning by the pool. That is why his father had called her a traitor. And yet everything had been going along normally until the wicked witch Hindrance had given them a potion that had cast a spell on them.

"Can you hear me, Jacob?"

The strange thing is that the earth is not shaking, the sea is not choppy and the room is not getting dark. Everything is exactly the same. Everything is suspended on his uncle's "Can you hear me Jacob."

Disjointed, fragmented images leap across Jacob's mind, anxious to piece themselves together into sturdy arrows capable of shooting down all his dreams. That is why he continues to shield himself so the "Can you hear me, Jacob" never comes true.

"It's a lie," he whispers. "It's all one big fat lie." He needs it to be. He needs it so that the scream of pain rising in his chest does not escape his lips. "I don't believe you."

And Eduardo Santillana does not contradict him. He simply mutters his disapproval. Bad words even Jacob knows you are not supposed to say because when his father says them, his mother gets mad.

"... all alike. Women are all alike ..." One after another, he qualifies them as fickle, incomprehensible, gossips and whores.

"... Any one of them can be what I call a 'tarterita,' which is nothing but a putrid combination of a tart and a señorita ..." It was as if he were talking to himself. As if a little boy were not there listening to every word he said. "... I've always said so. Why do you think I never married? That's why. Because you have to steer clear of women. You have to find a way to get along without them."

"I don't believe you. Mommy's different. Mommy. . . ." Even as he says it, Jacob's chin begins to tremble and he is unable to finish his sentence.

Uncle Eduardo falls silent. He was probably not counting on the child's sobs. He is crying noiselessly and his eyes are welling up with tears. They are the kind of sobs that sometimes leave you shaking and unable to get your breath.

"Come on, Little Pup."

But it is too late to staunch the flow. Stuttering, Jacob tries once again to talk to his uncle. "Wh . . . Why did you ss . . . say those th . . . things about Mommy?"

His uncle just looks at him, grimacing. He swallows and clears his throat once again. "Forgive me, Jacob. I've been a brute. I'd give anything to be able to just take them back."

And for the first time, Jacob thinks maybe Rosario was right when she said his uncle had been born without a guardian angel and was therefore a public danger.

"So . . . it isn't true." He is still clinging to the belief that his uncle might have been lying. Still hopes he'll take it all back.

Uncle Eduardo looks extremely uncomfortable. He probably has no idea how to back out of so many lies. He is looking around nervously and biting his lips, and he keeps banging the stick against his leg.

"Look, Jacob . . ." But he does not go on. He just stops there, after the "Look, Jacob." And once again he is muttering all sorts of unintelligible words.

". . . it's useless to try to whitewash so many lies. The best thing to do is face facts and move on."

He is talking to the air, avoiding Jacob's gaze. He probably cannot bear to contemplate the searching expression behind the fogged up glasses.

"I don't understand you."

Eduardo Santillana goes to him, takes off his glasses and folds him into his embrace. "Try to. Make an effort, Little Pup. What the hell am I going to do if you don't understand me?"

He sounds discouraged, as if all his strength had suddenly drained out of him. It is strange to see this uncle Eduardo, so defeated and downcast.

"You have to try to get used to the truth. Things are what they are. You can't fight them. Your mother loves Roger and she has married him."

A yawning silence fills the studio. It is even more sinister than the silence in the Pirates' Cave, where at least there were echoes. But this silence contains nothing but emptiness and pain. A stabbing pain that Jacob finds almost unbearable.

"And what about me? What am I going to do?" He asks it impetuously, violently, as if he is throwing in his uncle's face all of the instability he already senses. After all, he is somebody. A being with his own needs, and demands and hopes.

Uncle Eduardo presses Jacob's head tightly to his chest. "The same as you've been doing up to now: just live."

But the child rebels. Living is more than breathing and eating and getting dressed. Living cannot be so easy when everything is surrounded by death. He pulls abruptly away from his uncle, strides over to the window and yells, "No. I don't want to. How can I live without my mom?"

"You won't be living without her, Little Pup. I can promise you that."

Jacob's sobs grow louder and his chest is a runaway horse that cannot be reined in.

"You said she doesn't love me any more . . ."

"That's not what I said, Pup."

"Well, if she loves Roger, she can't love me."

In vain his uncle tries to explain that there are many kinds of love and he'll understand when he's older. But Jacob is not listening. All he knows is that his mother does not love him, the day is gray and the solitary boat in the bay has gotten away from its fisherman . . . and that his pain is much more than just pain: it is anger, hate, and fury. Suddenly, he grabs the paper saber and rips it to shreds, before turning to the general's hat and pummeling it into an amorphous ball of French newsprint.

"I hate them. I hate them. They're bad. They're all witches and evil spirits. All of them are, and I'll never play with them again. Not ever."

Breathless, he shakes his hair wildly, stomps his feet, his fists high in the air, and throws the sofa cushions onto the floor. "I won't show them the treasure or give them anything. They don't deserve it. They're all evil."

The day wears on in various shades of gray, as if it were nighttime. And Jacob's voice is becoming increasingly gruff and low until he sounds almost like an adult. "I want them all to die. Roger, and Mommy and Daddy, and Grandmother . . ."

He does not calm down for a long time. It is hard to calm down when your whole body is a mass of rage. But his sobs gradually grow farther apart and his voice, though still faltering, begins to sound like the old Jacob again.

"Come on, Little Pup. Let's dry those tears." His uncle holds a tissue to his nose, brushes his hair back from his damp face and kisses him on the forehead. "You still have me, don't forget. I won't leave you." Below, in the bay, the underwater fisherman can be seen swimming along the surface towards his boat. "Not ever."

And he hurries to explain that when Jacob returns to Paris it will be autumn, but autumn is still a long way away and, between now and then, a lot of things can change. He tells him he is not the only child in that situation and, if he puts his mind to it, everything will fall into place.

"Besides, I'm going to visit you in Paris."

So peace begins to reenter Jacob Santillana, between promises and kisses and the caresses of a beard that is now damp with tears. And between silences too. Silences like a field that has been turned into a mud puddle, but will surely dry out if there are enough red suns and blue dawns.

As he calms down, something deep inside Jacob tells him that all is not lost. As long as his uncle loves him, life will not be unlivable and the injustices will be buffered.

"You have to accept things as they are," his uncle repeats.

. . . You have to get used to them, there's nothing for it. You have to accept being abandoned by your mother and the birth of the "other one," and Roger's presence . . .

"Here, put on your glasses, Little Pup."

Jacob suddenly recalls how much his mother hated seeing Jacob put on his glasses. She would say things like: "There's nothing more depressing than watching a child do that . . . It is like watching an old person . . . No one can truly be a child when they are putting on their glasses."

Maybe his mother was right. Maybe kids who wear glasses can never really be kids.

Jacob shudders, takes a deep, rasping breath, and squares his shoulders. "I hope they all die," he repeats scathingly. And slowly, ever so slowly, he puts on his glasses with the very adult-like gesture that so pained his mother.

10

Duke is there under the bower, sniffing the air with his dry nose. He looks lethargic and sad, as if he too had succumbed to the deadening mists that had closed in on Jacob as his uncle was explaining his parents' separation and the impending birth of his half brother.

"Are you sure you'll come to Paris?"

"I'm sure."

"You won't leave me alone?"

"Never."

Jacob tries hard to believe him. And he wants to forget. Once you have managed to forget, you probably don't suffer any more. Maybe the future is contingent on this type of forgetting.

The sun has come out all at once and his uncle says they should take advantage of it. "So let's hit the water."

Down in the boathouse, Jacob sees the bow of the *Teresa*. He had steered the boat himself, a week ago now, when they were returning from the Pirates' Cave. His uncle had placed the tiller in his hands. When you think about it, steering the boat is not all that difficult. And he no longer finds it hard to skip rocks on the water like flying saucers, or hunt butterflies, or find matching pairs of stones for when he and his uncle play shoe store.

"We have to take advantage of this sunshine," his uncle says. And he scoops Jacob up in his arms to carry him down the steps.

"I guess Ruan will be coming around soon. This morning I sent him a message that he should come."

"How did you do that?"

"Through a goldfinch, remember?"

No, Jacob had forgotten that goldfinches fly to Venus and that his uncle knew how to speak the language of the birds nesting in the tamarind trees along the esplanade. The only thing he can recall with clarity right now is what he has just learned about his parents and Roger. So despite his uncle's efforts to cheer him up, Jacob feels weary, low, and exceedingly sad.

His mood does not lighten even in the water. There are too many disparate memories revolving around in his head to shoo them away as he should. On top of that, he feels terrible about destroying the paper saber and general's hat that Rosario made for him.

"Don't worry, Little Pup. Dots knows how to make those things."

"But it won't have magical powers."

"Who says?"

But Jacob cannot seem to get excited about anything. Even the prospect of Ruan's visit leaves him cold. His uncle is probably trying to get him to believe it to get him out of his bad mood. Then he'll make some excuse and Ruan will just keep on being a dream that never comes true. And so the morning is spent neutrally, among suppositions, portents and promises, all of which were probably invented by the painter to cheer him up.

His uncle talks to him animatedly about Coco, the skinny girl who wears Indian cotton tunics, and Paul, the ever-dozing Adonis who sometimes dreams out loud, and Lori, his diving buddy.

"You have to see her in the water, Jacob. She reminds you of a siren."

And when Jacob asks what "sirens" are, his uncle explains that they are hybrid creatures, half fish and half woman. In the old days, they would catch ships in the spell of their singing and cause them to run aground.

"They don't sing any more. They just dive. And they don't destroy ships either."

His uncle does not stop talking. He is probably trying to distract Jacob. He definitely wants him to go back to being the boy who explored the Pirates' Cave or accompanied him to the Garota bar to play with his friends. And then he asks Jacob what he thinks of Fabian.

"The sculptor?" But Jacob does not know how to define Fabian. He finds it strange the way the man wears white tunics, and moves in such an exaggerated way and explodes at the slightest disagreement. "I don't know."

"He's quite a talent. Too bad he's such a . . ." Maybe he can't find the word he's looking for, because he's biting his lip.

"Grasshopper?" asks Jacob.

"That's it. A grasshopper."

The day remains calm and the sun bores through the mist until it has evaporated completely. The beach appears deserted and the water, smooth and quiet, reflects the image of Jacob and his uncle, sitting on the side of the boat, while Duke howls nervously, waiting for them to jump into the sea.

"Look at that, Jacob."

At the end of the beach, behind the bushes edging the mountain slopes, a blinding light suddenly appears. "Now do you believe me?"

It is like the lighthouse, except it is coming from behind the thick foliage: a beam so bright it causes the child to see stars when he looks straight at it.

"What is it?" His voice is trembling as he forms the question. And there is no longer any trace of sadness in his mood, just fear. A fear that makes him grab hold of his uncle nervously.

"I warned you, Jacob. It's our visitor from Venus."

Dots comes out on the terrace, her hands twisted in her apron, her eyes very wide, and a tense smile on her face.

"He's here, Maestro. He's come." And she remains there, leaning against the railing as if the whole scene were completely normal.

Something is approaching from behind the glare of the beams: a semblance of a man, which is not fully realized, but rather a latent promise of one. It is a living being of some sort and it is clearly determined to advance in their direction.

"There is Ruan, Little Pup."

It is an incredible being wearing a diving suit with two inordinately long antennas.

"Ruan . . . ," breathes Jacob. "Ruan. . . ." He cannot quite believe what he is seeing and he is still consumed by terror.

His uncle is trying to calm him down, telling him not to be afraid. "Ruan's mission is one of peace."

Jacob remembers his uncle telling him that extraterrestrials have big heads and small bodies. And even though Ruan bears no resemblance to the child who had hydrocephalous, seeing him there—so stunted and with such a huge head—he is seriously considering the possibility that maybe the monster in his dream is one of them too.

Duke is barking wildly, but his uncle orders him to stop. "Anyone would think you'd never seen him before, Duke."

And hearing his firm command, Duke quiets down immediately. Then, tale wagging, he approaches the newcomer, licks his feet and whines submissively, as if ashamed at his own behavior.

"We've been waiting for you, Ruan."

The extraterrestrial nods wordlessly. Then he gestures towards Jacob, his movements slow, but unmistakable.

"Tell him to say something," says the child.

Ruan does not need to be asked twice. He begins to speak right away. He has a strange voice, deep and sonorous, as if he were speaking through a microphone, and his words are clipped and almost unintelligible.

"Can you understand him?" asks his uncle.

"No."

"He is saying you are a good boy, and you shouldn't be sad."

Jacob gulps down saliva, coughs and hurries to explain that he is not sad anymore and his uncle should tell Ruan so.

"Did you hear that, Ruan? Jacob is not sad anymore."

Ruan nods again and launches several prolonged noises into the air that could be laughter.

"He says that if you are able to recover your happiness, he'll take you with him to his planet some day."

"Alone?"

"Or with someone else. Whatever you like."

Jacob smiles. He does not want Ruan to think he is a sad boy.

"With you. I want to go to his planet with you."

"So now you know, Ruan. Jacob would like me to go with him."

Ruan continues to talk. It is a very strange language. Jacob has never heard anything like it before. It does not resemble any of the languages he is familiar with. But he can tell that everything he is saying is nice and promising.

"He's explaining that he went to visit the goldfinches along the esplanade this morning . . ." The argument is persuasive. Ruan is essentially corroborating everything his uncle shared with him this morning in his studio. ". . . and when he realized you were here, he decided to pay you a visit."

"How did he get here?"

"In his flying saucer. He's probably left it up on the road."

Sometimes Ruan's voice is interrupted by a cough and Jacob thinks it sounds very much like Quasimodo's cough. "Where is Quasimodo?"

"How do I know! He's probably washing the cars in the garage." His uncle does not seem overly concerned by Quasimodo's absence. He says Quasimodo and the extraterrestrial do not get along very well. In fact, they have actually argued on several occasions.

"About what?"

"Because Quasimodo gets in a foul mood and calls him fat-head. Extraterrestrials are very sensitive, did you know that, Little Pup?"

Ruan's words are gradually beginning to make sense. Maybe it is his tone, or the familiarity of some of the syllables, but if he really pays attention, Jacob finds he can understand parts of what he is saying.

Ruan is making connections, creating images, and acting out scenes. The flying saucer has, in fact, been left behind on the road, at the fork that leads to the lighthouse. He also says he cannot stay on the beach long, because his vehicle might be blocking the lighthouse keeper's way.

Jacob and his uncle move closer to him. Ruan extends his arm and shows them what he is holding in his hand. He explains to the uncle that he has brought something with him from Venus as a gift for Jacob. It is a stone. A strange material never seen before on earth. It is very valuable and apparently possesses magical powers.

"You are to keep it always, and use it only when you need it," his uncle explains.

Jacob does not dare touch Ruan's hand: it is of an odd, unexpected shape. It has no fingers and is shaped more like a fish's fin.

"Are you happy, Jacob?"

The boy just nods, too overwhelmed to speak. He thinks again what a shame it is that Quasimodo is not there to witness the scene. Suddenly, Jacob requires witnesses, ears that hear and eyes that see.

"Why don't you take a picture of him?"

"Don't worry. I'll draw him."

But Jacob is not satisfied with that solution. Drawings can be made up. Everyone knows uncle Eduardo has a huge imagination. What he needs is a good photograph that will amaze Pierre, and shut up his grandmother Katherine when she says there is no such thing as extraterrestrials.

"Go ahead and take the stone, Jacob."

"Are you sure it doesn't burn?"

Up close, Ruan's eyes are like crystals. He does not even have eyelashes and naturally he cannot blink. He does not have a nose either. He does have a huge mouth though. It has no lips and does not move, but it talks and grunts and sometimes it coughs just like Quasimodo. And it has a funny smell, like burning rubber, like something infrahuman.

"Do you like it?"

It is a marble-like stone, with bright reddish tones that radiate heat when they come in contact with his skin. Ruan explains that it is similar to all the stones on Venus. His flying saucer is made out of the powder from those stones.

"Ask him if he's going to come back."

His uncle replies that yes, of course he is. "He says he'll be here when you least expect him."

His confidence restored, Jacob becomes chatty. "I wouldn't ever call you fathead like Quasimodo. I promise . . ." But Ruan is leaving. He is retreating behind the bushes lining the foot of the cliff. ". . . and besides, I'm not afraid of you any more . . ." he yells after him.

Satisfied, Ruan raises one hand in a wave.

"Let's go, Little Pup. We have to turn our backs. Extraterrestrials don't like it when people watch them as they return to their flying saucers.

Dots is applauding from the terrace. There is no reason for her to applaud. After all, what she just saw was not a play, or a movie, or a TV show. But Dots and Quasimodo always react in unusual ways and you aren't supposed to pay too much attention to them.

"Goodbye, Ruan," he yells as he runs towards the water. His uncle takes off his glasses and advises him to leave the stone there beside them. Then, together, they jump into the sea.

"Let's go, Jacob. Swim with me." They splash each other, laughing, and dive under. And Dots' laughter smacks into them every time they lift their heads out of the water.

"Are you happy, Jacob?"

Jacob, panting, says yes, he is very happy. He is probably remembering the stone he has left next to his glasses, and the light coming from the grove of bushes, and Ruan's promise to take him to the planet Venus some day.

"I'm going to keep it in my shoe box."

"What are you going to keep?"

"The stone."

When they emerge from the water, Dots is no longer leaning against the railing. Only Quasimodo is visible, hunkering, lumbering and weighed down with fish.

"Want to see how I clean them?"

Jacob rushes to him, breathless, his hair dripping down his cheeks, and his eyes very wide without his glasses. "You know who came, Quasimodo?"

But Quasimodo pays no attention to the excited child. "Yeah. Dots told me."

"It's too bad you didn't see him."

Quasimodo coughs and shakes his head. "I haven't missed a

thing. I don't like fatheads." And he ambles over to the rock and squats down to clean the fish.

"Just ignore him, Jacob. Quasimodo is a party pooper," his uncle says.

A glimmer of promise is opening up along the beach. The gloomy speculation has disappeared, along with the suspicions, and sorrows, and painful memories. It even smells different since Ruan appeared to carry away the child's bitterness. There is no more hate left in Jacob. He no longer says "I hope they die," and rage does not stab at his chest when he thinks about the "other one."

"Have you ever been to Venus?"

"No, I've only been on the moon. But there aren't any extraterrestrials there."

"Will you go with me when I go?"

"Of course."

"And can we swim together in the sea on Venus?"

"Why not?"

"And will we discover some caves?"

"Naturally. Caves a hundred times more wonderful than the ones here on earth."

They are chatting as before, breathing in sun along with air and illusions, dreaming about stars at once remote and close at hand. They have reverted to the old Jacob Santillana talking animatedly with his uncle, leaving behind the ugly ashes that had momentarily threatened to submerse them in grime.

"I was sure that today was going to be a happy day."

"How did you know that?"

"It was a premonition. When I wake up, something tells me what it is going to be like. You can always predict happiness and sadness."

"Teach me how to predict them."

"It all comes down to looking around you. If the objects seem three dimensional, that's good. On the other hand, if they seem flat . . ."

Eduardo Santillana contemplates him curiously and then emits a deep sigh. "And then there's the sea. The sea will never deceive you. The sea is the great contact with what is to come . . . God help you if the sea is ashen."

"Today it was."

"No. Today the sea was a tin sheet. When the sea is a tin sheet, that's good."

94

Jacob's shivers when he recalls the fisherman swimming desperately to catch up with his boat. The image is so real that when he exhales, he can still feel a sob lingering deep inside his chest. "I want to be like you. Always."

"You are. I already told you that, Little Pup."

"But you don't have a grandmother, or stupid parents, or. . . ."

"But I do have a nephew named Jacob. Or have you forgotten that?"

Jacob thinks for a moment. Something his uncle has said does not quite fit. "But I don't," he replies. And he remains silent, staring at the floor, trying to figure out a way that he could have a nephew with his same name.

II

It had remained sunny all afternoon and was still warm at dusk. Later that evening, though, the weather had turned muggy, as if to resurrect the morning's unpleasantness.

There was so much excitement in the air. That afternoon, the stuffed owl in the studio had seemed to be staring at Jacob, as if he were trying to tell him something, and when the first star appeared in the sky, his uncle had pointed to it with his stick: "Take a good look at it, Jacob. It's the planet Venus."

It was wonderful to gaze at it from the studio. It glowed as no other star possibly could and it twinkled, just as if it were winking at Jacob. "Ruan ought to be back there by now," his uncle had commented.

"In his house?"

Eduardo Santillana had not skipped a beat. "Of course. Ruan has a home just like anybody else."

It was comforting to know he had friends out there, beyond the Earth. Especially a friend from outer space who had a deep, choppy voice and a special flying saucer made of reddish powder, just like the stone he had given Jacob.

Quasimodo had rushed them through dinner. His uncle had advised him to go to bed early. "It's been a long and emotional day, Little Pup. You need your rest."

Yet tired as he is, Jacob simply cannot sleep. Insomnia has set in just as it used to when he would dream about the big-headed monster, or when grandmother Katherine advised him not to look behind him because he might turn into a pillar of salt.

Ambiguous, overlapping images parade relentlessly through the child's head, jarring him awake: waves of vibrations and echoes, and flashes of daring feats and vindications and fears.

He can see himself discovering the treasure, or glimpsing the scarecrow from the road, or reaching out his hand to Ruan to take the gift being proffered. Now he is swimming alongside his uncle, scanning the seabed and being tickled by the algae. He is finding sea urchins and poisonous tomatoes. Or he is climbing the bluffs barefoot, or clambering up the tree up by the lighthouse, or steering the *Teresa*, or sitting next to his uncle sketching Quasimodo's stunted, deformed silhouette among the cliff rocks.

They are wisps of memories that never quite come into focus or evaporate completely. Traces of tangled evocations conspire to keep him awake. So he tosses and turns in his bed. The sheet slips off and the heat assails his pores as intensely as if he were sunbathing on the beach.

And then, like a blast of foul wind: the news. The lousy, rotten news. And it has not gone away despite all of the fun new things that happened during the day. So he cannot sleep. He cannot stop thinking. And he is sinking deeper and deeper into a morass of memories and grating images.

His eyelids do feel heavy though, and he thinks he may have dropped off to sleep for a few instants. But he wakes up right away. It is as if someone has shaken his shoulder or called out his name.

"Is that you, Dots?"

No one answers. He feels around for his glasses and turns on the light. Dots' bed is empty and the sheets have not been disturbed. Dots is not in the room and it is still nighttime. And suddenly, he is consumed with fear. He is afraid he might be alone in the house.

A strong murmur of voices suddenly penetrates his thoughts. Disjointed, anarchical voices. They are coming from downstairs. Maybe from the beach, or else the living room.

The racket intensifies as he becomes increasingly aware of it. Without a second thought, he jumps out of bed and heads for the stairs. The worst part is having to cross the gallery and see all those stupid pictures of Teresa. Allow them to make the skin on the back of his neck crawl as he passes by them. It suddenly occurs to him that Teresa is more than a dead memory. She is also a wall full of staring eyes and a name on the boat's prow.

Hanging on to the railing and striving to keep his balance, Jacob descends the stairs in his bare feet. He walks very slowly, on tiptoe, so as not to make any noise.

The hall light is on, but no one is there. The voices are coming from the living room and the terrace. A cacophony of voices intermingled with the dense aroma of bitter herbs. It is strange to see so many cigarette butts on the ground and so many half-filled glasses on the mantels and table tops. The smell makes him dizzy. They must not be regular cigarettes. They are probably the ones Coco smokes, because she sometimes smells like it does now.

He tries to avoid being seen. He flattens himself against the living room door. A jumble of half-naked bodies are squirming about on the sofas and rugs. The bodies look as if they might have been taken out of his uncle's paintings: they are a mass of incomprehensible gyrations, undulating movements, and slender, tanned shapes, or moving shadows in the dimly lit room. They are like legless grasshoppers trying in vain to jump.

No one seems to have noticed him and the tangled mess before him leaves him dazed, as if he were watching a movie in slow motion or a pyrotechnic game without any fire. It is all indistinct, like the precursor to a scene, or the portent of a vision, or a half-finished painting.

So this is how grown-ups play, he thinks: dry, seemingly hypnotized bodies rub their skin against others that have definitely taken a dip in the sea, because they are dripping with water and leaving puddles on the floor. It looks like a fun game, but not as fun as the one his parents played before the wicked witch Hindrance came into their lives.

Jacob suddenly feels an acrid taste in his mouth. He cannot understand what Coco is doing. He has spied her in between two men and two women, down on the floor, straining and swaying and gasping, as if she had been taken over by a strange vertigo.

"Coco. . . ."

But the only response is a shriek, a muffled cry that trails off amid more gasps.

"What's wrong, Coco?"

Maybe she is not playing. Maybe she has swallowed a match head and is about to die.

"Why don't you answer me, Coco?"

He pictures himself now, alongside Roger's swimming pool begging for help. Maybe Coco is dying just like he was, and nobody realizes it.

Frightened, he runs out to the terrace to find his uncle. Eduardo Santillana is probably down on the beach, swimming in the moonlight as some of the others are doing.

But a carpet of bodies is making it hard to get through and the bitter smell is making him dizzy. Something is affecting him. Something he cannot figure out. It is as if he is inside a dark tunnel and cannot see his way out. He is finding it hard to breathe. Just like that other time. And the child with the big head is back. He is right there in front of him, staring at him unseeingly. It could be a dream. Surely he is still in bed and nothing he is seeing is real.

"Help me."

The door to the terrace is blocked by Paul's body. The self-centered grasshopper with the baleful, glassy eyes, who sometimes snores when he is awake.

"Let me by."

But Paul does not answer. He just grunts and sways and stares at the ceiling as if his eyes were made of marbles.

"Move, Paul. I want to go out."

Paul does not budge. He is like a stick figure. *Sometimes Paul dreams when he is awake, know what I mean, Little Pup?*

He jumps over the motionless form, trying hard not to step on him. Then he sees Duke. He is under the magnolia, sound asleep with his paws in the air.

"Duke."

The animal wakes, sniffs at him, and licks his feet. And all at once, the fresh night air dispels the child's fears.

Duke follows him idly to the top of the stairs. From up there, the beach looks like an anthill swarming with naked bodies, glowing pale in the moonlight. A singular combat of gestures and cries overtakes the rocks and the lapping water. Fascinated, Jacob watches the game with the same enthusiasm as if he were observing a new landscape, detached from it all, even from his own life.

"Eduardo, look who's here," a voice calls.

And everything grinds to a halt.

"Little Pup. . . ."

Diffuse shreds of comments waft upward. Disjointed, even jubilant remarks dance before the child.

"What are you doing there, Little Pup?"

The phrase is repeated over and over, like gunfire, like waves.

His uncle draws near. He climbs the stairs. His almost naked body is damp and glistening in the whitish glow.

"Where did you come from, Jacob?" He is not angry, but he has a slightly bemused look on his face.

Jacob does not reply. He wants to tell him about Coco, about how no one noticed she was dying. But without knowing why, he is afraid his uncle will react just as his father did the day he surprised him playing savage beasts with his mother.

"Don't be afraid, Jacob," says his uncle, smiling.

And Jacob's concern about Coco's predicament vanishes in an instant. She is gone from his mind.

"I want to play with you," he says firmly. "I don't want to go to bed."

Eduardo Santillana raises him high off the ground. "You heard him. Jacob wants to play with us."

The faces are all running together. They are a blur, a mass of looks and smiles and waves. Only Lori, the siren, who dives into the sea after strange plants—the kind that looked behind and got petrified—comes into focus. "It's his right. We all have the right to play."

Seeing her there in the moonlight in her phosphorescent bikini, Lori really does look like a siren. "Come on, Little Pup."

He likes Lori. Likes her more and more. He does not care if his uncle tells him she is half this and half that. To the contrary, maybe the reason he likes her so much is precisely because, according to his uncle, she is not easily definable.

"Who brought you here?" his uncle asks.

"Nobody."

"Where is Dots?"

"I don't know."

"You should have stayed in bed," he says, sounding almost irritated for a moment. But he quickly recovers. "That miscreant must still be in the kitchen, sleeping it off."

He gives the child a horseback ride into the living room. Since Paul's body is still blocking the doorway, he jumps over him, imitating a brisk trot. "Hold on tight, Jacob."

It is not the first time his uncle has given him a horseback ride to cheer him up. "Giddy-up, horsie. Giddy-up." He whinnies and snorts and ends up running smack into the kitchen door . . . He is prancing and cavorting about just like a real horse, and Jacob is laughing so hard the tears fall from his eyes. His uncle opens the kitchen door with one kick and enters the kitchen, still trotting.

And there is Dots, sitting at the table, her head in her hands.

"I thought so." But he does not berate her. An empty bottle is lying on the table. "The old sot. As soon as I turn my back, she hits the bottle. And she always does it just when I need her most."

He takes her by the hair and raises her head. Dots' eyes are closed and her mouth half open. A foul odor assails Jacob's nose.

"I told you, Pup. Sometimes she likes to bend the elbow. And there she is, totally soused." Then he yells for Quasimodo and orders him to see to his mother and put her to bed.

They return to the living room. There are no longer supine bodies everywhere you look. Lori has probably taken charge of clearing the room. A resuscitated and drowsy-looking Coco is there to greet them. She executes a couple of dance steps.

"She's such a show-off," his uncle comments. "She's absolutely clueless. One day she dressed up like a water sprite and announced she'd just come out of the sea. Everybody knows water sprites are river creatures."

But Coco does not even acknowledge the insult. She does not even seem to remember that she was dying just a very short time ago. She reaches out to Jacob, hugs him, and asks him whether he would like to take a puff of her cigarette.

"You have the right, Jacob. We all have the right . . ."

And when his uncle knocks her aside, she begins to cry. "The world is so screwed up," she repeats obsessively. "The world is pure shit. Absolute, pure, unadulterated crap."

"Don't pay any attention to her, Jacob. She has no idea what she's saying."

But Coco continues to protest. "In a world where death didn't exist, you'd be fighting to die, just like you fight to survive now."

"A brilliant discovery!"

Coco whines and smokes. She throws up her arms and tells Jacob his uncle is heartless. He makes no effort to understand her and that's why she is so messed up.

"Just ignore her. She's drunk."

"Like Dots?"

"No: this one doesn't drink. She smokes."

"Does tobacco make you drunk?"

"Sometimes."

But Coco is no longer beside them. She is sashaying about the room, her arms wafting in the air, imitating the ballerinas Jacob has sometimes seen on TV.

Below, on the beach, a simmering stew of naked forms is still riding the moonbeams. Some of them jump into the water and the sea sends up spurts of silver light.

His nephew still astride his back, Eduardo Santillana proposes a swim.

"Isn't it late?"

"It's hot out."

Jacob does not even take off his pajamas. And the laughter continues and the scent of magnolias intensifies.

"This is the best, Little Pup."

Each stroke creates tiny moons on the surface. Jacob has never seen anything so outrageous. He thinks about all the things he has to tell Pierre. He probably has never had the chance to swim like this, in the middle of the night, surrounded by people playing strange games, in the care of a man like his uncle Eduardo.

When they get out, his uncle takes off his wet pajamas. "You might catch cold." He instructs him to stretch out on the rocks. "They're warm, right?"

Someone is commenting that he looks like his uncle. "He's got your physique. Your shoulders, your thighs . . . your chest and your . . ."

It is Fabian, the sculptor, who likes to hang out in the Garota Bar wearing white tunics and gold ribbons in his hair.

". . . A real Cupid," he continues.

But Jacob has no idea who Cupid is and he is upset when his uncle shoos Fabian away, because now he cannot ask him.

"Go do your faggot routine with someone else, okay? Leave my nephew alone."

That Jacob understands. At least he knows the word exists. He's heard it too many times from his father to miss it. Probably Fabian is one of those beings his father detests. In that case, Jacob feels inclined to admire him.

He's tall and youthful, with an erect and supple build. From the back, he could pass for a woman. Fabian is not fazed by the faggot remark. To the contrary, he must have liked it because he laughs and has a self-satisfied look on his face.

"Don't be alarmed, maestro. I know the boundaries." And he holds out his glass to Eduardo for a refill.

"You've already got a barrelful of whiskey in you."

But Fabian protests. "So now you're going to be our great redeemer. As if we didn't know how you soak it up like a sponge."

"But I hold it better than you do. And besides, I don't assault people of my own gender."

"And what does that have to do with it? Tit for tat."

His uncle relents. "The last one. Understood?"

Fabian moves off. He stretches out languidly at the water's edge and allows the waves to lap at his feet. Then he chugs down the contents of the glass, amid burps and hiccups.

A hush falls over the beach. Someone has announced that the maestro is going to sing. Probably uncle Eduardo's friends admire him as much for his voice as for his paintings. With his guitar in hand, he is able to generate quite a bit of enthusiasm. So Jacob, now dry, sits down close beside him. He does not want anybody else to take his spot.

A few isolated couples, still entwined, are leaning up against the rocks to hear better. Others have raised their faces to the moon, as if they are tanning in its rays.

"Will you sing with me, Jacob?"

He is very sleepy now, but he says yes. Lori, the siren, holds out a glass to him. "Come on, Little Pup. Have a sip. You'll sing better."

His uncle laughs at Lori's gesture. He's never objected to his nephew having a good time.

An unexpected wave has just crashed onto the sand, and the duet begins: *Save your kisses for me. Bye bye, Baby bye, bye . . . don't cry, Baby, don't cry. . . .*

And all the eyes around them are no longer watching the moon. They are watching the two of them, spellbound and suddenly serious.

When the song is over, his uncle hugs him close, tickling him with his beard. "What do you think of my nephew?"

Eduardo's friends applaud. They tell him he did a fine job and request an encore.

Lori gives him a kiss. "You deserve it for being such a good singer." Then she announces that, from now on, he will be the group's mascot. And though Jacob does not know exactly what the word means, he can tell it is something very, very good.

"So now you know, Jacob. From now on, you're our mascot," echoes his uncle.

Jacob tries to smile but his lips suddenly feel rigid and refuse to obey him. The beach is spinning around. He does not know what is happening. All he knows is that he is very happy, and his uncle loves him, and his uncle's friends love him, and he will never forget this moment as long as he lives.

Filled with wellbeing, Jacob closes his eyes and settles into his uncle's lap. A strange fluttering sensation is creating whirlwinds in his head. The guitar is still playing and Eduardo Santillana's voice does not falter. Now his songs are full of Neptunes, of plaintive siren songs and devious nymphs, of terrible rage and promises never uttered.

And finally, just before dawn, Jacob succumbs to sleep.

12

He wakes up late. He can tell how late it is by the quality of the sounds. They are not the usual morning sounds, sporadic, hollow and reverberating. The ones Jacob is hearing now contain echoes of midday, like when he has been down on the beach for a long time and the morning is about to become afternoon. Without intervals of silence or the beating wings of early-rising seagulls.

From his bed, he hears the far-off groan of motorboats, nearly drowned out by the wind and the waves. If he listens hard enough, he can even hear the murmur of the far-off village, already well into its daytime routine.

All at once, Quasimodo's voice can be heard talking to his mother, most likely from the rock where he cleans the fish. Dots must be on the terrace, because her voice sounds close by.

Stepping out onto the balcony, he sees her by the magnolia tree, sweeping the floor with slow, bobbing motions, like a buoy. She is probably mad because she drank so much the night before. She definitely looks as if she is in a sour mood. She is talking about him, about Jacob. She is saying that he is much too young to be dragged into such debauchery, and it is absolutely absurd that his uncle has allowed him to swim in the moonlight, and he is making a big mistake by allowing the child to get mixed up with those disgusting pigs he calls friends.

"Orgies are not for children."

And Quasimodo is saying it is her fault. "You were supposed to have been there when he went to bed."

Dots defends herself. She says she had no way of guessing that Jacob was going to wake up unexpectedly. She'd left him snoring before, and he'd never had an inkling of the commotion that went on.

And she launches into a diatribe against Coco, against Paul, against Lori, and especially against Fabian . . . "That devil, with all his fancy fairy ways . . . They're nothing but a gang of godless, depraved animals, and homos to boot."

Quasimodo laughs. He laughs so hard he starts to choke. "Your problem is you're jealous." And he coughs again, with the cough that sounds so much like Ruan's. "You're not going to deny that you'd like to join in yourself."

But Dots defends herself. She says no. It is one thing to drink, and quite another to take drugs. "For your information, I've never taken any kind of drug in my life."

It is a long exchange, full of shady areas for Jacob, but he has now been alerted to what goes on at Can Boig every night.

Then they fall silent, because his uncle has appeared at the living room door. He says he has received a telegram that a certain Mauricio Belarmino will be arriving shortly.

"Will he be staying the night?"

His uncle says they should prepare the guest room just in case.

It has been a rainy morning and the rocks beyond the breakers look damp. Everything smells of earth and mud, like the puddles where the crickets breed.

"Who is Mauricio Belarmino?" calls Jacob from the balcony.

Seeing him there, his uncle says he should come downstairs. It is almost time for lunch.

In the living room, the damp aroma is gone. The whole house smells of magnolia and there is still a trace of the strange odor of bitter herbs from the night before.

"Who is Mauricio Belarmino?"

Eduardo Santillana looks at him with a grin and says he is an old friend. "He's a journalist. Do you know what a journalist is?"

Jacob knows very well what they are. They tended to show up in hordes when his uncle was least expecting them. Cameras in tow, they would spend the entire day asking questions: Did Eduardo Santillana live alone or with someone? How come he had never married? And, what was his opinion of Picasso, or Dali, or Miró? (apparently there was an endless list of famous painters who were not called Santillana). Was he in favor of abortion, and divorce, and the pill and homosexuality and nudity . . . ? All of these matters were nothing but gibberish to Jacob, but they came up incessantly in the interviews.

"Will he ask you the same old questions?"

His uncle's mouth twitches and he says no, Mauricio Belarmino is different. "And if he comes to Can Boig, it's so I can ask *him* questions."

Jacob is disconcerted by this answer. Something beyond his grasp is going on with his uncle this morning and he guesses it must be related to the impending visit.

"How do you know that?"

"I know him very well."

There is a certain edginess in the way he talks about the journalist's visit. It is almost as if he is dreading their meeting.

His uncle was never this touchy when it came to other journalists. Sometimes he even seemed to find them entertaining. He would air his opinions with the same abandon as when he was skipping rocks like flying saucers. And it was as if he intended for them to be distracted by the ripples they left in their wake. "It's my way of confusing them, know what I mean, Little Pup?"

Some of them would react: "But just now, you said . . ." Yet they never were exactly sure what the maestro had just said, so they would inevitably end up twisting the idea around until it worked to their advantage.

Jacob delighted in witnessing those exchanges, especially when his uncle would start to hand out candy, which would leave them openmouthed. "The trick is to turn your answer into another question. It's a skill, Little Pup. They get all flustered and stop acting so aggressive. They all have their Achilles heel and it is usually as big as a cathedral. There are no exceptions."

"What questions are you going to ask him?"

"None."

The magnolia leaves are shiny with dew. The leaves are clean and polished and, as they move, they seem to be made of plastic.

"So why is he coming?"

Eduardo Santillana taps the stick against his leg and repeats that Mauricio Belarmino is a friend of his and sometimes friends feel an enormous need to interfere in one's private life.

Jacob was very concerned about the matter of the Achilles heel. His uncle had explained to him that Achilles was immortal except for his heel, and as soon as his enemies found out about it, they had quickly finished him off. "How?" And Eduardo Santillana said they shot him with an arrow. "Sort of like what I do to the journalists, you know, Little Pup?"

They usually took photographs of him too: now with the walking stick, now with the dog, now with his nephew. There were journalists of all ages and from all over the world, but Eduardo Santillana never answered their questions in any language other than his own. Even though he spoke several languages, he did not feel like switching. "When they come to my country, they can speak my language," he would say.

Most of them liked to trot out the word *democracia*. How

would you define it, maestro? And the maestro would say it was just a word that began with D and, interestingly enough, ended with CIA, and the journalists were never quite sure whether he was in favor of democracy or against it. Then they would ask him about his politics and his views on the Communist Party of Spain and General Secretary Carrillo, and the upcoming elections and President Suárez . . . Uncle Eduardo usually responded that artists had no business getting into politics. As far as he was concerned, all those people jockeying for power could make their own bed and lie in it. His only ambition resided in his paintbrushes, and if Spain became too stifling, he would take his brushes and go elsewhere.

Then the journalists would start sermonizing. They would tell him being apolitical was a right-wing posture and being on the right was tantamount to being a traitor to the fatherland, because what the people needed was an egalitarian, Marxist-style socialism that would send the rigid, rotted, Francoist institutions straight to hell.

His uncle would let them go on and when they were finished, he would applaud and say they had done a very good job and if they kept on like that, they should probably form a brand new party of their own. Because in the end, Spain was the country of political parties and Spaniards loved having input from foreigners. He also assured them that he envied their capacity for enthusiasm and when they reached his age, their blood would probably simmer rather than boil, so they should make the most of it now. And when they asked him how old he was, Eduardo Santillana would invariably reply that he had just turned 2,000.

Indeed, most of the interviews ended in disaster. The journalists would get huffy and to retaliate, would often steer the conversation towards subjects guaranteed to touch a nerve. Some even dared to probe the subject of Teresa. Apparently, everybody knew that Teresa had left Eduardo Santillana before he had achieved international acclaim. "So what happened between you two?

Eduardo Santillana always kept his cool when they asked him that question. "She took a disliking to my dog," he would reply. "She put me between a rock and a hard place really. She said: It's either me or the dog. And I said, Well, the dog then . . ."

"Did you get a telegram?"

"It's right over there."

It is crumpled up at the base of the magnolia tree. Jacob does not dare touch it. It's enough just to see it there, already damp, the ink running on the page. He wonders now if his uncle will treat Mauricio Belarmino the same way he treats the other journalists who get on his nerves. Like the time he called Duke over and rubbed his hand along the dog's back and asked him to shake hands with the delightful gentlemen who write for foreign newspapers . . . because they have prodigious memories that require no refreshing. If they took notes it would be worse because then they would make even more mistakes . . ."

In any event, Jacob is not overly concerned about the visitor his uncle is expecting. He knew now that, from here on out, his uncle would never leave him—he had given his solemn promise—and whenever the moon came up, he, Jacob, would never be tired.

Dots could grouse all she wanted to. She could say it wasn't right for a child to have breakfast at lunch time and dinner at bed time. Because the painter had said, in front of everybody, "I don't want you to have any bad memories of your uncle, Little Pup. From now on, you go where I go."

Lori had seconded it. Jacob had been developing a real fondness for Lori for some time now. She was not anything like the sirens from before. The ones that drove the sailors mad. The siren that lived inside Lori was cheerful and sincere, and went out of her way to make his uncle happy. "Do you like to play with us, Little Pup?"

Sometimes she took him to her house. She had shown him her collection of Spanish crafts and she let him play with them while she and his uncle went upstairs to talk. She even told him she would leave them to him when she died. "So you'll remember Lori the siren, Little Pup." And once Jacob asked her if she could hurry up and die, because he really liked everything in her house. But then he felt badly about it and said no, she should keep on being alive. And in reward, Lori bestowed a kiss on his forehead and say that come what may, Jacob would always be their mascot.

"Is he coming soon?"

"He should be here in about an hour." He is frowning as he says it. He is staring out at the sea and the damp railing leaves marks on his hands. "He probably got caught in the rain. He's had to travel a long way," he adds.

It is not unusual for people Jacob does not know to visit from far away. People who speak all different languages and do not seem to affect the calm and pleasant routine of Can Boig. Most of them are buyers. People who admire Santillana the painter and want to visit his studio.

Uncle Eduardo usually tried to avoid them. He said he could not sell anything without speaking to Mr. Raimundo. Apparently, Mr. Raimundo was a very important man. At least, he was the only one who could tell his uncle what to do. He determined the price of each painting after researching the market in Paris, New York and London.

But Mr. Raimundo had not returned and the painter tried to steer clear of his own buyers to avoid any discussion. "Tell them I'm not here. Tell them I'm not in Spain at the moment," he would order Quasimodo.

Sometimes, if the visitors became very irate, saying it was not right that they should have come all the way across the ocean only to have to go back without having visited the painter's house, his uncle would grab Jacob and hide with him in the chamber of secrets. "Show them the studio," he'd tell Quasimodo. "Just tell me when they're gone."

He always said that meeting new people made him nervous and he hated making inane conversation with a bunch of gawking idiots. "Better the devil you know . . ." he would add. And they would hole up together while the visitors explored the house at their leisure, until Quasimodo came to tell them that everyone was gone and they could come out now.

It was fun to be alone in the chamber of secrets with uncle Eduardo. There was always something new to discover. But what Jacob liked best of all was to wrap his arms around his uncle's neck while the visitors were in the studio. He would press his forehead into his beard to keep his voice from carrying. It was like playing hide-and-seek from the grown-ups. "Don't give us away, Jacob. Hold your breath." And the two would remain like that, intertwined, frozen, Jacob's breathing ragged, and their hearts beating as one.

In those moments, his uncle would reveal to him the true secrets of the sea. It was fascinating to hear his murmured stories. Clearly, Eduardo Santillana loved to talk about the sea: its reactions, its cruelties, its bounty. How it would get rough whenever the sirens seductively combed out their tresses and sang their famous toxic melodies. How Ulysses had to tie himself to the mast of this ship to avoid the trap that Leucosia, Ligeia and Parthenope had laid for him. And how he had to cover the ears of his men too keep them from falling under the spell of the daughters of Achelous. "When it comes down to it, sirens are just like other women, which is why they're so dangerous."

And Jacob would hasten to assure him that he would not have to tie himself to any mast to keep from falling—"Because when I grab onto a tree, nobody can make me let go, not sirens, not anybody, did you know that Uncle Eduardo?" So if he were ever in a position of having to defend himself against one of them, all he would have to do would be to climb up a pole and that would be that.

But his uncle was adamant that he should never let down his guard. "Women have their wiles and their tricks," he said, and he re-iterated the part about how any one of them can be a "tarterita."

It was clear that uncle Eduardo did not like women. He was constantly advising Jacob to be on his guard against them when he grew up. They were all dangerous, harmful, spiteful. . . .

"Even Lori and Coco?" Jacob had asked. And that was when his uncle explained that neither Lori nor Coco was quite like other women. It was very difficult to pin them down exactly. "They're even more hybrids than the sirens, you know, Little Pup? Half this, half that," he had explained, moving his right hand from side to side as if his wrist had been dislocated. "They're mimetic creatures like the walking stick you found that afternoon, but they are not totally women."

Jacob did not find this assessment fair, at least when it came to Lori. Maybe it was true of Coco, but Lori . . . No one could deny that she had the voice of a woman and she definitely moved like a woman. And he had even caught her more than once, looking at his uncle the way his mother looked at Roger.

His uncle went on to say that sometimes the sea was female and sometimes it was male. "You'll understand some day, Little Pup." And he explained that when the sea fumed with rage and hurled foaming waves against the rock formations, there was no ques-tion that it was female. But when the wind licked at the surface to smooth its waters, and the rocks dried without difficulty, then the sea was male again. Basically, the Mediterranean Sea was fickle, very capricious and erratic. "That's why you have to see it as more female than male."

With a sudden stab of fear, Jacob had asked, "But you're not go-ing to change, right Uncle?" And his uncle had replied that he'd never been a sea.

A brusque sound that is not coming from the sea begins to poke at the gray calm. "He has arrived," says uncle Eduardo.

Quasimodo is moving lethargically in the direction of the

house clutching the cleaned fish. "Step to it, Quasimodo. Let's get a move on."

But having said that, his uncle does not move. He is gazing at the magnolia tree, the puddle at its base, the white lounge chairs, which have been put away to protect them from the rain. Then he moves towards the railing.

"We have to go out and greet him," he mutters, as if to himself. Yet he makes no move to do so. He just stands there, leaning against the railing, his back to the door, rhythmically striking the walking stick against his leg.

And without knowing why, Jacob recalls the day they had shut themselves into the chamber of secrets and his uncle had begun to describe a sick, pockmarked sea that resembled tiny white horses atop the thick, ash-colored water. It was an infected pus-filled sea. It could be just one big boil created by the atavistic outbursts of history. And he added that this might be because the sea was very old and once in a while it rebelled against its own advanced age. So much trash has accumulated inside it, that if it doesn't toss it all out, it will rot.

"When you said the sea could be sick, is that like today?"

His uncle does not reply. He probably has not even heard him. Distracted, he seems focused solely on what is happening below, in front of the house. First Duke's barking is heard, followed by the booming voice of the newcomer.

"Barking at me—at *me*..." Then hurried, firm steps can be heard and, abruptly, the journalist's sizable frame appears on the threshold.

"So there you are, you scoundrel." He moves towards the terrace, arms outstretched, his stomach bulging with enthusiasm.

His uncle smiles, tosses the walking stick on the table, and the two men embrace, striking each other over and over on the back.

"A sight for sore eyes, maestro."

The reunion fills the terrace with warm words and lively expressions. "So here's the famous..." And "Who would take it into his head to live in the middle of nowhere..."

Eduardo Santillana seems happy. He is no longer regarding the sea as if it were full of pus. The arrival of Mauricio Belarmino has caused his frown to disappear and the terrace seems to be wakening to fresh air and exotic aromas.

"So, you've been in France?"

Mauricio Belarmino laughs. His laugh is also larger than life and overflowing, much like his voluminous frame. "I've just come from there."

Everything about him is huge. His voice, his body, his folds of skin, his sweat.

"You were expecting me, right?"

It is not so much a question as a statement, issued with a sort of hard, unyielding complacency.

His uncle nods and offers him a chair. "There's been a lot of rain, but the northerly dried everything out."

Jacob has remained standing before them, waiting for his uncle to "ask." At least that is what he had said he would do. But his uncle does not ask anything. He is going to let the journalist start. Sometimes his uncle likes to do the opposite of what he says he's going to do.

Jacob can sense something out of the ordinary brewing between the two men. They seem to understand each other without saying a word, and the silence deepens and spreads. The only sound is the large man catching his breath, and the rhythmic tapping of the stick against his uncle's leg. It is like watching a boxing match without punches flying or anybody falling.

"I've come to tell you, in case you hadn't heard . . ."

"Tell me what?"

Mauricio Belarmino opens his eyes. They are small dark slits, with two or three folds in the eyelids. "So you don't know?"

"What is it that I'm supposed to know?"

The journalist flushes, his cheeks taking on a moist plastic sheen just like the magnolia leaves. There is a brief, almost imperceptible moment of hesitation. Then Mauricio Belarmino inhales deeply and tells his uncle that Teresa's husband has died.

13

Angry words had filled the air, cutting, wounding words, as if the two men were divided by a longstanding resentment. And it had all started when Mauricio Belarmino told his uncle that Teresa's husband had died.

At the exact same moment, Quasimodo had come in to say that lunch was ready, but nobody had moved. It was as if Quasimodo had not spoken at all.

The journalist was insistent, "Did you hear what I said, maestro? Teresa's husband has died. It happened at the French Riviera. I was with him. One minute, he was standing there sipping a martini, and then he simply dropped dead."

A couple of bumblebees were buzzing around the magnolia and his uncle raised the stick to shoo them away. When they were gone, the painter took a bloom in his hand and brought it to his nose to inhale its perfume. "It happened on the *Poseidon*, right?"

And when Mauricio Belarmino assented, his uncle had confessed that he had read about it in the newspapers. And with false bravado, he had said what a shame it was that such an important New York financier should have met his end. By dying, Richard had made yet another terrible misstep.

Mauricio Belarmino was curious as to why the painter had not gotten in touch when he found out about it, but uncle Eduardo made no reply, because an ant nestled among the magnolia petals caused him to sneeze.

The painter had then launched into a prolonged diatribe against Richard, Teresa, Purita, the Italians, Flora . . . even attacking Mauricio himself for joining a yachting expedition in such disagreeable and fickle company.

Mauricio had opened and shut his mouth several times, as if he would have liked to interject something, but uncle Eduardo did not give him the chance. His indignation was growing by the second. "A collection of undesirables . . . parasites the whole lot," he was saying. "I can't understand how a human being of your caliber would choose to rub elbows with such cretins." Mauricio Belarmino had responded that Richard was not like Eduardo thought. And the painter had snapped back that he did not think anything at all, because ever since he had left with Teresa, Richard, for him, was nothing more "than a fucking money launderer for a two-bit whore."

Uncle Eduardo seemed upset, very upset. And when the journalist chided him for talking like that in front of the child, his uncle had retorted that he never kept secrets from his nephew and the way things were going, Jacob would do well to learn a few choice words, ". . . because otherwise the world would eat him alive—just like it did to me, you get that, Mauricio?"

His uncle's fury had mounted, intractable and brusque, like a sudden vindication or a catharsis long overdue.

It was pitiful to see Mauricio so cowed by his uncle's assaults. He was gulping in air and clearing his throat noisily, as if his body fat were rising up and pooling there.

The worst part was when he said, "Come on, man. Don't get all worked up like that. Maybe Teresa will come visit you, now that she's free."

His uncle had taken a deep breath and retorted that he had never been fond of leftovers and if Teresa ever showed her face at Can Boig, he would leave.

Quasimodo, still standing in the doorway, had not dared to repeat that lunch was ready. He had just stood there, arms crossed, his good eye shut, awaiting orders. But the discussion had become increasingly heated. "I'd be willing to bet a good deal of money that you still think about her . . ." And Eduardo Santillana had started violently, rattled his stick against his leg, and retorted that those days were dead and gone and it was better to bury them with candles and incense, just as he had done.

The journalist had raised a hand to his chin and scrutinized the man opposite him, as if he could vanquish him with his gaze. "So am I to understand that you've buried Teresa forever?"

Eduardo Santillana had not replied. He had hoisted Jacob up by the armpits and set him down on the table between them. "This little leprechaun has helped me bury her," he asserted.

The days passed, and it had seemed as if the battle was going to rage forever, but just when the tension seemed to be reaching the breaking point, everything changed. Mauricio and uncle Eduardo no longer argued. They contemplated the sea together. They spoke in whispers and winked whenever Jacob approached, as if they were planning a surprise for him.

The journalist finally departed and the days that followed were like a never-ending party for Jacob. In the evenings, they usually dined at Perico's Tavern, along with all of his uncle's friends, of course.

Perico was a very unique character, small and round, with a florid face and a very bald head. His voice sounded like a trumpet and whenever he addressed Jacob he yelled at him as if he were deaf.

"So here we have the mascot." The first thing he does is give him a piece of candy, and then he seats him in between his uncle and Lori.

"What will it be this evening?"

Lori orders for him—she says men don't know anything about children's diets—and Jacob agrees with her recommendations, since he and Lori have been friends for a long time now.

Perico likes it when the painter dines at his tavern. It is tucked away among the narrow side streets and, according to his uncle, it used to be a stable. Perico is a very clever man and he knows how to get ahead. The only bad thing about Perico is his wife. Every time she appears in the kitchen doorway, he shoos her away, tells her she has no business being out there. She is an unkempt, gawky sort of woman. A Cinderella-stepmother type who clearly is not good for the reputation of the place.

"I married her because I felt sorry for her," says Perico. "Nobody else would have anything to do with her."

And Coco looks at him in disgust. "Please, Perico. Don't pretend to be so magnanimous. Everybody knows you married her for her money."

It would seem that, once upon a time, Perico had been a fisherman—a sea dog—who had taken advantage of the influx of tourists to make a career change. "If I had to make a sculpture of Perico, Fabian likes to say, it would be shaped like a jug."

Perico loves to tell stories about the village, especially stories that have something to do with Visitarana, the witch. "You should have seen her when she was young. She had a perfect figure."

Paul opens his eyes. He is always entertained by Visitarana's adventures, as recounted by the tavern owner.

"And how come you know all about it?"

"Because I was her victim . . . More than once I saw her slathered with putrid ointments, heading for Castillo beach."

Jacob is also fascinated by these stories. And although some of the words go right over his head, every time Perico mentions Visitarana he is immediately on alert, anxious not to miss a single crumb.

Perico knows a lot of things. "He's a clever jug," admits Fabian. He is an absolute repository of information about the local lore. Most every night they make him repeat the same stories, replete with insinuations, compacted fears, and daring brushes with fate.

He speaks of the "witches' Sabbath" and how Visitarana, naked and smeared with ointments, would mount a donkey—because she could not find a ram—and ride to Castillo Beach, next to the cemetery, to meet with the devil and report her evil deeds and spells. She would light a huge bonfire and call upon Beelzebub with piercing shrieks and lewd gestures.

"Who is Beelzebub?" Jacob inquires.

"Who do you think, Little Pup? The devil."

Paul is restless. Paul is never as awake as when Perico is telling stories about Visitarana.

"And what did they do?"

"Well, when the bonfire was burning brightly, the devil would appear in the form of a dashing young man."

"Without horns?" asks Coco.

"You could barely see them under his curls. Same with the tail."

"Yes, but what did they do? Jacob persists.

The "clever jug" regards him with some hesitation, exchanges a glance with his uncle, and replies that they did things children should not know about.

Once again the embarrassment and shame of being a child, and letting his hair drop over his cheeks so no one will notice his humiliation.

"Come on, Little Pup. Have a drink."

As always, it is Lori who comes to his rescue, smoothing the way for him, somehow helping him overcome his status as a mere child.

And Jacob takes a sip of the drink because, according to his uncle, you have to start very young if you're going to build up a tolerance for the stuff life throws at you.

"She was evil. So evil no one in the village wanted to have anything to do with her. So she took her revenge."

"How?" Paul chimes in once more.

"She would make rag dolls and name them after people. Then she'd stab them with needles and knife blades."

"For what?"

"The next day her victims would wake up with angina, or bruises, or even gaping wounds."

Jacob was astounded to learn that Visitarana did such things. She must be a very wicked witch indeed. Maybe as bad as Hindrance.

Somebody in the group proposes they all go down to Castillo beach, with Perico, for a reenactment of Visitarana's witches' Sabbaths. "The night is clear and it will be Saturday in less than an hour." And that is where they head as soon as dinner is over.

"Don't be frightened, Little Pup. It's all just a big spoof," his uncle assures him.

But Jacob wants it to be real, so that when he gets back to France, he can tell Pierre something completely new and different, something neither of them ever knew before.

"Don't forget the cassette," admonishes Coco.

And Fabian says he has not forgotten it. He always has it with him so Coco can dance.

Fabian finds it very entertaining to watch Coco dance. He says she looks like some kind of vestal virgin. But everybody else makes fun of her.

The truth is, Jacob thinks Coco looks ridiculous when she raises her arms, fluffs up her hair and throws her head back to begin her dance. "You're such a show off," his uncle often told her. "It's irritating." But she would just tune him out and keep on dancing—wild, gelatinous and wistful—until she finally dropped to the ground to die, just as she had the night Jacob stumbled upon the grown-up games in the living room at Can Boig.

Sometimes Coco and his uncle fight. Jacob is not sure why. Their squabbles are short but cutting. His uncle tells her he cannot tolerate so much sappiness in a dyke like her, and seeing her dance is like watching a garlic clove dressed up like an onion. And Coco retaliates by calling him a miscreant, a sewer rat of a painter.

Now she is warning him that Lori is tiring of him just as Teresa did, but tonight, Coco's rebukes fail to get a rise out of uncle Eduardo. He merely says, "We shall see about that." And ultimately, he adds, if Lori gets tired of him it will be no great loss.

"Hear that, Lori? Live and learn. . . ."

Lori laughs, She is probably happy to be on Castillo beach. Perico has accompanied them. Paul asked him to come. "I want you to tell us exactly what happened on this beach when you were young."

And Perico explains, with a wealth of detail.

But tonight, the beach of the old time witches' Sabbaths is not being used for spells. It is being used to play jellyfish, cops and robbers, kidnapped princesses, and prisoners and guards . . . Perico takes charge of distributing whisky and cigarettes that smell of bitter herbs and Jacob, from his perch up in a tree, is in charge of announcing all that is going on below: "Guards to port. Jellyfish to starboard." Just like a real lookout.

It is a new game. It is unlike any he has ever played before. It is fun to watch them chasing each other from his perch high in the tree. It is like uncovering an anthill and watching the insects bustle about, sinuously and nervously, all confusion and exhilaration.

"Careful everybody. Fabian is jumping the cemetery wall," yells the child.

And Paul chases after him, grabs him by the tunic, tearing it. Then they fall to the ground in a heap, like two sea urchins stuck together.

It is a joyful night, full of surprises.

"Let's go, Jacob. Come down out of that tree," somebody yells.

Suddenly they are all playing savage beasts. Even Perico has joined in the game. And Jacob jumps up on his uncle to claw at his face like a panther.

14

It was very late by the time they returned to Can Boig, because the sun's rays were already visible beyond the cape of the bay. Lori was with them in the car. She was going to spend the night with his uncle so he did not have to take her home. She said she could help the painter put his nephew to bed. You could not rely on Dots. Most of the time she was completely out of it by that hour, already in bed and snoring violently. Try as you might, it was impossible to wake her.

Fortunately, Dots no longer made remarks like, "This is no time to be putting a child to bed." Or, "Who would even think of a child your age gallivanting around like a grown-up?" And of course she never again reproached his uncle for dragging his nephew into his own base existence. Indeed, she seems to have gotten used to Jacob's new life and she sometimes even forgets herself and inquires, "How did it go last night, Little Pup?"

Sure, sometimes the child has huge dark rings around his eyes, but nobody really notices because of his glasses. That is why Dots has even been known to comment that the air at Can Boig must be doing him some good, because he has put several pounds on his slight frame since his arrival.

What continues to exasperate Dots are the frequent nighttime gatherings at the house. They always leave behind a total disaster, after which she has to spend the entire morning sweeping up the rubble on the terrace and in the living room.

"Here come the raving hordes," she always mutters when his uncle is out of earshot. And then she retreats to the kitchen to "forget" what lies ahead.

The gatherings usually begin after dinner at Perico's Tavern or the Garota Bar. The group arrives back at the house keyed up, gushing that their true home is the painter's house and where would they be if he weren't so generous.

"Come on, Little Pup. Give me a hand." Lori has a way of asking for things that makes it impossible to refuse her.

So Jacob helps her. They want to play "talking table" again. It's a pretty boring game, but they always get very keyed up about it. The first time he had played it was quite a while ago now, at Lori's house. Lori says the game is called a séance and it is not the table that is talking, but rather the dead, speaking through it.

So he had asked Lori if any of it was really true.

"I've told you a thousand times, it is the dead who are speaking."

"Really and truly?"

"Really and truly."

The first time, at Lori's house, he had found it all very hard to believe. "Come on, Little Pup. Ask a question." Jacob had not dared. He was hesitant to talk to a table. But Lori had insisted. "Go on, silly. Nothing bad is going to happen to you."

Then she told him the dead were anxious to communicate with the living and tables liked being intermediaries. She went on to explain that the voice itself was not heard. Something like a current was established and the message was transmitted through a sort of Morse code.

The "Morse" thing was a little strange. There was a Morse for yes and a Morse for no, another for numbers and letters and one for countries and places. It was all a matter of being completely silent and concentrating very hard on what you were doing.

"Is everybody ready?"

The grasshoppers say yes and his uncle takes his place beside Jacob. "Okay, Little Pup. Who would you like to speak to?"

Who else was it going to be? It is always the same. The only dead person he knows is his grandfather. The rest would be historical figures he has never actually seen before. The bad thing about grandfather is he always says the same old things: how grandmother Katherine is boring and Jacob is a smart boy, and Paris is really too big a city for his taste. He basically always just agrees with Jacob and that gets tiring after a while.

Lori smiles. She has situated herself by the sliding glass doors to the terrace. She says she likes it when there is a crescent moon. The terrace is deserted because all of the guests—even those not participating in the game—have gathered in the living room.

Fabian reaches out to stroke Jacob's pinky finger. "One of these days you're going to have to lend it to me so I can sculpt it."

But uncle Eduardo frowns and tells him to leave the child alone. "If you're looking for pinkies, I suggest you go find out where they might be for sale."

Fabian rolls his eyes, raises his hand to the ribbon on his forehead and nervously arranges the sleeves of his tunic. "You have such a dirty mind," he protests.

"Ready?" asks his uncle.

"Ready."

And the séance begins. At first it is all expectant glances, hesitation and sighs.

"Silence," his uncle orders.

The table rocks and the tension grows. No one is joking now. Lori clears her throat and his uncle shoots her a withering look.

"Spirit, express yourself," Eduardo Santillana says finally.

A slightly mocking smile at play on Coco's lips abruptly freezes. The table has expressed itself.

"Are you there?"

A rap on the floor means yes.

"Do we know you?"

Again, yes.

"Do you want to speak with us?"

Another rap.

"Who would you like to speak with?"

The preambles are always slow. You have to find out the name by process of elimination.

"Fabian?"

No.

"Coco?"

No.

"Jacob?"

No.

"Eduardo?"

The table says yes. It is unmistakable and definite.

"Go ahead then. Tell us who you are."

The table does not move. It simply waits while those seated around it start going through the alphabet. "Tap when we say the first letter of your name. It is not A or B or C . . . it seems as if the name the table wishes to reveal does not start with any letter.

. . . E, F, G . . .

Silence.

. . . I, J, K . . .

But when they get to R, the table reacts. It is a clear R, as unmistakable and definite as the yes had been.

"Okay, next letter."

And they start all over again: . . . G, H, I . . . another rap.

There is no doubt about it: the name begins with Ri—.

"I was expecting this," says Coco. "I was sure Richard was going to want to speak with you."

Eduardo Santillana frowns, bites his lips and, once again, his beard looks like a reddish, tousled pompom.

Fabian raises his voice sententiously. "Just a moment, friends. This is burning hot. Let's see, spirit, or whatever you are. Tell us once and for all if your name is Richard."

The response is unequivocal and the yes fills the room with foreboding.

"So, Richard."

Somebody, Paul maybe, lets a tiny giggle escape, more caustic even than Coco's was. It is an impertinent chuckle, but terribly contagious.

"You heard him, maestro," exclaims Coco. "Teresa's husband would like to speak with you."

Lori's face is contorted. She looks as if she is scared. She turns to the painter in distress, sees how pale and agitated he is. His hands are rigid, the veins bulging out in zigzagging lines.

Fabian persists: "Go for it man. You'll never have a better opportunity to give him a swift kick in the gut."

Eduardo Santillana does not blink. He is staring down at his hands. It is as if he cannot lift them off the table. As if the act of pulling them away from the wood surface would be as damaging as ripping off his skin.

"How interesting," continues Coco. "Richard just checked out and he's already causing trouble . . ."

His uncle swallows, squares his shoulders and pushes back from the table.

". . . It's really just a delicate way of reminding you how he dicked you," adds Coco.

She says it angrily, as if the insult was to make up for something Jacob does not quite grasp. For an instant everything stops dead. Even the magnolia on the terrace stops emitting its perfume.

Shrinking down into himself until he is little more than a shadow, Jacob can tell that something terrible is about to happen. He feels it coming as he watches his uncle, breathing heavily, lean over the talking table. A genuflection, a grunt and a grip on the wood are all it takes. The pedestal is in the air and uncle Eduardo looks as if he is raising up a trophy, rather than a table. He carries it out onto the terrace. The star-filled night rains down its silence and damp on the upended table.

"He has definitely gone crazy this time," remarks Coco.

And Lori signals for her to be quiet. "Shut your mouth."

But it is too late to turn back. There is fire in Eduardo Santillana. The fire of a dead man who wants to live again. The fire of a memory that—between the snide remarks and sheer tedium—has been consuming him for years now.

Still breathing heavily, he slams the table over and over again on the terrace floor. Then he grabs his walking stick and begins to lash out at the air, wounding it. His cries rouse the night, causing it to take up his wail.

"Out," he screams. "All of you. Get out of this house now."

The blows are hard and violent, and the air is filled with a painful keening, as if each strike were drawing blood.

Afterward, when they are all gone, Eduardo Santillana falls onto the divan in the entry hall, his elbows resting against his thighs, hands hanging down, and his head bowed.

Crouched in the stairway, Jacob dares not approach him. He has never seen his uncle so unlike himself or so full of despair. Fear has pervaded his body, freezing him in place. He does not know what to do, where to turn, or what he should say or not say. He only knows that his uncle hurts. He has broken a table and has kicked all his friends out of his home.

As he makes his way to his bedroom, he seems to detect a certain smugness in the eyes of all those Teresas—, as if his uncle's violent outburst had somehow been in homage to her.

Beyond the bedroom window, he can see the moon, no more than a sliver casting a faint glow on the lighthouse.

15

The incident of the preceding night is still festering in the house. Quasimodo has attempted, without success, to repair the table. Despite his best efforts, it will never be the same.

"So yesterday we heard from Teresa's husband . . . Well, that's all we needed!" says Quasimodo. "I wonder how your uncle's taking it."

The servant's sarcastic tone immediately puts Jacob on his guard. He doesn't like the way Quasimodo seems to accept what happened just like that. "The truth of the matter is, it was a pretty nasty joke."

"It was not a joke," protests Jacob. "I heard it too."

Quasimodo lets out a guffaw and turns his good eye towards the bespectacled child. "Don't tell me you believed all that stuff about messages from the great beyond."

"Lori says it's true."

"Well, maybe it is then, but what happened last night was a joke. A nasty joke."

"Why? Why would they do that?"

"To drive your uncle bonkers. He and Richard were good friends . . ."

Like every other morning, the breeze coming in through the window carries the scent of magnolias, but the terrace is empty. His uncle has shut himself in his studio and no one has seen him. He did not even want to have breakfast with Jacob.

" . . . that's why. Because it was his friend Richard who stole his girlfriend right out from under him, did you know that, little guy? And that is something a man never forgives."

"Well . . . he has more friends."

"The old ones were more refined."

"How do you know?"

"I have a good nose, little guy, that's all it takes," says Quasimodo, bringing his thumb to his nose. "The friends he has now are nothing but a bunch of nobodies who give themselves all sorts of airs."

"Lori too?"

"Lori most of all. Let me tell you a little secret: Lori is just trying to take Teresa's place, but nobody can take Teresa's place. No siree, nobody can."

"I like Lori."

Quasimodo glues the broken pieces together, wiping off the excess glue with a cloth, and turns his good eye to survey his work.

"She's a good diver. I'll give you that. She also has a nice chassis, no question. But Teresa had class and Lori is just a deviant little harlot."

Jacob wants to know what Quasimodo means when he says class, and the part about being deviant. To him, Lori is a nice girl who treats him kindly and is always trying to please his uncle so he does not get bored.

"What does chassis mean?"

Quasimodo shakes his head and his mouth curls, as if he is about to burst out laughing. Then, waving his hand dismissively he says, "Bah. Just forget it."

But there is so much Jacob wants to know.

"And Teresa? What was she like?"

He anxiously awaits the response. Teresa both fascinates and worries him—especially after last night. It is sort of like what happened with Roger, except Roger is not a woman.

"I can't really describe her . . . She loved your uncle."

"So why'd she go away with Richard?"

Quasimodo shakes his head, emits a strange exclamation and throws up his hands as if to shake loose the memory.

"Some people say she married Richard for money. Others are convinced that your uncle grew tired of her. But none of that is true. I know. The night before she left, I overheard their conversation in the studio."

Quasimodo pauses, perhaps afraid the child will go and squeal. Then, with a mysterious look, he begins to speak rapidly, as if someone had wound him up. "Teresa wanted to get married. She could not stand for people to think she was something she wasn't. But your uncle didn't believe in marriage. Well, you know how he is. He always says he'd sooner drift across the Mediterranean alone in a boat than get married."

"... *Stay away from women, Jacob. Any one of them can be a tarterita* . . ." And as he said it, his face had hardened and his eyes had seemed fiercer than usual.

"Besides," continues Quasimodo, "he hardly had any money at the time. He was just beginning to make a name for himself as a serious painter when Teresa got married. American customers began to roll in over night. It was nice to see it happen."

Maybe that is why he would take every opportunity to say that splitting up with Teresa had brought him good luck. "... *There's such a thing as negative influences, Jacob. Very negative.*"

"Your uncle did not realize, or maybe he did not want to accept, that he owed his sudden fame to Richard. Do you understand what I'm telling you, little guy? Everybody knows that Richard and Teresa have been his principal dealers. Maybe that's why he detests him so much."

Jacob cannot possibly grasp the nuances of the story. He has only understood that his uncle detests them. He shrugs. All of these dealings and conjectures are too much for him to get his mind around. What sticks is little more than a couple of vague maybes, a few flickers of stray motives.

What upsets him most is that his uncle has been carrying around so much sadness all because of Teresa. That alone is enough for him to think she deserves to be turned into an enchanted rock just like Malabrun and his henchmen.

"It's probably best you don't understand me. It's too complicated for you anyway." He turns back to the table as if it were actually possible to fix it. Jacob is not concerned by what Quasimodo has told him. There will be time later to figure out what seems incomprehensible to him now. Anyway, when grown-ups talk in code like that, the words just dissolve and scatter without a trace. Only the outlines remain, and occasionally certain dense suspicions that settle to the bottom of his thoughts like sediment.

"I think Teresa is a witch," the child says abruptly. "And uncle Eduardo told me she's even more beautiful than Visitarana was when she was young. And he also says all beautiful women end up being witches."

"Have you met Visitarana?"

He had seen her the day he and his uncle had gone up the street by the church to sketch. It was after he had heard the explanation of the witches' Sabbath and the rams. They were standing next to a house with a balcony full of sweet-smelling flowers and she had crossed their path without warning. "That's her, Jacob. That old lady is Visitarana."

She was hunched over and draped in black like all the women in the village and her head was covered with a black scarf.

"She lives there, across from the flower balcony."

At first glance, she looked just like all the other women, except she was more stooped and her nose was bigger. The witch had passed right by them and entered her house through a red doorway.

Of course she had no shadow and Jacob regretted that he had not brought his paper saber with him.

But his uncle told him not to be afraid because, ever since she had gotten old, her magical powers had diminished notably. "Besides," he had reiterated, she doesn't stick pins in dolls to take revenge on people any more."

"I met her one afternoon," he tells Quasimodo.

"Where?"

"Near the church."

"What did you think of her?"

"I wasn't scared at first, but then . . ."

"What happened?"

"She gave me the evil eye."

It had been a bad day for Jacob. No sooner had he arrived home than he had stumbled, hitting his knee on the edge of the step. It had begun to swell up, so Dots had to resort to home remedies to make sure the spell Visitarana had put on him did not cause any additional harm.

Behind his uncle's back, she had made a poultice of used tobacco from the previous night's cigarette butts. First she had boiled it with a sprig of rosemary. Then she mixed in some mud and manure, added some red pepper, wrapped the whole mess in gauze and applied it hot to the child's knee. You'll be safe now, she had promised, and she implored him not to tell his uncle so as not to alarm him.

The worst part was at dinner, when his uncle ordered that all the windows be opened up because the house smelled like shit. Jacob was about to tell him the truth, but Dots' index finger signaled him to remain silent and uncle Eduardo never did find out about the episode.

"What kind of evil eye? How do you know?"

"Because a lot of things happened to me that day."

That night he'd lost a tooth and as if that weren't enough, he had dreamed about the child with the big head again.

But his uncle was delighted he'd lost a tooth in his house and had suggested that they hide it under his pillow so the tooth fairy would take it and leave a gift in its place.

"What kind of things?"

"I bumped my knee and my stomach hurt and I lost a tooth."

"Those are just coincidences. Visitarana is nothing but a poor, wretched old lady."

But Dots said just the opposite: "She's as toxic as a sea tomato." And Dots knew the whole story. She'd known her ever since she was almost as beautiful as Teresa.

"Yesterday, Coco said it was Visitarana who made uncle Eduardo get so mad, because she gave him the evil eye too."

"That's ridiculous. Coco is jealous of your uncle. That's why she goes after him like that."

"You should've seen him when he picked up the table. And when he started to hit all over with his walking stick."

"He must've been drunk."

"Like Dots?"

"Oh man . . . maybe not that much."

The same night, the tooth fairy had come and taken away the tooth, leaving a five Euro bill in its place. "Hang on to it, Little Pup. You never know what might happen. You're probably going to need it one day."

Jacob had never had so much money before. Elated, he had picked up the bill and placed it in the treasure chest.

Then his uncle had turned to the subject of his birthday party. "We're going to go all out. It will be the best party ever."

"Do you think he'll still want to have my birthday party after what happened last night?" he asks now.

"It's still a week away. He'll have gotten over his fury by then."

But one look at him in the entry hall, erect, severe, and frowning, is enough to know that even if the fury was receding, he was still tormented by misery.

"Good morning, Little Pup."

Jacob answers in a tiny, timid voice, unable to move.

"Aren't you going to give me a kiss?" his uncle continues.

The child runs over to him and gives him a hug. But it is a mechanical hug, nothing like before.

His uncle turns his attention to Quasimodo. "You should have just tossed it into the sea," he observes, gesturing towards the table. "It's worthless."

Quasimodo mouths an unintelligible response and his uncle insists that when things lose their utility, they should be thrown out. He also says that the servant's biggest fault is frittering away his time on little things that never come to anything.

"I'm giving you fair warning. From now on, there will be no more séances in this house. And you can just throw that damned table out, so I don't have to look at it again." Then he takes Jacob by the hand and leads him down to the beach.

There is something disagreeable about their surroundings. Nothing looks the same as it did the night before, when the night was enthralling, perfumed and star-filled. Now, everything seems shrouded in mist and it would not be at all surprising if it suddenly started to rain.

"We didn't say a proper goodnight yesterday," comments his uncle. "I didn't even realize when you went to bed." Duke rushes over to his master, licks his feet and flutters around him as if he is afraid to make him angry. "When you see me like that, just ignore me, Jacob. Sometimes I drink to much and I act like an ass."

He brandishes the stick, tracing circles in the air, and continues, "The truth is we humans are pretty stupid. We drink so we can feel happy and then we end up sad . . . or worse yet, mad."

Jacob thinks he should say something, but nothing occurs to him. Maybe he should propose a game of shoe store, or flying saucers . . . or maybe he should mention Ruan.

"I dreamed about you last night, did you know that, Little Pup?"

"About me?"

His uncle tells him about the dream. He says that Jacob had suddenly grown a reddish beard, just like his own. "Everybody was getting us mixed up. Even Duke thought you were me."

Jacob smiles and rubs his chin. "But it's not true. I don't have a beard."

"Maybe you will in a few days."

"How? With chalk? That's not like having a real beard."

"No, another way."

And as if the beard had something to do with his birthday, he starts telling Jacob about the party he is planning. "We'll have fireworks and balloons, and snacks . . ." And suddenly the old uncle Eduardo is back, the one who looks like Jacob.

"Have you invited Ruan?"

"No, but I'll get a message to him today."

"How?"

"How will I do it? I'll go into the village, climb a tamarind tree and give the invitation to any old goldfinch."

"Will it arrive on Venus on time?"

"It will get there in no time. I've already told you."

On special occasions, when the day is very clear and the atmosphere free of clouds, it is possible to pick out Ruan's planet even in the daytime. But the day is overcast and try as he might, the child cannot catch a glimpse of the star.

"The weather will probably clear up tonight and you'll be able to see it." He places his stick on the child's shoulder. "Let's go, Little Pup. I invite you to take a spin in the boat with me."

On days like this, despite the glare, Jacob does not need a towel or a hat or anything to prevent sunburn. His skin is dark and toughened and his eyes have grown used to the water's reflection.

"We're off, Little Pup."

And once again, the groan of the motor, the smoke and the smell of gas. Once again, his uncle's fragrant mixture of saltwater, tanned body, and cologne. Every day, Jacob unconsciously waits for the chance to breathe in that smell. It is nice. It helps him forget about the world of his parents, Roger, and grandmother Katherine.

"Hang on tight, here comes a big wave."

Once they have left the protection of the bay behind, one big wave follows the next and the *Teresa* is rocking violently among them.

"Faster, Uncle."

"Yes sir."

His uncle adjusts the lever and the boat takes off, splashing as the waves strike it. Occasionally the bow jumps atop the surface, lofty and proud, only to smack down loudly on the other side, as if to break the keel.

"Faster."

When the sea gets like that, spirited and snappish, the crags turn to gray from all of the seagulls perched on them and the atmosphere seems to contain nothing but air, empty sky, and compact clouds.

"Where are we going?"

Uncle and nephew regard each other squinting, Jacob's glasses caked with salt, their smiles lopsided, and a spark of mischief playing at the corner of their mouths.

"Where do you want to go?" shouts his uncle.

"Wherever you want to."

"Let's go then: we'll head towards the future, towards hope and freedom . . . And above all, Jacob, don't you ever, ever think about looking behind you . . ."

16

Mr. Raimundo had finally returned. He showed up at Can Boig on the eve of Jacob's birthday. He came bearing so many packages his car seemed more like a delivery truck. "These are for your birthday," he had advised Jacob. And he had added that his uncle was going all out for his birthday party. It was going to be an event fit for a prince.

Mr. Raimundo was nice. He seemed younger than his uncle and he also wore glasses. He assured Jacob that he too believed in witches, and when Jacob told him how he had bumped his knee because of Visitarana, he had crossed himself several times and said it was better not to say her name out loud. "Witches find out everything and if she realizes we've been talking about her, she is perfectly capable of causing more trouble." So whenever Quasimodo started to say how Visitarana was just a normal old woman and how all the things people said about her were ridiculous lies, Jacob quickly crossed his fingers, just as Mr. Raimundo had taught him, and spit on the ground so the witch would not hear.

It had been an exhilarating afternoon. Eduardo Santillana and his administrator had festooned the terrace with streamers, colored lights and strands of silver flowers trailing all the way down the stairs to the beach.

The sky was clear and the rain that had taken them by surprise a few days before—when he and his uncle were out boating towards freedom, hope and the future—had moved on.

Even before dark, the planet Venus was already shining brightly, shot through with orange hues, as huge and resplendent as a far off sun. And Mr. Raimundo had assured Jacob that it was shining extra brightly so he would know Ruan was planning to attend.

He also said his uncle had told him a lot about Jacob and considered him an exceptional child. Thanks to his presence, Can Boig had changed a lot. "You can be proud of yourself, Jacob."

That afternoon, Mr. Cusi arrived to install a portable buffet table down on the beach and a short time afterward, Perico showed up with a brigade of waiters to set up tables, chairs and place settings.

The whole house was in an uproar that afternoon. Huge boxes of prepared food were brought in. Dots was busy grousing: all the tumult drove her crazy. "I often think your uncle is a little daft. Imagine inviting half the village just to celebrate a birthday."

But, since Dots was always grumbling about something or other, no one paid her much attention. Occasionally, she would plant herself in the living room doorway, hands on hips, her eyes announcing violence from underneath the half-closed lids. "Your uncle has never made such a fuss, not even when Teresa was here." But she had quickly corrected herself: "Of course, he didn't have any money then either." And as if to make up for her displeasure, she had taken a healthy swig out of the nearest bottle.

Although Jacob still has not gotten out of bed, he can tell from the intensity of the light filtering in through the balcony railings that the sea must be calm, smooth, and painted with sparkling diamonds. The beach and the terrace are silent. Every little sound is magnified in the still of the early morning.

He wonders if his uncle is still in bed. Though he usually rises early—sleep is for marmots he often says—after such a hectic, boisterous night, anyone would have trouble getting up.

An unpleasant episode had occurred right at dusk. It was when his uncle had confronted Dots and forbidden her to drink. "At least not until all the guests are as drunk as you are. Are you paying attention, Dots? Only then will I allow you to get yourself good and plastered."

And he had instructed Mr. Raimundo to keep an eye on her: "I'm holding you personally responsible for whatever happens."

Everything else proceeded as smooth as silk.

A tremendous lethargy has taken hold of Jacob. He is having fun remembering it all. Calling to mind each individual detail of the party, one by one. It was a grandiose affair. Streaks of light shot upward only to burst apart into a thousand colors. Rockets were launched into space at such speed it seemed as if they might reach the planet Venus. They were luminous balls of light that discharged noisy sighs, like someone suffering from a bronchial infection, before shattering into a rain of stars. And an aroma of perfumed gunpowder blanketed the beach.

Dots' voice is booming now, just as the fireworks had boomed last night. She is telling Quasimodo that Perico is a filthy slob. He should have cleaned up the beach while he was gathering up his place settings. From her grouchy tone, you can tell she is cleaning up the mess Perico has left behind. Furious, she curses her bad luck. She reiterates that she is tired of serving in a house full of lunatics and, since the maestro is still so out of sorts, she is going to pack her things and find a new boss.

"And you tell me who in the hell is going to take you in," replies Quasimodo.

"Lots of places. One thing for sure: there's no shortage of houses."

"Have you taken a good look at yourself in the mirror lately, Mother?"

"Why you little . . ."

They must be half-joking because all of the sudden they both burst out laughing. Jacob is aware that Dots and her son spend hours and hours trading barbs. They both know that their options are limited, so they accept what they have because, when it comes down to it, who else would take them on? And besides, both of them—bless their hearts—are fiercely loyal to uncle Eduardo. And though they might pretend otherwise, they also enjoyed the birthday party. Dots' scabs almost seemed to recede when the Bengal lights silently exploded, lighting up the beach, the water and the rocks.

The fireworks show lasted for a long time but, before that, there had been other sorts of entertainment. His uncle had spared no expense. They had tossed balloons, had circle dances and sack races and broken open enormous piñatas packed with candy. They had distributed snacks and Coca Colas to all of the villagers milling about and sampled the enormous birthday cake that Perico's waiters served with six candles on top for Jacob to blow out.

And there were presents for him too. Lots of presents. The first one was from his uncle. He had given it to him first thing in the morning just as Jacob was getting up. "It's from the dream I told you about." It was a beard, a real beard, a curly reddish beard just like the painter's. "Do you like it, Jacob?"

The beard is there now, on the night table, its strap shortened because it had been a little too big for him.

Jacob jumps out of bed and opens the door to the balcony. The sky is clear and Dots and Quasimodo are no longer out there. They have probably gone back to the kitchen with all of Perico's trash.

He looks at the kite Lori gave him. "Your uncle will teach you how to fly it." Jacob had been delighted to see Lori back at Can Boig. In fact, all of his uncle's friends were there. It was as if no one even remembered the incident of the broken table. "Know what, Jacob? Kites fly really high, higher even than the seagulls." But when he had asked her whether they flew as high as Ruan, she had said no, only goldfinches could fly like Ruan.

"Good morning, Jacob." Mr. Raimundo is standing on the adjacent balcony, still in his pajamas, his bespectacled face turned towards the child. "What a good night's sleep. We're nothing but a couple of lazy-bones."

"Have you seen my uncle?"

"He went out in the boat early this morning," responded the administrator.

"Why didn't he tell me?"

"You were sleeping."

He does not like it when his uncle goes off in the boat without him. Sulking, he tells the administrator they should have wakened him.

"He didn't want to disturb you."

The most spectacular scene of all had starred Ruan. Though he did not notice exactly how he had gotten there, Jacob had suddenly spied him on the beach, bathed in light and surrounded by a group of astonished earthlings, who were eying him with distrust.

His uncle had hurried over with Jacob in tow, and everybody could see how Ruan had handed him his present. It was a quiver full of arrows. So you can dress up as Cupid, the extraterrestrial had said in his cavernous voice. And from that moment on, Jacob was treated like a god. The god of *love*, stressed Fabian.

They stripped him right down, draped a loincloth around his middle with a big bow in the back, placed the quiver and arrows over his shoulder and seated him on a throne, bow in hand, so that the guests could parade before him.

It was very flattering to be a god. Especially when the guests took turns laying birthday gifts at his feet. There were so many packages, he barely noticed when Dots presented him with a new paper saber.

Perico gave him candies and chocolates and told him that there was a surprise tucked inside the giant cake. It was a miniature flying saucer, with antennae and wheels, and a mechanism in the belly that made it fly. When Ruan saw it, however, he said his vessel was very different and, to prove it, some day he would let Jacob visit him and see what real flying saucers were like.

"There's your uncle now."

The *Teresa* can be seen rounding the bend. His uncle is steering the boat standing up, his shoulders thrust back and his erect frame strong and solid. He is smiling.

Jacob rushes down to the terrace and Mr. Raimundo follows shortly after. It is a little off-putting to observe Mr. Raimundo, who has changed into his swimsuit. He does not look anything like his uncle. The skin hanging on his gaunt frame seems dull and lackluster and calls to mind a cured ham.

"How did you like the bash, Little Pup?" The old Uncle Eduardo is back, quick-witted, indulgent and commanding. "I wanted to take you with me this morning, but you were fried."

The silver strands, the little lights, and the garlands of flowers, now slightly wilted, are still draped across the terrace. Some of them are a little charred where the swaying lights burned the paper.

"When did Ruan leave?" Jacob asks. He had disappeared all of the sudden, when Jacob was not looking.

"Extraterrestrials have that power. When they get tired of people, they simply vanish."

"How is it done?"

"If you figure that one out, I'll give you my walking stick."

Mr. Raimundo laughs and exchanges a couple of glances with his uncle that Jacob does not catch. His uncle is sending what seem to be affirmative signals, as if something he had been wondering about had been confirmed.

Uncle Eduardo has a mysterious air about him. Something Jacob would like to figure out, but does not know how. A couple of times, his uncle lapses into silence, as if he is not there. He just stares out to sea, his eyes fixed and blank, like a blind man's.

The bay looks different too. There are very few boats and, although the sea is calm, he gets the sense that it has suddenly become perilous, as if it were full of hidden cracks and on the verge of collapsing in on itself.

The *Teresa* is moored at the jetty and Jacob focuses his gaze on the obsessive swaying of the hull. An inexplicable sense of despondency has suddenly washed over him like an epidermal liquid that niggles at the soul and debilitates the body.

Mr. Raimundo dives into the water. He says it's warm and Jacob and his uncle should join him. Jacob has the sensation that everything is coming at him from far away. It is as if something is preventing him from registering what is going on around him.

Jacob suddenly understands that the whole morning is hurting him. The feeling has welled up inside without warning, just as the boat carrying his uncle was coming into view. Everything hurts: the wilting paper flowers, the singed strands and lights, the stray pieces of trash tucked among the rocks along the beach. Even the magnolia, looking ridiculously like a nymph because of all the fallen garlands draped around it, is wounding him. Everything is somehow out of place.

"Are you going to finish my portrait?"

"We won't be having a session today."

"Why not?"

"Because I'm tired," his uncle replies simply.

And he sits at the water's edge, cross-legged like a Buddha, his gaze fixed on the sea. "That's the direction if you're coming from France," he says, indicating the islet.

"No," replies the child, "it's how you get to the cave."

"But if you pass the cave and keep going, you'll get to France."

And he squints, as if straining to see the far-off country beyond the cave. Afterward, he remains silent for a long time, as if words were bothersome, an unnecessary disturbance he would prefer to avoid.

Way out against the horizon, the waves are being whipped up into whitecaps.

"It's a ship," says Jacob.

His uncle has stood up nervously, as if Jacob's mention of a ship has propelled him to his feet.

"Are you sure?"

"Look at it."

It slowly comes into view. A white and yellow ship, the bow rising high above its massive hull. It is headed cautiously towards the village, skirting the cape and, from the beach, it looks as if it is on a straight course for the islet.

"It's coming here."

Under normal circumstances, the arrival of a ship would not cause any stir at all. Jacob has seen a million of them coming into the bay. But this is different. This one has bypassed the islet and is headed straight for Can Boig.

"It's going to run aground," the child warns.

But his uncle smiles and says no, it won't because the captain is very experienced.

"How do you know?"

"I know him."

"Were you expecting him?"

"Perhaps."

Mr. Raimundo emerges from the water, his back to the beach, watching the ship. Then, walking unsteadily—he does not have his glasses on—he approaches his uncle.

"Is that him?"

Eduardo Santillana nods. His face has gone pale under his tanned skin. In fact, it really does not look like his face at all.

"I'll let Quasimodo know," says Mr. Raimundo, quickly draping his towel around his shoulders.

Jacob is still hoping that the ship will continue on into the bay, but the bow has not veered in either direction. It is definitely headed straight for them.

It is a stubborn ship. A ship that refuses to capsize. His uncle has told him a thousand times that there are few navigable channels among the crags ringing the beach. "Any old lunatic captain can easily run aground there." So he cannot comprehend why his uncle has remained impassive, has not signaled for the captain to stop.

"This captain knows exactly what he's doing," he murmurs.

Then, he excitedly explains to the child that there is a deep channel between the rocks and only the most experienced navigators are able to maneuver through it successfully.

"Can it get all the way to here?"

"It can," his uncle affirms.

As it draws nearer, the ship begins to come into focus. It is an enormous yacht, svelte and graceful as it moves through the water.

"No question about it. He is a good sailor," his uncle repeats.

A French flag is flying from the mast and Jacob recalls vaguely that Richard had dropped dead unexpectedly on a yacht called the *Poseidon*.

Tanned forms are scurrying about on the deck. The crew is hard at work, loosening moorings, working crank handles and tackles and pulleys. When the siren sounds, the engine dies down. Now the chop-chop of air hitting water can be heard, and the clanking sound of the windlass as the anchor is lowered. Soon, muffled voices are audible.

"Are they friends of yours?" asks the child.

But his uncle does not reply. "We have to wait. We just have to be patient and wait."

A cacophony of voices carries across the water. People are crowding around the ladder as dinghies full of bodies are launched. And

Jacob suddenly glimpses a familiar form, rolls of fat girding his shirtless form, his booming voice reaching the beach easily, as if he were using a loudspeaker.

"Here we are, maestro," he yells from the water, waving his hands and causing the small boat to sway dangerously.

Eduardo Santillana does not move a muscle. He has remained standing, rigid, tense, his jaw clenched and his beard trembling slightly. The child is watching him fearfully, trying to guess at things that quickly slither from his grasp, so surreal is the scene before him.

"Mauricio Belarmino has returned," he murmurs.

Time is moving so quickly, it seems to be devouring everything in its path.

The beach is filling up with bodies, with strange people Jacob has never seen before. Men and women who rush up to his uncle, embrace him, and then step back to search his face with anxious, smiling expressions. But none of them look like Lori, or Fabian or Coco.

"It's about time."

"It doesn't seem possible . . ." ". . . back at Can Boig . . ."

A gray-haired man with vague eyes looks at Jacob. "Who the hell is that?"

"Relax. He's not my son." his uncle replies.

Everything is confusing, disjointed. Nothing is as it should be. Even the silver strands still suspended gaily from the terrace seem phony, as if they might have been celebrating the birthday of a very old man.

A dark-haired woman is standing before uncle Eduardo, her back very straight, her gaze direct, almost defiant. Then she sways towards him and he catches her in his arms to keep her from falling.

PART TWO

CEIBO

17

A brutal, pitiless wind is blowing across the district. It had started before dawn, while they were still sleeping, and has snaked across the water, shrieking and irate, whipping up whitecaps and foams.

It is a tenacious wind, olive and leathery, and it paints an iridescent coating across docks, puddles and ditches, sweeps stray branches from the cliffs and provokes a certain melancholy in humans. *"Don't ever look back, Jacob, never, never . . ."* But on days like today, Jacob cannot seem to suppress his nostalgia, especially since Teresa's arrival.

He definitely does not like the "present" Can Boig has to offer. It is as if he were a prisoner of the stupid *Poseidon*, which is still anchored off the beach, filling his mind with murky premonitions and strange somersaults. Every once in a while, a wall of water will slap heavily into the bow, raising the hull high before it comes crashing down to the surface again and the sea bursts open like a balloon. When the wind blows like that, the crew hastens to cover the decks and batten down the hatches.

"Hurry up, Jacob. Duke is waiting for you," says Dots.

Sulking, Jacob hunches down into the big chair in the living room, and stubbornly crosses his arms in front of him. "I don't want to go out. It's cold."

Despite Dots' efforts to change his mind, Jacob has decided to stay put in the house.

"Your uncle is going to get mad if you don't obey him."

"Let him."

"So you don't mind giving him a bad time."

Well, his uncle has done the same thing to him hasn't he? Starting when Princess Kilsa—resurrected and reincarnated in the form of Teresa—had arrived by sea in a yacht called the *Poseidon* to cast a spell on his uncle and tear him away from Jacob.

He had sensed it immediately, the minute he saw her appear on the beach. There would be no more portrait sessions on Clavileño, or night swims in the moonlight, or walks to the lighthouse, or treks along the coastline in search of petrified plants . . . No more sharing a meal elbow to elbow or singing duets, and no more all-night parties on the beach and playing savage beasts . . .

"Well that's a fine way to thank your uncle for all he's done for you," continues Dots.

She had changed too. And Quasimodo. And Mr. Raimundo. Dots had changed so much that if Jacob hadn't met her before Teresa came, he probably would have thought she was really mean: just one big scolding machine like his grandmother Katherine.

"The problem with you is you're jealous."

"Of who?"

"Who else? Teresa of course."

"I don't get jealous of witches."

He is staring at the magnolia as he says it, as if the key to any possible jealousy would be there.

"Are you saying Teresa is a witch?"

Lori had insinuated something similar when his uncle had forbidden her to set foot in Can Boig. "From now on, things are going to change. Teresa has come back and I'm planning to rebuild my life . . ." So an indignant Lori had retorted that he should go ahead and commit suicide. "You men act so blindly. You're perfectly capable of seeing clear water where there is nothing but a pool of shit." And when she said that, his uncle had told her to go straight to hell and absolutely forbade her to talk about Teresa like that. "One more word out of you and I'll deck you."

It was painful to say goodbye to Lori. Jacob remembers the moment as if it were yesterday. "Goodbye, Little Pup," she had said, sobbing. "Make sure that rotten bitch doesn't run roughshod over you." And she had taken all her things because—according to her—his uncle didn't want to see her face around there anymore.

After Lori left, it became clear to Jacob that her departure had eliminated a crucial aspect of his existence. In a way, having Lori by his uncle's side had served as a shield against any attack or detour. Lori was his safety net, the promise of stability, the conviction that things would go on as they were.

"You should be ashamed of yourself, Jacob. If your uncle ever gets wind of what you're thinking . . ."

"Let him."

When she had glimpsed him on the beach for the first time, Teresa had faked a smile that did not go with the tears falling from her cheeks. "So this is your nephew." And she had walked right over and given him a kiss. Her lips were cold and her body emitted a sweet perfume like crushed violets. "And what, may I ask, is he doing in Can Boig?" And his uncle had explained that he was spending the summer there. "Well, where are his parents?"

Now his uncle was going to tell her how his mom has married Roger, thought Jacob. But he had merely explained that Jacob was a great kid and very good company, and he'd be returning to France when school started.

There were a lot of strange people all over the place too. Busybodies who wanted to "know," to "hear about," to "understand the situation." "So your brother is the father? And whatever possessed you to be the babysitter?"

The worst one was a tall, fat lady with a scar on her forehead and a neck like a man. "What's the matter with your eyes? So little and already wearing glasses . . ." Uncle Eduardo had offered vague explanations, saying Jacob's father wore them too . . . The fat lady's name was Purita and she seemed to be best friends with another lady named Flora. "Is Dots still here? And Quasimodo?"

Then there was the marquis: stuck up and shifty, and full of anecdotes to spice up the evenings: "The year I spent in Casablanca . . ."

Mauricio Belarmino was acting very self-satisfied. Every time he saw Teresa and the painter together he would say it was about time the hostilities had ceased.

Mr. Raimundo was a bit of a wild card. Although he participated in the evening gatherings, his uncle would sometimes feel compelled to remind him that he was still an employee. "Raimundo, please go into the kitchen and tell Dots we would like to have paella tonight."

Then there was the Italian couple. Two colorless individuals of indeterminate age who apparently belonged to Rome's high society. "What are those lights doing there?" the wife had asked. And his uncle had told her about Jacob's birthday celebration the previous day. "So your name is Jacob," exclaimed the husband, adding that Jacob was a Jewish name.

"You're not being fair. Teresa is a good person. And she really loves your uncle," Dots insists.

"But she married Richard."

Dots flinches and shakes her head nervously. "Leave Richard in peace. The past is the past. Richard is dead."

"But the other night Richard wanted to talk to Uncle Eduardo."

"Nonsense. The dead can't talk."

"That's what you think. Lori says they can."

"Through tables?"

"With or without tables."

No one is going to get that notion out of his head. It is as if everything Lori ever said is engraved in his mind.

"Well, maybe they can talk," Dots concedes. "But that isn't the point. Now Teresa is free and, if your uncle wants to, she has the right to marry him."

Jacob hunches down into the chair and looks out at the *Poseidon* again. It is a squalid, leaden ship swathed in tarps and the chill air. Dots calls it Teresa's house, but the truth is, Teresa and her friends spend most of their time at Can Boig.

Restlessness had set in almost immediately after their arrival. It was necessary to get out, spend time in the village or visit places on the other side of the mountain. And according to Teresa, in order to make sure Jacob maintained an appropriate schedule, he should stay home with Duke, Quasimodo and Dots. That is why Teresa is no longer just a bunch of pictures that make the hairs on the back of his neck stand on end whenever he walks through the gallery, or a name painted on the side of a boat. She is a real face and a concrete form. Someone who speaks, and gives orders and makes decision designed to upset Jacob.

There has been a little bit of everything since her arrival: rosy western skies with orange clouds. Glassy raindrops beating down on the sea, until it looks like a huge colander. Dark, gloomy, worn-out mornings. Bright sunlight that turns seagulls' backs to silver and human bodies brown. Clear moons and hazy moons. Star-filled skies and overcast skies that even block out Venus.

But most importantly, new voices have usurped the old ones, the ones Jacob knew, admired and liked. The new voices have different accents and cadences. They were shocked that Jacob was allowed to interfere in the goings on of the adults. "That's no way to raise a child, Eduardo. You shouldn't let your nephew stay up so late. You shouldn't let him eat whenever he feels like it. A child needs routine, discipline, order . . . If you keep on like this, your going to turn him into a *ceibo*."

And when his uncle had asked her what in the hell a "ceibo" was, Teresa had said it was the cockspur coral tree, the national flower of Argentina, whose bright red flowers bloom before its leaves come out. And that would be a shame, don't you think? There's a time for everything."

So Mauricio Belarmino, who fancied himself a poet, improvised

144

a ditty, which Jacob has still not forgotten. "Bright red flowers—on Argentine trees—bloom so radiantly—before its leaves. Isn't that pretty?"

And that was how the guests started to call him "Ceibo." *A stupid word*, he thought. A word worthy of Teresa. When it came down to it, all those things were like poison bubbles. Bad ideas designed to gradually drive him and his uncle apart. One stupid remark after another, to destroy the understanding they had shared . . .

"No," Jacob shoots back. "Uncle Eduardo will never marry Teresa."

"What would you know about it, child?" says Dots dismissively.

"He told me a long time ago. Uncle Eduardo doesn't lie."

A gust of wind causes the magnolia tree to shudder as if it were being pummeled, and Jacob thinks the tree must be feeling a lot like he is.

"You know what I think, Jacob? You're homesick. It's an ill wind that's blown it into you. That's what your problem is. Once the weather clears, you won't feel so bad."

But Jacob protests. He grumbles. He says that if the choice is to live the way it has been since Teresa got there, he would rather go back to France. "I'm tired of you, and Quasimodo, and Can Boig . . ."

His eyes are brimming with tears as he says it, because despite everything, France is not a pleasant prospect either. Not just because it is where Teresa came from, but mostly because no one is waiting for him there.

"What did I tell you? You're homesick, pure and simple."

Dots is not entirely off base. The truth is that ever since the *Poseidon* anchored in front of the beach, Jacob's life has become flat and crippled. Nothing has been the same, not even the village.

Indeed, to Jacob the village was the Garota bar, Perico's tavern, the beach of the witches' Sabbath . . . And his uncle's friends—Fabian, Paul, Coco, Lori—who joked around and played with him.

The friends his uncle has now like to say things like, "What are we going to do with Ceibo? Shall we take him with us or leave him at home?" Until Teresa chimes in, "Well, we're definitely not going to take him . . ." and children this and children that . . . , until Jacob feels just like a toy that has fallen on the floor and been trampled on over and over.

"You heard me. Duke is waiting for you. He wants you to play fetch with him," Dots suggests for the second time.

His uncle was the one who had invented the game in the first place. And before he left, he had said—as if it were a big deal—, "When the weather clears you can go out and play with Duke. You remember how. Just spit on the stick, throw it as far as you can, and he'll bring it back to you."

Spit on the stick. Who knows how long it has been since Jacob played that game. Duke is no friend of Teresa's either and ever since she arrived, he hardly ever prances around his uncle any more.

"I'm tired of spitting on the stick," he tells Dots. "I'm tired of playing shoe store, and painting and everything."

"Come on now, Jacob. That's no way to behave. What would your uncle say if he could hear you now?"

One afternoon, Teresa had gotten hold of Jacob alone and had dumped the whole sermon on him. She said his uncle loved him a lot, but he was turning him into a little monster. "Children do not drink, or smoke, or swim in the sea at night. So, from now on . . ."

"From now on" meant restriction and dictatorship and the constant, "That's enough, Jacob . . ." "Dots is waiting to feed you . . ." or "It's time to go to bed now . . ." or some other stupid thing.

Until one day, fed up with so much meddling, Jacob decided to stand up to her. "You're not in charge here," he had told her. Furious, Teresa had gone to his uncle to complain. And then the painter had decided to take her side. "I don't want to hear you using that tone of voice with her again, do you hear me, Jacob? I forbid it."

So the child understood that she was behind his uncle's irritable mood. *She is a rotten bitch*, he thought. *She's a witch* . . . And he decided to put an end to her evil spells once and for all.

Without stopping to think, he had run up to his room while the guests were visiting with his uncle in the living room. He had grabbed the magic saber, determined to make use of its magical powers. Running back down the stairs and into the living room, he had raised the blade high in the air and pronounced the magic words: "Kans, Kins, Kuns, Kilsa, Katapum, Kalen . . ."

The voices in the living room abruptly had stopped abruptly. A huge silence invaded the room. Then Purita the fat lady had said, "Do you see what I see?"

Uncle Eduardo had been unable to suppress a chuckle. He had gone over to the boy, still smiling: "What the hell are you up to, Little Pup? You're not trying to cast a spell on us . . ."

Jacob had not replied. He had spit on the floor and brandished the saber again. "I'm trying to defend you against that one," he had said, indicating Teresa. At which point, his uncle had cut him off sharply. "Go up to your room right now and don't come back down."

That was the night Jacob had decided to leave Can Boig forever. The saber did not work. Nothing was stronger than Teresa's powers. He had walked out onto the balcony, stared out at Venus and implored Ruan to help him. Begged him to come down and carry him back to his house. He was practically screaming the words, but there was no response. Then he thought he would be better off finding his own means of escape. He would take the boat and head for the Pirates' Cave. No one would find him there.

It was a chilly night, but the burning feeling inside had kept him from shivering. Darting from shadow to shadow, he had reached the jetty. He had tried to untie the boat's cover, but his fingers were clumsy and slow, and his hands were not strong enough.

A thousand times he tore at the canvas. He had jumped up and down on it. But the canvas was strong and his feet had slipped every time he jumped.

He had finally given up and walked over to the beach, exhausted. Up above, in the living room, his uncle's guests were laughing. They were discussing him, saying that Jacob was a charming little boy and the nickname Ceibo fit him perfectly.

"The main thing is, I'm sick and tired of Teresa," he says now. And he adds that if uncle Eduardo decided to marry her, he was going to be as miserable as Prince Kalen.

"But how the devil did you get it in your head that Teresa was a witch?"

"My uncle said so."

"When?"

"I don't remember, but he told me so."

"That would have been before. Things are different now."

But by Jacob's standards, witches do not change. They never stop being witches, no matter what.

"Sooner or later she's going to end up just like Visitarana."

"Leave that woman in peace and please stop saying her name out loud," exclaims Dots, crossing her fingers in the shape of a cross. "It's bad luck to talk about her." But what has brought Jacob bad luck has been Teresa's evil deeds.

The morning after his failed escape, Quasimodo had found him stretched out on the beach in a cold sweat, his forehead burning with fever. "It was her," he kept repeating in his delirium. "It was her." He was sure Teresa had caused his illness to keep him from getting away.

Uncle Eduardo had tucked him into bed himself. "You've given us a good scare, Little Pup. What got into your head? Spending the night outdoors, like that."

They had called the doctor, since his fever was very high and, according to Dots, he was drifting in and out of consciousness. Apparently, the big-headed monster had not stopped tormenting him the whole time and, to make matters worse, a pillar of salt had invaded his body.

He had spent several days in bed with a sore throat and sick to his stomach. His uncle had very nearly called his parents, because the doctor had said if he did not improve by the following day, he might have to go to the hospital.

But his parents were not notified in the end and Jacob had emerged from the whole episode five pounds lighter, half an inch taller, and with his hostility towards Teresa noticeably stronger.

"She brings me worse luck," says Jacob now, "and people say her name out loud all day long."

"If you're talking about when you got sick—for your information, young man, that was your fault, not Teresa's."

"That's what you think. When I went into the living room with the saber you gave me, Teresa gave me a weird look and I knew right away something bad was going to happen to me."

"Anyone would get sick after what you did."

"I didn't do anything. All I did was fall asleep on the beach. She did the rest."

"You're being insolent . . ."

"And then after I got better, I got stung by a wasp. Did you forget that?"

"And what does that have to do with anything? I've gotten stung by plenty of wasps. Who the devil hasn't been stung by a wasp some time in their life?"

"Well that one was sent by Teresa."

"It's just a coincidence," insists Dots.

But Jacob does not give in. He is all too familiar with the way witches operate. It is not for nothing that he has had to put up with the wicked witch Hindrance's influence day in and day out.

In any case, one good thing about Jacob's illness was it made his uncle start paying attention to him again. He had even slept in his room at night, stretched out in Dots' bed in case Jacob needed something.

The first day he had started to feel better, they had sat up talking for hours, until the sunrise took them by surprise. It was just like in the good old days, with no thought for how late it was or that he was a little kid who had to be in bed by sundown.

It was a happy, fun-filled night. Uncle Eduardo had talked about jellyfish, comparing them to women just like before. And he had made shadow puppets on the wall, and told Jacob stories about princes who turned into toads and princesses into frogs, and he had even assured him that the tiles on the village housetops really were flying carpets.

And for the first time since Teresa had started hanging around, Jacob felt free of her and her nasty, tricky ways.

That is why, in order to prolong his uncle's presence, Jacob had made up a lie. "You know what, Uncle? Yesterday Princess Kilsa came to visit me. She isn't bad anymore. Now she's good."

That seemed to make his uncle very happy. He had said, if that was the case, they were all going to be very happy, and very soon he would take him out on the *Poseidon*—"so you can see the coast from the deck of a big ship, Little Pup."

But no sooner had Jacob's health improved, than the old patterns were restored and they were back to square one. Teresa was adamant: *Such things are for adults, not for children . . .* And off they went, leaving him alone with Dots and Quasimodo, and with his own particular sadness, full of nostalgia and longing.

He had had no choice but to suck it up and stay home alone, dissecting his memories and conjuring up images of an increasingly uncertain future.

"Haven't you noticed that she has a shadow?"

"No," replies Jacob.

"Well, you would do well to pay more attention. Maybe it will convince you once in for all that Teresa is not a witch."

Dots' point is a clincher. And the truth is, Jacob was lying when Dots asked him about it. He has seen Teresa's shadow more than once. It is long, and delicate and harmonious, a pleasing kind of shadow, like Lori's and Coco's. But Jacob also knows that the exception proves the rule and appearances can be deceiving.

He had been convinced of this after—in a fit of good will and to make his uncle happy—he had decided to talk to her and make an effort to be nice. It had happened a short time after his illness, after he had told his uncle that Princess Kilsa had become good.

It was a sunny day. The two of them were alone on the beach, sitting under the umbrella his uncle had ordered set up for his nephew so the sun would not harm him during his convalescence. In an excited voice, Jacob had told Teresa all about Ruan. How he had visited Can Boig, and his cavernous voice and his cough that sounded just like Quasimodo's. He told her about the trip to the Pirates' Cave with his uncle and filled her in on the enchanted rocks ringing the entrance.

Teresa had listened intently and, for a few minutes, Jacob had even started to believe she might be a normal woman. So he had opened up to her completely, holding nothing back. Becoming more emboldened as he went along, he told her about his astral visits on Clavileño's back and the games on the witches' Sabbath beach. And he had even confided how, one time, he had climbed Roger's apple tree and flown exactly like Peter Pan.

His excitement growing with every word, he had failed to notice the severe expression on his listener's face. He told her about the moonbeam path, the one reflected on the water. "The fairies always put it there so they can go for a walk."

Then Teresa had asked him if he really believed in fairies or if he was just spouting off fantasies. And he had replied that he really did believe in them, except he had never seen them because boys see fairies less often than girls do, so one day Rosario had dressed him up as a girl so he might have a better chance of coming across one.

Teresa's tone had changed abruptly. "But that is an aberration," she had said, her frown deepening. "You should never dress like a girl, Jacob." And then she had started to say mean things about the Spanish nanny. She said the way Jacob was being raised was a disaster. There were already enough faggots in the world, why fan the flames . . . And to reinforce her argument, she had blasted the stupidity of certain people who encouraged children to believe in such ridiculous things as extraterrestrials, and fairies, and enchanted rocks. She said it was high time they put an end to such saccharine and pernicious child-raising practices. Boys should be raised like boys and they shouldn't be allowed to be soft, like little girls. She went so far as to suggest that playing shoe store with matching stones was the stupidest thing she had ever heard in her life. She absolutely could not believe his uncle Eduardo had invented such a game, because she had always considered him to be an intelligent person.

That is when Jacob had understood that Teresa was, in fact, a witch, even though sometimes she managed to pretend otherwise. So he had taken off for the house as fast as he could and shut himself in his bedroom, in order to escape her influence.

The rest had followed in rapid succession: the straw that broke the camel's back. It had all started the same afternoon when Jacob—feeling desperate after having put up with her insolent comments and running away leaving her alone on the beach—had gone out onto the balcony to gaze up at the planet Venus and implore Ruan to come to him.

He had seen them right away. They were pressed against each other next to the magnolia tree, their lips joined as if they were kissing, but in a special way . . . He thought about the song his uncle liked to sing—*Save your kisses for me . . .* —and he told himself his uncle could never sing that song again because he had not saved his kisses for Jacob. And it was all because of Teresa's wicked spells.

Furious, he had shut himself in his room and thrown himself onto the bed, trying to think of a way to calm the frantic beating of his heart. He had suddenly remembered Visitarana's black arts and how she would take revenge on the people who were bothering her, and it occurred to him that he might be able to do the same thing.

Taking a cork he had hidden in the shoebox, he draped it in some rags Dots kept in the chest drawer, knotting one of them to form a head. He stuck two nails in it for the arms and two more for the legs, and he told it that its name was Teresa.

Then he found a pin and began to poke the doll all over with it, just as Visitarana had done: "So you'll learn. So you'll suffer. So you'll just die and get it over with . . ." Totally absorbed in his task, he had failed to hear his uncle calling him from the terrace. "So you'll blow up. So you'll get old overnight. So you'll forget to breathe and suffocate. So the devil will take you away and you get indigestion. So you'll throw up and your stomach will fill up with diarrhea . . ."

He was sweating with pure anticipation and his vision was clouded with excitement. It was like discovering a new world, in which revenge could be reduced exclusively to spells and one's wellbeing was contingent only upon hate.

He had stopped abruptly, because he thought he heard a scream . . . Panting heavily, he had pressed his ear against the window, but there were no more sounds. He looked at the doll and thought it, too, was moaning. "I'm glad," he had murmured. "I'm glad." And he stuck it again. "So you'll lose your voice and turn blind. So you'll get mumps and measles and all the sicknesses in the world . . ."

And he felt happy. So much happier than the night he had played savage beasts. "So the worms eat you and your stomach swells and your face looks like a frog . . ." And when the doll began to fall apart completely, he had tossed it on the floor and stomped on it until it really was in a sorry state.

Then the door had swung open and Dots was standing there. "What the hell are you doing, Jacob? Can't you hear your uncle calling you?"

Jacob had just stared at her, his eyes radiant and his face flushed with excitement and surprise. "Is she dead?" he had asked.

Dots had stared at the rags on the floor, flabbergasted. "What is that?" He had said it was nothing, but Dots had wanted to know. "What kind of game is this?"—and when Jacob did not answer— "What did you just ask me? Who was supposed to die?"

Frightened, Jacob had taken off down the stairs and rushed out onto the terrace. There was Teresa with his uncle, safe and sound, smiling, and her eyes, greener than ever, drilling into his.

That night, Jacob had been unable to touch his food. Neither his uncle nor Teresa had noticed his lack of appetite. And naturally, that night he had dreamed about the big-headed monster and Dots had had to wake him up because, apparently, he was screaming like a banshee.

Now Dots moves closer to him and tries to caress his hair. "Tell me the truth, Jacob. What were you doing that afternoon with the cork and the rags?"

"Nothing."

"I bet you were trying to copy Visitarana."

"No I wasn't."

The wind is still blowing hard and the magnolia is so bent over it looks as if it might snap any minute. "If this hurricane lasts much longer, it's going to topple the magnolia," remarks Dots.

But Jacob does not care whether the magnolia falls over or not, or whether the sea suffers, or whether the whole house blows down. The only thing he cares about is that the image of Teresa be wiped out. By any means, at any cost.

18

Now that the wind died down, the *Poseidon* has stopped rocking and the waves are lapping gently at the hull.

Still sulking, Jacob watches the night fall across the beach, the sea and the terrace. The stars come out one by one, their glow producing mysterious, asymmetrical, patterns on the bluffs. As the evening wears on, the brambles and the bald areas expand until the lighthouse has bathed everything in its light.

It had been a boring and hostile afternoon, very much like the evenings he had spent at grandmother Katherine's house. Maybe that is why Pierre suddenly comes to mind. And for the first time since coming to Can Boig, Jacob misses him terribly.

"You need to brush your hair, Jacob," Dots yells from the kitchen. "Your uncle will be back soon."

Before—thinks the child—*his uncle never worried about brushed hair, or brushed teeth, or a stained shirt.* Which is why he would rather his uncle found him just as he left him when the wind was still blowing: his hair all mussed up, submersed in gloom and wandering bored and listless about the living room, Duke by his side.

"And wash your hands."

"They're not dirty," he responds furiously from the sofa. At the sound of his voice, Duke cocks his ears, as if he just smelled a rabbit.

If only Pierre were there. Maybe he would be able to think of a way to put an end to Teresa and her hateful friends once and for all. The ones that call him "Ceibo" all the time and tell his uncle he should change his ways with the boy. But Pierre is far away—terribly far away—and Jacob has the impression that nothing and nobody is going to help him ward off the terrible sense of isolation taking hold of him.

If only he could make contact with Richard . . . Richard died, and the dead—according to the grown ups—like to help the living, especially when they are called upon in a desperate trance. But his uncle has banned the séances in no uncertain terms, making any possible dialogue with Richard look more and more complicated.

Surely Richard has no idea what is going on between his wife and Jacob's uncle. Quite possibly, no one has told him that the minute he died, the first thing Teresa did was head straight for Can Boig and leave the yacht anchored day after day in front of the beach.

Someone needed to fill him in about all this. When it came right down to it, the dead had a right to know these things. The dead—at least this is what Jacob has always heard—are holy and should be worshiped the way you do a guardian angel and Ruan.

He thinks back to Richard's failed attempt to communicate with his uncle through the table. He probably wanted to say something about Teresa. Maybe he wanted to warn him about her evil nature and advise him to be on his guard against her and try to avoid her witchcraft. But his uncle not only refused to accept this, he got mad at everybody, as if Richard's attempted communication were merely a joke in bad taste.

He suddenly remembers Lori. She will help me. Lori is good. She is not a traitor and she does not get tired of things the way his uncle has. Besides Lori talks to the dead through tables. He will ask her to arrange a session at her house . . . And when the table asks Jacob which dead person he would like to speak to, he will not have to haul out his grandfather again. *I'll talk to Richard. I'll tell him everything*, he thinks.

He also still has Ruan. All he has to do is climb a tamarind tree and tell a goldfinch to get a message to him. The only problem is figuring out a way to get to the village.

But once he takes an idea into his head, Jacob rarely lets anything get in his way. Trying to seem very casual, he finds Quasimodo in the dining room, busily juggling plates, silverware and glasses.

"Quasimodo—"

The servant grumbles, says he's very busy and he has to hurry, since his boss is about to return.

"I want you to take me to the village."

The plates are balanced on Quasimodo's arm, and he leans his elbow on the table.

"Right now?"

"No. Tomorrow."

"What do you want to go to the village for?"

Jacob shrugs.

"Well, you better give me a better explanation than that or else you'll be staying home."

Jacob hesitates, takes a deep breath and finally decides. "I want to climb a tamarind tree."

"That's silly. The things you get into your head. As if there weren't trees all over the place right here."

"Tamarinds are different. They're full of goldfinches."

"And what do goldfinches have to do with anything?"

"They can fly to Venus."

Quasimodo squints his good eye in confusion. He lays the plates on the table and bursts out laughing.

"Who told you that goldfinches fly to Venus?"

"Uncle Eduardo."

Quasimodo nods. He seems to hesitate for moment, not sure what the child is getting at. "Well, if your uncle says so, it must be true."

"Uncle Eduardo never lies. You know that. And he promised me that all the goldfinches in the world have visited Venus."

"Okay. So what does that have to do with it?"

"I want them to take a message to Ruan."

"That fathead? Why do you want them to take a message there?"

"Ruan is my friend and I want to see him."

"You shouldn't take advantage of your friends."

"I'm not. I just want to see him so he can take me back with him."

"Back where?"

"Where else? To his planet."

"And what will your uncle say when he finds out you've gone to another planet?"

"Nothing. I doubt he'll even care."

The car's engines can be heard outside, returning from the village, and Duke rushes impetuously to the door to greet his master.

"Well, that's enough talk, kid. They're back."

But Jacob does not budge. "Will you take me to the village?"

"I'll take you."

"Tomorrow?"

"Tomorrow."

Dots is still issuing commands from the kitchen. "Brush your hair, Jacob. Wash your hands. Smile. Don't act like you've been to a funeral . . ."

Jacob acquiesces. He no longer cares whether Dots jumps on him. Quasimodo's promise has made him feel more relaxed. He runs obediently up the stairs to his room. In a short time, he will have to go down to the living room, scrubbed, clean, and brushed. He will have to greet all the guests: say *buona sera* to the Italian couple, shake hands with the marquis, put up with Flora's inspection, listen to Purita's eternal jabber about where she got the scars on her face and undergo an obnoxious once-over from Mauricio Belarmino, who has become insufferable ever since he took it upon himself to throw Teresa and the painter back together.

And when it came to Mr. Raimundo—he had also lost out when Teresa arrived. Now he spends his whole day making sure nothing is missing and everything is going smoothly and the meals are "on schedule."

More than once Jacob has heard him discussing this with Dots. "We're going to have to turn Can Boig into a bourgeois household . . ." "The maestro thinks Teresa is absolutely right when she says we were living like heathens before she arrived . . ."

Mauricio Belarmino is another story. He has got it made. "I'll never be able to thank you enough for all you've done for us," he tells uncle Eduardo. And with that as his excuse, he has started to boss everybody else around.

But the worst part of all is Teresa's stare. Ever since he made the doll to give her the evil eye that did not work, Teresa has not stopped staring at him, as if she knows full well what he had in mind.

It went beyond what you might expect. Teresa "knew" and "was aware of" and "found out" things the way only half-human, half-immortal beings can "know," or "be aware of," or "find out."

Once, Jacob tried to ascertain the extent of Teresa's powers of divination. But the only thing that became crystal clear to him was just how much everyone enjoyed calling attention to Jacob's unfortunate situation and the understandable tendency to turn into a ceibo. "My sister-in-law has married someone else, you know?" his uncle had explained. And Mauricio Belarmino had lost no time in remarking that children of divorce tend to be rather peculiar and you had to keep a close eye on them, because they had a proclivity to latch on to any sort of deviant behavior.

Then Purita the fat lady had launched into her own story, speaking of deviant behavior. Laughing hysterically, she said her husband had the bad habit of "doing it" with a man. "You heard me right. If it had been a woman, at least . . . But no, the guy had a beard and everything. Isn't that the limit?"

And she would draw near the painter so he could observe the scars her husband's male lover had given her when she threatened to report them to the police as perverts. "He hit me with a bottle, the slimy pig. A bottle—right in the forehead . . ."

Even if it was "the limit," anybody could tell from a mile away that Purita loved telling the story. "I caught them cooing all over each other like two little turtle doves. Imagine my trauma: two sodomite pigs making love. Can you imagine anything more ridiculous?"

The same day, he had asked Quasimodo what the word sodomite meant and Quasimodo had just stood there incredulous, staring at him with his good eye. Where in heaven did you come up with that word, boy? He said he heard Purita say it. And Quasimodo had gritted his teeth as if he would have liked to send her straight to hell. A woman like that would turn anyone into a fag . . ." But he stopped there and Jacob could only figure that fag and sodomite were similar words.

Quasimodo also said that a sodomite was someone who came from Sodom. Lot's city? he had asked. And Quasimodo had said yes. Apparently everybody who lived in the city were *that* word his father repeated whenever he saw Jacob cower in the face of danger.

Next, Jacob had wanted to know what Purita meant when she said her husband was "making love." According to what he had heard, love was not something you could impose or force on someone, much less make. He thought love was something you felt. But Quasimodo had dodged the question, saying Jacob should do him the favor of changing the subject because such topics were not appropriate for children.

Through his bedroom door, Jacob can hear Mr. Raimundo telling Dots what to do. "Make sure Quasimodo does not announce dinner until the soufflé has risen and is at just the right point," he is admonishing her. Then Jacob hears him move towards the dining room to survey the table and make sure Quasimodo has placed the candles in such a way as to create a "decadent" yet "nostalgic" atmosphere. And Flora, Purita's friend, will be right there behind him, making sure nothing is out of place and dinner goes smoothly.

Jacob has already figured out that Flora is actually little more than Teresa's handmaiden. Teresa takes advantage of her every chance she gets: "Flora, check on the boy . . . Flora, tell Dots to keep an eye on the roast. Ten more minutes in the oven is more than enough . . . Flora, the ice tastes like a dirty freezer. Tell Quasimodo he should scrub it out with bicarbonate . . ."

Teresa was not the only one either. It seemed as if everybody treated Flora like their gofer. And even though they said thank you, they would make fun of her as soon as her back was turned. They said Flora would stoop much lower than that—in fact, she would sell her soul to the devil—as long as they let her ride on the *Poseidon*.

Yet Flora also seemed to hold Teresa in very high regard for whenever Jacob—unable to contain himself—showed any hostility towards her, Flora rose to her defense, claws bared: "You're not being fair, Jacob. Teresa is a good person and that's why your uncle loves her: because she's such a good person . . ."

Until one day, Jacob had told Flora straight out that Teresa did not love anybody. He said Teresa only thought about herself and made fun of her whenever her back was turned. Flora had turned every shade of red and said it was hard to believe he could be such a liar. She said Teresa never spoke ill of anyone, much less to their backs . . . And just because of what he had said, his uncle had made him stand in the corner, and would not let him play spit on the stick and fetch with Duke for a whole hour.

Since then, his uncle never puts Jacob to bed anymore. It is as if he wants to punish him for everything he has said about Teresa. Which is why, when he sees him at the bedroom door, just back from the village, Jacob feels his heart in his throat.

"I've come to speak with you," uncle Eduardo says, his expression severe, adding that Dots has filled him in on his behavior that afternoon. "Things cannot go on like this, Jacob. Children need to go out and play. It's not healthy to sit inside all day like a stick of furniture."

"It was windy."

But his uncle said a little wind never hurt anybody.

"You know I love you, Little Pup. That's why I don't like it when you act the victim."

His uncle would never have spoken to him like that before. He had never ever reproached him. Before, he would have stroked Jacob's head and told him whatever he did was well done.

"I know I've been a little hard on you, but the truth is you've deserved it, Little Pup. When children get rebellious, they have to be disciplined."

Before he would have said, "You'll have enough on your plate when fall comes." That is why it hurts even worse now, to hear his uncle say such things.

"I don't like to punish you, Jacob. I swear I don't."

Before, the only punishments had been meted out to the petrified pirates or Princess Kilsa. His uncle had never so much as suggested that some day he might punish Jacob too. That is why he taught him to skip flat stones like flying saucers.

"I hope you understand, Little Pup."

Jacob does not reply. Miserable, he throws himself on his bed and presses his face into the pillow.

"You are definitely not the same, Jacob."

His uncle's statement does not seem at all fair to him. He is the one who has changed. But he dares not say it.

"Do you hear me, Jacob? It's as if you aren't anything like me any more."

Hearing that, Jacob takes off his glasses, because he can no longer contain his sobs.

"Come on, Little Pup. What will our guests think if they see you crying?"

He is not crying. It is one continuous sob, a violent, suffocating wave that causes his chest to swell and will not allow him to speak. The pillow is drenched with tears and his nose is a fountain.

His uncle sits down on the edge of the bed and tries to gather him in his arms, but Jacob's body has gone suddenly rigid and his uncle soon tires of struggling with him.

"Come on, Little Pup. Don't you love me any more?"

Jacob is on the verge of saying no, he does not love him any more. But he knows it is a lie and his uncle would know it too. He just sobs, with a sound much like an adult would make. His mother had sounded like that when Jacob surprised her all sprawled out on the bed, and she would try to cover up her sadness.

"I'm begging you, Little Pup. Tell your uncle what is wrong."

Little by little, the child's body relaxes. "I want to go to Venus," he says. It is the only thing that occurs to him.

"So you're crying because you want to go to Venus."

"No," he corrects him. "I want to go to Venus because I feel like crying and I don't want your friends to make fun of me. At least I can cry in peace there."

Eduardo Santillana bites his lips and allows a small chuckle to escape. "But Venusians don't like it when people cry. What will Ruan say when he finds out you know how to cry?"

Jacob inhales deeply until a deep sob catches in his throat. "But you said when days die, they don't come back, and I helped you bury them."

"Did I say that? Maybe I did . . . But I still don't understand the thing about Venus."

"And you said I wouldn't need the stone from Ruan because I'd always have you."

"And you do have me."

"No I don't." He says it angrily. It is a furious, cutting retort. "Besides, I'm not the most important thing to you anymore."

"Who told you that?"

"You did. You have Teresa. She's the most important thing."

He is no longer crying. He has stood up and is reaching for his glasses.

"It's not the same," he exclaims. "Nothing is."

And he shakes his head, stubborn, sulking, indignation pouring out of him. Eduardo Santillana contemplates him coldly.

"Now I know what's going on with you."

"No you don't know," replies the child. "You can't know. If you did know . . ."

"If I knew what?"

"Nothing."

With a dignified, contained gesture, Jacob opens the closet and extracts the stone from Ruan. "I'm going to take it with me wherever I go," he says. "I won't ever leave it here again."

His uncle grabs him by the shoulders, obliging the boy to face him. "You don't need the stone. I told you, I'm here."

But Eduardo Santillana's voice does not match his expression. He is trying to look serious, but his lips are twitching mockingly and the words sound mechanical and totally lacking in sincerity.

Jacob senses something new in his uncle. It is something he cannot quite put his finger on, or gauge, or define, but it is awakening a jumble of opaque, confusing sensations in him.

"Relax, Jacob. Nobody can take your place."

And Jacob's secret yearnings allow him to rekindle his hope.

"Will I have to eat in the kitchen?"

"No, Little Pup. Tonight you will join us in the dining room."

19

It had been an awkward meal, fraught with tensions, furtive glances and patronizing remarks. "We really missed you, Jacob. Too bad you couldn't go into the village with us." Masks, placating remarks, anything to buffer those nebulous fears that been threatening a storm for several days now.

Just one look at Teresa's caricature of a smile, Flora's ironic expression and the marquis' clueless and mildly curious look, or Purita's and Mauricio Belarmino's watchful gazes, and you could see the discomfort behind the veneer of civility.

Sometimes an inexplicable sixth sense can explain many things and that is what made Jacob feel so uncomfortable in the midst of all the playacting. It is as if his uncle had issued a general recommendation: *We need to handle Jacob with kid gloves . . . He's a little vulnerable . . . We have to be careful not to hurt his feelings . . .* The slightest hint of affability, therefore, struck him as condescending, as totally perfunctory, pure duplicity.

Mr. Raimundo had also contributed his two cents to the recently launched "best buddies" campaign. There was no earthly reason for him to have spent half the night talking about the treasure Jacob and his uncle had discovered in the cave or the importance of shadows for human beings. No reason at all for the dog and pony show when he had stepped in front of a lamp so every last person could see that he had a shadow.

Sometimes, without warning, the group would lapse into silence. Gaping expanses of air would soak up every last trace of naturalness and, despite all efforts to avoid it, would inevitably lead to the wrong conclusion.

Close-mouthed, ill-at-ease and listless, Jacob had contemplated his uncle warily, because deep inside, he knew it was all nothing but a cheap show. That is why whatever was said seemed to hang in the air with no obvious target. Remarks were tossed out randomly, in no rational order, like aimless insects buzzing about your ears, being bothersome and pesky just to prove they were still around.

They had talked about the *Poseidon*. About how much Jacob was going to enjoy going aboard and sailing along the coast. "You've never seen anything more impressive," Teresa had predicted. And Jacob had thought again how Teresa acted as if she owned the whole sea, just like Princess Kilsa. And they had talked about the political situation, the famous march for freedom, the Marxist plague that had pervaded the country and nascent terrorism in the north. All matters for serious, boring people, including words Jacob had never heard before.

And naturally, certain unfortunate topics had also come up: quick flashes that rocked the more or less hypothetical status quo: "I've always said a six-year-old child is nothing more than an emotional embryo . . ." Teresa had reacted to that by giving Purita a swift kick under the table signaling her to change the subject, since such remarks might hurt young Jacob's feelings.

So Flora, always on the ball, had backed Teresa up by saying that there were children, and then there were children, and Jacob, for example, was a stellar example of an intelligent boy, a mentally sound boy . . .

It had not been difficult for Jacob to intercept the looks the two women had exchanged or his uncle's relieved expression.

Teresa had immediately broached the topic of flowers and how ridiculous they looked when condemned by people to be nothing more than insipid bouquets. "Don't even think about putting flowers on my grave," she had said. "I would not hesitate to rise up from my coffin, just to brush them off."

Then the marquis had wondered how such an obviously vital woman could even consider talking about graves. And the Italian woman seconded the thought, gushing that Teresa must certainly be immortal. She, for one, was sure the goddess Thetis had dipped Teresa in the River Styx at birth, just as she had done with her son Achilles.

Eduardo Santillana had applauded and then raised his index finger: "Be very careful though. If Thetis dipped Teresa in the River Styx, she must have been holding on to some part of her . . ."

So that meant Teresa, like Achilles, was vulnerable in the heel. While everybody was chuckling at the notion, what was left engraved in Jacob's mind was the thought that Teresa could die because of her heel.

Later, they had gone out onto the terrace because after all that wind, the night had turned calm and the sky was full of stars. Uncle Eduardo had grabbed the guitar right away and asked Jacob to sing *Save your kisses for me.*

He had complied without enthusiasm, almost huffily, but Teresa had listened contentedly and told him what a great job he had done.

Then Jacob had said he was tired and his uncle had taken him up to bed himself. "Sleep well, Little Pup."

But Jacob was not at all tired. It had just been an excuse because a plan had occurred to him during dinner, and he was not about to miss his chance for anything in this world.

The idea had popped into his head all of the sudden, when Mauricio Belarmino had remarked that the truth is spoken only in one's absence and, as a journalist, he would sometimes give a good deal to have an invisible cloak. That way, he could lurk in the privacy of people's homes and discover what they were really about: "I'm so tired of all the talk about sincerity and honesty and self-realization, and all the other crap everybody spouts off about, but nobody believes," he said. "It would be quite something to see a few of those paragons of virtue in their everyday routine. We'd soon find out what becomes of all their sincerity and honesty rubbish then."

And that is exactly what Jacob is hoping to obtain: an invisible cloak so he can go back downstairs and listen in on the grown-ups' conversation. If—as he was promised—Ruan's stone possesses powers far superior to those of the paper saber, there should be no problem obtaining one.

So as soon as his uncle has left the bedroom, Jacob leaps out of bed and opens the balcony door. The terrace awnings have been pulled down, but you can tell the houseguests are nearby from of the murmur emanating from behind the cloth.

"Ruan, listen to me. Ruan . . ."

Heart thumping wildly, he calls out to him in a low voice so no one will hear him, clutching the stone in one hand. ". . . Can you hear me Ruan? I want to go down to the living room when they can't see me, so I can find out if my uncle is tricking me or not."

But Ruan does not answer and the sky is serene and full of twinkling lights.

"Please, Ruan. Give me an invisible cloak." He says it breathlessly, his eyes shut fast and his hand all sweaty. "A cloak so I can hear what they really think." He remains like that for a while, quiet, expectant, his face upturned, and the lighthouse beam winking at him.

Then the wondrous thing happens. As soon as he opens his eyes, an immense trail of light shoots across the sky from end to end only to fall right behind the lighthouse, very close to Can Boig.

And Jacob knows it has been sent by Ruan in answer to his plea. It is as if he were saying, *You can go on down, Jacob. No one will know you are there*. The realization makes his chest swell with pleasure. At last Ruan has seen fit to answer him.

Still holding the stone, he opens the bedroom door and heads determinedly towards the living room. It is mostly dark. They are taking their coffee on the terrace. Uncle Eduardo and Teresa are sharing a lounge chair facing out towards the lighthouse, their backs to the house.

Jacob is no longer afraid. He knows Ruan is helping him. Knows that, even though it might not look like it, he has lent Jacob a special cloak to make him invisible to others. Not even Duke, stretched out at Purita's feet, seems to have noticed his presence.

Cautious, he does not dare to venture out onto the terrace. He remains in the living room, sandwiched between the frame of the open glass door and the closed curtain. From this vantage point, none of Teresa's friends can be compared to his uncle's old friends. They are more like his parents' friends, or Roger, and maybe even a little bit like his grandmother Katherine. Especially Flora. They all say the same things in the same kinds of voices. They are repulsive beings who do not hesitate to point out that Jacob was being deformed by such a permissive environment. Eduardo Santillana has been far too indulgent. He has gone too far, and if Jacob keeps on the way he has been, impetuous, demanding, and bossy, he is going to end up like a carnival freak: a child who has deviated from all the logical rules of nature.

And to reinforce this thesis, Mauricio Belarmino insists: ". . . Do any of you consider it normal for a child of six to be so head over heels in love with a grown man?"

His words cause chuckles all around. "Come on, Mauricio. Don't be such a doomsayer," retorts his uncle.

But Purita the fat lady backs him up: "Who's to say my husband's tendencies didn't start early on in his childhood, precisely because of a situation like Ceibo's?"

And the Italian lady jumps in, "It is true—most of our afflictions start in childhood."

The marquis also has something to say. "There've been worse cases, my dear Eduardo. Just allow Mauricio to tell you what he knows."

And Mauricio launches into the same stories Jacob has heard on other occasions. Ambiguous refrains he does not understand about high school, and certain teachers, and the idiotic behavior of certain students . . . They are vague, meaningless references, but suddenly they seem to attach themselves to him: to his circumstances, to his passionate feelings for his uncle, to his desperate need not to lose him.

"And I can assure you that it was not a strictly platonic love affair," continues the journalist. "It was the scandal of the season." And he quickly daubs at his forehead with his handkerchief because the sweat is running down his cheeks and probably tickles.

Mauricio Belarmino knows a lot of stories and he does not pull any punches, so when he tells the story about the boy who was perverted by his teacher, he does not leave out a single detail.

Eduardo Santillana looks around, as if afraid Jacob might be able to hear them.

"Come on, Maestro. Don't get all worked up," says Purita the fat lady. "Ceibo is asleep. You don't have to watch what you say."

And Jacob shrinks back, clutching the curtain with rigid hands. Teresa is next. She says it is fortunate Jacob is not there right now and, though she does not rule out that he may have fallen in love with his uncle, the real problem is the child needs affection, because no one has shown it to him before.

"Do you really think Jacob has fallen in love with me?" asks the painter, seeming almost pleased.

And kissing him, Teresa responds that it is very hard not to fall in love with him. It is the most natural thing in the world to fall in love with Eduardo Santillana.

Jacob's stomach is churning with anxiety. The curtain is suffocating him and the heat is making his eyes blur. If only he could understand what he is hearing, but all he can do is absorb the sense of it, because the grown-ups speak a different language than he does and it all seems to skitter out of reach before he can truly grasp it.

"Be that as it may, I can promise you one thing, my dear Teresa. He is not a dangerous rival."

But the journalist says he does not agree. Sometimes the ones who seem the most innocuous are the ones you have to worry about the most. Eduardo Santillana would do well to be cautious, because certain tendencies can mark a man for life.

"You are carrying this way too far," retorts his uncle. "Jacob is not in love with me, at least not in that way, and it has never crossed my mind that I might pervert him . . . Teresa is right: he just needs affection. When it comes down to it, he is just another victim of our screwed up lifestyle. A poor uprooted soul who everybody has simply brushed off as if he were a fly."

But Teresa insists that no grown-up should give in to the whims of a child and she cringes whenever she thinks of all the things his uncle let him do before she arrived.

"He was happy," his uncle shoots back. "Why deny him that?" And he laughs. He repeats that Jacob is innocent. He has never seen the sordid side of things. The child is completely guileless and he, for one, is convinced he has not caused the boy any harm.

The voices blend. Everybody has something to say. It is as if one of the mountains had crumbled and rocks were raining down on the terrace. Teresa asks for silence. She says no one can understand a thing anybody is saying. And then she returns to the subject of guile in children. "Don't think they are such little angels. Some are better than others, but they all have an arsenal of wickedness inside them."

Agitated, she stands, walks over to the railing, and stares out into the night just as if it were daytime, completely sure of herself, the beam from the lighthouse illuminating her features. Eduardo Santillana walks over to her and puts his arm around her waist. They remain standing in that position, their backs to the others, as if the islet had hypnotized them.

A pungent smell permeates the curtain. A smell reminiscent of the bitter herbs Coco used to smoke. "Imagine letting Jacob ingest alcohol . . . ," Teresa is saying. And his uncle says he only drank a little bit: just enough to make him happy. But Teresa is adamant, ". . . and smoke. Imagine the kind of future you were laying out for him!"

The Italian man interrupts them. He says that the future is always an unknown and one cannot extrapolate too much just from tobacco.

But Jacob hardly hears what they are saying, The smell of the curtain is making him dizzy. He can hardly breathe.

Somebody mentions Ruan. He realizes this because they are saying something about Venus and Mars and the moon, but he does not understand what the word galaxy means or grasp the sense of their conversation.

"Imagine for a moment that an extraterrestrial comes to our planet and, wishing to analyze our soil, he grabs a piece of cow manure. Who is to convince him it is not a treasure?" asks the Italian, smiling. And he repeats ad nauseam that everything in this life is predictable, precarious, and intangible.

Jacob's body is coated with sour sweat. And fear. A jolt of fear that makes him tremble. He does not trust the invisible cloak any more. His legs feel weak and he is no longer plagued by the need to know. What plagues him now are the questions. The monstrous questions the grown-ups have raised and he cannot solve.

Still squatting and on tip-toes, he lets go of the curtain. He notes with terror that the distance between the plate glass window and the door to the hallway has grown. When he came into the living room it had not been that far, that is for sure. Or maybe it just seems that way because Ruan's cloak has lost its invisible powers.

Trying not to make a sound, the child creeps softly along the edges of the room, step after step. His legs hurt. It is hard to walk like that, his heels touching his thighs, and the fear of being caught sabotaging his breathing.

It takes a long time to get to the stairs. Back on the terrace, they are all still talking, laughing, and the motley assortment of voices drifts off pointlessly into the night.

When he finally gets to his room he sees that Dots' bed is empty. His heart still thumping wildly, Jacob slides under the covers without undressing, and tries to think.

20

Through one, barely cracked eyelid, the child had observed Dots to make sure she was sleeping soundly. He was still sweating and his mouth was completely dry.

He had decided not to wait for Quasimodo to wake up. Afraid he might oversleep, he had gone down to the garage as soon as he was sure everyone else had gone to bed.

It had been a long, soundless, exhausting vigil. The hours had dragged on interminably: superfluous hours, out of sync, devoid of rhythm or relief. He had had to fight off sleep with all his might, especially as dawn neared. He had pinched his face several times, wiggled his legs and even jumped up and down once or twice, just like he used to when he would gallop along the hillside with Duke.

He had finally heard Quasimodo's footsteps approaching the garage. The servant was carrying the basket for purchases in one hand and whistling, just like his uncle did whenever he got into the car. No sooner had he lifted the garage door, than he had noticed the boy curled up on the floor.

"Well, look who's here."

Quasimodo had forgotten all about their agreement and Jacob had been obliged to refresh his memory. "Stubborn as a mule, aren't you, boy? You're still set on climbing the tamarind tree?"

But the tamarind is no longer on Jacob's agenda. The conversation between the grown-ups had called for a change of plans.

It is a clear morning. The sun is pale and the sky empty of clouds or mist. It is a virgin morning, fresh and new. Maybe that's why the mountain flanking the village looks so stodgy and ancient and cheerless.

Beyond the bluff to his right, Jacob glimpses the sea, cold, calm, and so smooth it seems almost fossilized, and even the rocks casting their shadows on the water's edge seem old to him.

"I'd like to bet you've never gotten up this early before."

Jacob lets the question hang and Quasimodo just keeps on whistling. He is oblivious to the child's distress, convinced this expedition to the village is just another whim. Some sort of pig-headed mutiny to shake off the boredom that had set in when Can Boig turned into a respectable household.

Jacob absently pats his pocket. He is no longer carrying Ruan's stone. He is not entirely sure why, but after overhearing the adults' conversation, the stone seems to have lost some of its value. In its place is the five Euro bill the tooth fairy left under his pillow when he lost his tooth.

"I warn you, once we get to the village, I won't be able to babysit you. I have a long list of things to buy and no time to waste."

"It doesn't matter. When I'm finished, I'll wait for you at Lori's house."

"At this time of day, you'll probably find her asleep. Anyway, I'm not sure your uncle would approve."

"He doesn't have to find out."

Quasimodo shrugs and coughs slightly. Then he clears his throat and resumes whistling.

"If you don't tell him . . ."

The village gradually comes into view around the mountain. From the highway, it looks stunted, its church rising up from the center of the horseshoe. Next Jacob can pick out the pine forest, the wall of eucalyptus trees and the plain of cork oak.

There is the usual morning bustle as they enter the village proper, half-castrated sounds that dissolve into the smell of the sea. An early riser after some sea air is launching his boat into the water. A body, half-lethargic from sleep and last night's drinking, leaps out of the vehicle's path. Cars line the street, parked up on the sidewalks so as not to disturb the morning traffic. But what Jacob notices most of all are the empty terraces, the closed bars, the trash accumulated in the nooks and crannies of the wall along the water's edge.

It is the first time Jacob has seen the village at this hour and it seems like a different place entirely. You might say it is like a poor copy of the village he has gotten to know. Even the tourists look different. They walk slowly and uncertainly, as if trying to prolong a time that cannot be prolonged, or start a day that is not primed to start yet. Hybrid creatures with aimless expressions, disconnected from their surroundings, as if they were out wandering the streets with no plan or goal other than to start amassing bodies out there, at an hour when bodies tend to stay hidden behind the gates, within the protection of four walls.

There is also a lot of dust—on feet, in hair, on outfits—probably the product of yesterday afternoon's windstorm. And a lot of uncombed beards and heads. And the infuriated eyes of an old man, maybe because he is ashamed he is so old . . .

"We're there, Jacob."

In the center of the village everything is different. The noise level rises, steps quicken, and bodies converge at market stalls. The car pulls up next to a row of boats recently moored high up on the beach. Quasimodo has friends among the seafaring men and always finds a special spot where he can leave the vehicle.

The cacophony of noises grows: squealing tires as the cars make their way through the multitudes. Babes in arms bellowing, dogs barking. And griping. Lots of griping. Vendors griping about customers. Customers griping about the vendors. A woman griping about being a woman, as if that were frustration enough. And a man griping about the way women whine . . . And there is laughter too, and random exclamations.

There along the beachfront, fishermen are blowing into mugs of milk, no doubt to vanquish their hangovers and the overpowering exhaustion of catching and selling fish. They stare into their mugs as if it is the only thing that enables them to go on.

"We'll meet right back here in two hours," Quasimodo warns him. "Don't even think about making me wait."

Jacob says yes, he'll be there, and runs off, disappearing into the crowd of people milling about beyond the market. He finds the narrow side street that leads up to the church. It winds steeply upward like a tunnel between the houses. Jacob knows this street very well, because he has often come up here with his uncle, seeking the highest point in the village.

The first time they had reached the little square up above, his uncle had explained that the church was from the Baroque period. "I'll take you in there one day so you can see it."

When Jacob asked what it was used for, his uncle had responded that it was so the tourists would visit it and tell everybody that Spain was full of art.

It was there, near the church, where he had first encountered Visitarana. Jacob remembers her as a scurrying bundle, black and hunched over, making her way towards a red doorway. "That's where Visitarana lives," his uncle had told him. And he had been sorry he had forgotten his paper saber.

That was the afternoon he had tripped on the step as soon as they had arrived home . . . The afternoon when he had gotten diarrhea and lost a tooth.

It is clear to him, however, that no matter how powerful a witch Visitarana might be, she could never be as evil as Teresa. Which is why, Jacob feels a certain degree of sympathy for the old lady.

Although the street is very steep, the coolness of the narrow passageway helps to mitigate the weariness. It is pleasant to breathe in this marine atmosphere, so full of possibility.

But the street soon ends in a three way fork and Jacob cannot remember which one he is supposed to take. He picks the middle one. It is the steepest of the three, but it might also be shorter.

The village sounds gradually recede as he climbs. He can barely hear the vague reverberations of barking and voices. On either side, still sleeping, are whitewashed hovels featuring twisted, uneven windows in patterns he has seen a million times, reproduced in his uncle's paintings.

One house has been adapted to serve as a storefront. Instead of a front door, counters set behind large windowpanes reveal cheap clothing confected from garish, multicolored fabrics, embroidered espadrilles and long, crudely fashioned chains braided unevenly in a way that screams handmade. Antique books and used objects are displayed on modern tables, along with handkerchiefs, bikinis, towels, postcards.

"Out of my way, kid."

A tall, severe looking woman hurrying up the pebbled street nearly bumps right into him. She is carrying a huge green water jug on her head and barely avoids dumping it all over him.

He would like to stop the woman, ask her where he is. But even though she is barefoot, the woman is moving up the hill with the nimble grace of a deer. Jacob's is feeling increasingly uneasy. He is afraid he is lost. He suddenly realizes that nothing around him resembles the streets he walked with his uncle.

Then something arrives to comfort him: it is the scent of flowers. Surely the same flowers he and his uncle saw that afternoon across from Visitarana's house. The church cannot be far away. The brusque, deafening clang of church bells confirms it.

Jacob does not understand why the church has a belfry. In fact, he does not understand exactly what a church is. His uncle's explanation had done nothing to elucidate the matter.

He remembers Rosario telling him once that people went to church when they felt like being good. She said God lived there. But when Jacob wanted to know who God was, a scandalized Rosario had taken her head in her hands and asked hadn't anyone ever told him about God before. And Jacob had said sometimes, at school. So Rosario had explained that God had "created us and without Him, neither you nor I, nor anyone else had any purpose on earth."

But then Jacob's parents had said she shouldn't be filling the child's head with such strange ideas, and no more talking to him about God. There would be time for that when Jacob was older and able to decide for himself. It was better to leave him alone and not try to manipulate his beliefs. That's why he had not been baptized yet. It was very serious, very serious indeed, to interfere with children's consciences. They could end up deformed. . . .

Rosario had been very angry that day. She had even stood up to his mother, her boss: "And meanwhile, what? Are we supposed to leave him without food or schooling? Not take care of him until he's 'older'?" And she had launched into a tirade against modern fads that forgot all about God and—to keep from deforming consciences—ended up deforming the most undeformable principles: "A crime, that's what it is, Jacob. That's what they're doing to you, you poor little wretch. It's a real crime." And to make sure he would at least have a vague notion of who God was, she had said that on the day we are born, God gives each of us a guardian angel to protect us. So when Jacob was still with Rosario, he never went to bed without reciting, "Angel of God, my guardian dear . . ."

But the truth is, he has not recited it since coming to Can Boig, because neither Dots, nor Quasimodo, nor his uncle have told him to say his prayers.

There is the church, adjacent to the flowered balcony. Comforted, Jacob contemplates the house where people go when they want to be good. It is open and every time the door moves, a strange odor of perfumed dampness wafts out onto the square. Adjacent to the stonework flanking the entrance is a high wall with a built-in bench. Below, the tile roofs cascade downward towards a calm sea still lost in the dim morning light.

Jacob would like to go into the church to see if God really does live there like Rosario said. But he is a little intimidated by the darkness he glimpses whenever somebody pushes the door open. Besides, his uncle has assured him that churches have been put there for tourists to visit, and he is no tourist. That is why he dares not enter. They might throw him out and then his uncle would give him a good dressing down.

He walks resolutely over to the red door. It is closed and the slightest of cracks can be observed between the glass and the frame of the tiny window in the whitewashed façade.

He reaches down and pats his pocket one more time, just in case.

The bill is safe and sound inside. Uncle Eduardo himself had told him not long ago, "You never know what might happen, Little Pup. Put the money away in your treasure box."

Well, what might happen *has* happened and that is why Jacob had not hesitated to retrieve the bill. His father always used to say that money will open any door. And five Euros is a lot of money.

Encouraged, he knocks on the red door and waits for a response, as the flowers covering the balcony nearby silently emit their perfume. Finally the window high above him is thrown open and he hears a high-pitched, raspy voice. "Who's there?"

Jacob looks straight up into the old lady's face.

"Open the door," he yells from below.

And just in case, he crosses his fingers and repeats the magic words his uncle taught him.

"What do you want?"

"To talk to you."

"I'll be right down."

It does not take her long. From close up, there can be no question whatsoever that the hunched over, toothless old woman dressed all in black is a witch. She has taken off her head scarf and she is almost completely bald. What wisps remain are pulled back into a thin bun at the nape of her neck. Behind her, the room is nearly empty. There are no owls, or cats, or broomsticks. The fireplace is at the far end of the room and, in the center, a there is a table with two stools.

Visitarana moves to one side. She does not smile, she just looks. It is probably the first time a child has ever visited her. Maybe that is why she seems so perplexed.

"Now I've got it. You're the French kid at Can Boig. The painter's nephew."

Jacob says yes and holds his nose because Visitarana smells bad. It is the typical witch smell. A cross between moldy and dried out, as if it were coming from a dried-up well, mixed with a combination of rags, stale food, and feet used to tromping in manure. It is nothing like Teresa's smell, which is all violets, and lavender salts and expensive soaps.

"I'm your friend," Jacob rushes to assure her. "I've come to see you because I'm your friend."

Visitarana frowns. "What are you after, boy?"

Jacob pats the bill again and hesitates for a moment, wondering if he should show it to her right off or wait.

"As far as I can recall, your uncle has never darkened my doorstep."

The remark intimidates Jacob a little, but he tries not to show it.

"I like the way you smell," he tells her. "I like it better than how Teresa smells."

Visitarana cocks her head slightly and stares at him, unsure how to respond. She is apparently satisfied by what she sees, because she tells Jacob to sit down.

"Since you're here, you might as well make yourself welcome."

At that moment, the witch Visitarana does not seem as sinister as she did the first time he saw her, when she was scurrying along the street towards her house. Underneath it all, she is just like any other old lady, even if her nose is a little hooked and she keeps moving her jaws as if she were chewing something soft, maybe even her own lips.

"Go on. Say what you came to say."

Jacob gulps down saliva. He clears his throat, then takes a deep breath. "I want you to teach me how to be a warlock."

The words are out there, suspended over the wooden surface of the table, cloaked in decisions, and daring, and desires that cannot be suppressed.

"I should tell you that I have money," Jacob continues. "A lot of money. It's in my pocket. If you teach me how to be a warlock, I'll give it to you."

Head in hands, Visitarana closes her eyes. As she presses her fingers against her face, the wrinkles deepen and the skin stretches across her cheeks revealing a forest of hairs, folds, and dark stains.

"How much money do you have?" she asks, without looking at him.

"Five Euros."

The old lady smiles. It is a beatific smile. The smile of someone who has just discovered a gold mine.

"That is a lot of money indeed."

Emboldened, Jacob persists: "I brought it for you. It will all be yours if you turn me into a warlock."

Visitarana continues to chew on air, but she does not reply.

"Where do you keep the owl, and the broomstick and the black cat?" Jacob has always been told that old witches had all of those things in their houses.

174

Their gazes meet, cautiously, perhaps slightly disconcerted.

"What makes you think I have those things?"

Jacob shrugs.

Visitarana sighs. Then she says, "Being a warlock is not a very pleasant job."

Visitarana seems put off by Jacob's questions. Perhaps she is afraid Jacob might be planning to take over her position as official witch.

"I don't want to take your job or anything. I just want to make a pact with the devil so I can get revenge on a bad person."

"Who is it?"

"Her name is Teresa."

Visitarana's head bobs up and down and then she stares at the wall for a moment, her eyes narrowed as if she is trying to recall something. "I know her," she says tersely. "A very beautiful woman."

"So were you, right?"

"Yes," the old lady responds with a nostalgic expression. "I was indeed."

She acknowledges this calmly, the way one might acknowledge the night, or silence, or boredom. In all likelihood, Visitarana already knows she is not the only witch in town anymore, even if Jacob never does make a pact with the devil. She is probably certain that Teresa is copying her and her powers are much stronger than the ones the old lady has managed to retain.

"That's why you became a witch. They say all the beautiful women end up like that."

Visitarana folds her hands on the table before her. The sight of her black, chipped fingernails is a little nauseating. She has thin, bony hands, full of veins and dark spots.

"Why do you hate her so much? What has she done to you?"

"She stole my uncle."

And they look at each other searchingly once more.

"Hate is a terrible thing, little one. It's worse than a toothache."

She is probably remembering her own. The hate that made her stick pins in those dolls. She is probably seeing herself in the maelstrom of the witches' Sabbaths, back when the village was just a remote place high in the hills, inhabited only by the locals, with no tourism to speak of.

It is hard to imagine the village of Visitarana's youth. The sea would have been empty of motor boats, pedal boats, and yachts anchored in front of Can Boig, or the seawall, or tied up in dry dock. And there would have been no lines of cars, or junk shops tucked into winding side streets, or expensive cafés that looked more like seedy dives, or bars with bottles of whiskey on the tables.

It would have been mostly deserted, devoid of tensions, rivalries, and shining mirrors and transistor radios blaring all kinds of music from behind windows and doorways. There would have been no television antennas atop the tile roofs. And its festive atmosphere would have had a different feel altogether: a more innocent, less brazen dimension, centered around local customs and not confected around foreign stereotypes.

"So you believed it?" asks Visitarana after a protracted silence. "You really believed I was a witch?"

Jacob opens his eyes so wide his glasses slip halfway down his nose. "Once you even put a spell on me to punish me, don't you remember? I passed by your house and you gave me the evil eye."

"What happened to you?"

"I tripped on a step in front of my house, then I got diarrhea and then my tooth fell out."

Visitarana's head continues to bob, and she finally says, "And of course, it was all my fault . . ."

A tremendous sadness takes hold of Visitarana's face. A sadness Jacob would like to erase.

"Well, if it wasn't you, who was it? Teresa hadn't gotten to Can Boig yet."

Visitarana continues to nod slowly and deliberately. "I see," she repeats. "I see."

And silence once again pervades the room. Visitarana chews, sucks her lips in and puffs out her cheeks as if she would like to say something, but is not quite sure. Then she seems to come to a decision: "I hate to disappoint you, little one, but I've never been a witch."

She says it somewhat ashamedly, as if not being a witch were a defect. "I've never seen the devil. I've never slathered my body with filthy oils. I've never ridden atop a ram, nor have I stuck pins in dolls to hurt people. Yes, I know what they've told you. It's all a lie. Perico invented every last bit of it. He has spent his entire life destroying my reputation. He never forgave me for what I did to him when we were young . . ."

Shaking with emotion, she extracts a grimy handkerchief from her sleeve and blows her nose hard.

"I know his damned fairy tale very well," she continues, her voice cracking. "Perico took it upon himself to repeat it every chance he got. Perico is an evil man, little one, very evil. He always has been. Even when he was barely three feet tall."

And as someone had wound her up, she told him about her childhood and about Perico's nasty tricks. How he would surprise her on deserted street corners when no one was around to protect her. The lies he told people to make himself sound interesting: a real hero. How later on the filthy pig had participated in the looting, when civil war broke out.

"As if that weren't enough, he killed a poor unfortunate stranger. Accused him of being a fascist. And then he sets himself up as an upstanding man. I'll tell you what Perico is, little one: an opportunist, a repugnant snake who changes his colors like other people change their shirts."

Her sobs were getting louder as she spoke. Several times now, she has had to dry her tears and blow her nose with the handkerchief.

"If you want to see the devil, you don't have to go far, little one. Just have a look at Perico. That's what he is: a devil. A poor imitation of Satan . . ." She sobs and moans and Jacob is beginning to doubt that Visitarana is really a witch. *Witches don't cry*, he thinks. *Witches are never ashamed of what they are.*

"No one is more bourgeois than Perico now that the tide has turned. Disgusting old man. And to think I nearly married him."

There is no way a witch could be as helpless and miserable as Visitarana is now. It is absolutely impossible.

"It all started when I left him at the altar. I had come to realize I hated him, and I told him so, just like I'm telling you now: 'I hate you, Perico.' And I added that I'd rather die than lie in his bed and if he wanted a wife he could go straight to hell to find one, because no girl in her right mind would ever agree to marry him. There you have it: he ended up with the dumbest girl in the village."

She shudders and blows her nose again.

"He swore he would take his revenge and he made good on it. I know the whole story about the witches' Sabbath, little one. I know it well. He has proclaimed it to the four winds, especially since the tourism started up. The tourists love that kind of thing. *If you want to see a real witch, I know where one lives . . . I'll show you for a buck . . .* And he'd point me out to people. Did he ever. *There she is*, the bastard would say, indicating my front door, and then he'd take off back down the street before I could dump the chamber pot on his head."

Jacob listens in silence, his spirits dampened, his eyes glued to the woman's handkerchief, all his hopes gradually slipping away.

"You have no idea what it's like to be smeared like that, little one, God save you. No matter how hard you struggle, how hard you try, there isn't anything or anyone who can remove that brand on your forehead. I've been wearing it for years."

She slowly settles back down. She is no longer crying. She just sighs deeply. "There were times I wished I really was a witch. I'd have given most anything to wreak my revenge on that man."

"Maybe if you wish for it really hard, you'll be able to."

"No," says Visitarana. "It's no use. Besides . . . revenge is ugly, very ugly."

Once again, Jacob pats the bill in his pocket. He suddenly realizes that it is of no use to him. The only thing he wanted to get with it, he will never be able to get.

"I'm sorry, little one. I really am sorry, but I can't help you."

Jacob stands up. He looks at the table, he looks at the cold fireplace, and he looks at Visitarana. And he thinks to himself that it is a real shame there is no owl, or cat or broomstick in the house.

21

Back out on the street, the sun's burning rays are beating down on the tile roofs of the village. It is a white hot, aggressive sun that filters through the gaps in the walls and forms strange patterns on the pavement of the shady streets.

The child's eyes are burning. He is exhausted and miserable: completely worn down. It had been very painful to learn that Visitarana was not a witch at all. In a way, Jacob had been banking on her being one. That is why he had been so irritated with Quasimodo when he had said that everything that had happened to him was mere coincidence.

He still has Ruan, however. All he has to do is climb a tamarind tree to make contact. His feet heavy and his legs aching with tiredness, Jacob reaches the esplanade and pauses in front of the Garota Bar. It is depressing to see the tables abandoned outside, empty and in disarray. At dusk, those same tables wake up from their forced slumber and fill up with customers. So looking at them now, so skeletal and abandoned, evokes a strange feeling of nostalgia and homesickness.

They look like yawns, or sighs, or voiceless complaints heard by no one. Jacob walks towards them, as if in a trance. Maybe the tables will fill up by magic as he approaches. But it is hopeless. No matter how many times he shuts his eyes, then opens them up really quickly to witness the miracle, the tables are still empty.

He suddenly remembers Lori. The first time he ever saw her was here, on the raised deck, sitting at his uncle's table. "Take a sip from my glass, Little Pup . . ." And he would be filled with an agreeable sensation he has not felt ever since Lori left.

It hurts to discover so many memories clustered around an empty table. It hurts to think he will never sit there again, surrounded by friendly faces. But what hurts most of all is knowing that, beyond the rocks enclosing the bay, the stupid *Poseidon* is still anchored. And that Visitarana is not a witch after all . . .

The sea is close by, below the patio deck, slightly agitated, shooting up sparkling drops flying whenever its waters crash into the posts that sustain the floor. At this hour, very few people are swimming on the adjacent beach. Perhaps a fisherman or two, or a maid taking advantage of her bosses' laziness to take a quick dip before they rise.

If only Visitarana had been a witch . . .

Jacob wanders down to the beach, forgetting all about the tamarinds. All he can think about right now is finding a place to sleep. His knees are buckling and his head feels heavy, just like the way the child with hydrocephalus must feel. After all, he had stayed up all night. That is why his body is collapsing like a closed accordion. All because he wanted Quasimodo to bring him to the village so he could implore Visitarana to turn him into a warlock.

But Visitarana had not been able to help him, because she never was a witch at all.

In the shade under the patio deck of the Garota Bar, he finds a dry, spongy hole in the sand, quite close to the water's edge. It does not matter that flies are buzzing around the hole, devouring filth and foul-smelling scraps. Visitarana smelled bad too, a lot worse than Teresa. And yet Teresa is a witch and Visitarana is not.

So he does not hesitate. He nestles into the spot as if it were his bed at home. He has an overpowering need to sleep, to close his eyes and forget everything else. It is the only remedy he has to forget that Visitarana is not a witch.

In the distance, he sleepily observes the black islet, the other end of the horseshoe, the lighthouse. He thinks he might even have caught a glimpse of the *Poseidon*. And as sleep overtakes him, he has time to promise himself that he will never, ever return to Can Boig until the *Poseidon* weighs anchor and leaves Spain forever.

And so Jacob sleeps, thinking about Visitarana, and the departure of Teresa's yacht. Suddenly, giant hands are lifting him high in the air and a cavernous voice is assuring him he will soon be aboard Ruan's flying saucer. *When we get to Venus, we'll destroy Teresa's yacht from there.*

But Teresa's yacht is as indestructible as she is. Perhaps it has a vulnerable heel . . . So Jacob hurries to explain that boats do not have heels, only keels. *It doesn't matter,* Ruan says. *We'll destroy the keel then.* And he fires a battery of laser rays against the *Poseidon* that make short work of the ship. *Now I can go back to Can Boig, can't I, Ruan?*

No. Ruan is not exactly Ruan. He somehow resembles grandmother Katherine. *How's your English, Jacob? Have you been practicing at your uncle's house?* Jacob is terrified at the sight of her.

Where am I? His grandmother says he is with her in Paris. *Why? I don't want to live in Paris. I want to live on Venus.*

There is nothing for it. Children like Jacob always live in Paris with annoying grandmothers who criticize everything and are constantly saying that life with an uncle like the painter would traumatize anyone. *So there you have it, Pigeon. From now on, you will not be going back to Venus.*

Jacob hates it when they call him that. He has never liked it. And so he screams at his grandmother, warning her that if she mentions that word one more time, he's going to jump into the sea so the whales can eat him. But his grandmother only laughs. *Since when does Paris have a sea?* The river, the sea: it's the same thing. *I'll jump into the Seine then.* And his grandmother says fine, he should go ahead and jump, and he'll just have to see who will take care of him when he catches a bad cold, because she is not planning to. She has enough problems with her broken leg, a divorced daughter, her son-in-law Roger, and the bothersome child they are expecting. *So you'll have to figure it out on your own, Pigeon.*

But she changes her tune right away because Rosario is wringing her apron and Rosario's aprons have always had a tremendous influence on the family. *You shouldn't talk that way to the child. It could really damage him.* And when his grandmother sees Rosario so worked up, she thinks this really is not a good time to risk losing a hardworking girl. So she says Rosario is right. It is important to talk gently to children and she won't call him Pigeon ever again.

Rosario tries to wipe his face with a sponge. *Good children always wash, right Jacob? You have to wash your face, and your hands, and brush your teeth.* But Rosario seems to be taking a lot of time washing his face. *Why? Why does it have to be clean?* And Rosario insists, *You have to wash, you have to wash, you have to wash...*

"Stop it."

It is not Rosario. It is a starving dog that smells like fish and is busily licking his face.

"Go away."

But the dog does not leave. It probably likes the way the child's cheeks taste. Still half asleep, Jacob stands up and dries his face with the back of his hand.

"Get out of here. Go away."

He does not know how long he has been sleeping, but judging from the look of the village, it must have been several hours. The sun's progress indicates that it is definitely well past noon. It is a torrid, swaggering sun that pelts the rocks with heat and leaves an aura of siesta in the air.

Jacob has not eaten and the hunger invading his stomach feels as if it were biting him. Instinctively, he feels around for the cash. He will buy ice cream. He will buy the doughnuts his uncle calls *churros*. All the things his uncle used to buy him before Teresa started interfering in their lives.

The Garota Bar is probably full by now, because he can hear footsteps on the deck, and conversations, and the scraping of table and chairs. And he can hear the owner, Mr. Cusi's, sharp, penetrating voice. "A beer . . . A coffee . . . Right away . . ."

Little by little, the voices start to make sense. Mr. Cusi sounds all worked up. He is talking about a lost child—probably kidnapped . . . "The family is looking for him desperately . . ." Then he launches in about all the abductions around the country. "A shame, a crying shame . . ."

And Jacob thinks he would not want to be in that child's shoes. What awful luck it would be to be lost among unfamiliar faces and nasty kidnappers.

It does not take him long to notice the change that has taken place in the village while he was asleep. Although it is still not the village of the evenings, it is definitely not the boring village of this morning either. It is probably about the time his uncle—before Teresa came—would invite him into his studio to continue the morning session. "Are you tired, Jacob?" And he would say no, so his uncle would not think he was a little kid who had to take naps. But he had just woken up from a very long nap. A nap with no lunch, no bath, and no painting sessions.

As he walks along the beach under the deck, his legs no longer feel heavy and he has no trouble negotiating the filth he encounters along the way. The flies are still obsessed, buzzing all over, and stirring up a foul smell with their wings.

Back up on the esplanade, he finds a stand selling churros, ice cream and Coca Cola. "Would you like an ice cream, young man?"

"Chocolate," says Jacob. And he hands over the bill.

After he has bought the churros and the Coke, he only has a few cents left. But Jacob does not mind. It is nice to look about the village with a full stomach. If you follow the road to the left, you get to Lori's house. It is the area he knows the least, but he likes it. He supposes he likes it more than the road towards the right, which leads to Can Boig.

Viewed from the embankment to the left, the village looks less subdued. Although the sun continues to bully fans and awnings, people have resumed their afternoon routines. Later on, after the sun has set, the same people as always will emerge from behind the closed doors and shuttered windows. The ones that like to paint the town and liven up the bars.

Jacob pauses occasionally to contemplate the sea. There is something fascinating about the way the water beats against the seawalls, splashing up foam and silver bubbles and drenching the cornerstones. The rhythm of the waves is continuous and gradually crescendos as the night, though still a long way off, begins to nudge the afternoon towards sunset.

Offhand remarks can be heard here and there. Words pronounced without much conviction. Prattle intended mainly to stir up a breeze: "Do you think it's going to rain?" "Have you been fishing?" "Are you using traps or nets?" The barges rocking gently in the water smell of sardines and herrings, and the nets draped over the retaining wall are waiting to be mended so they can be taken out to sea again.

The road to Lori's house is long. Longer than Jacob remembered. He gradually leaves behind the cluster of houses at the center of the horseshoe, but the road does not end.

Tired, Jacob climbs up on the seawall to sit, his legs dangling in empty space. Where he is sitting, the crash of the water is less aggressive and he does not get splashed.

"What are you looking at?" It is a tiny voice that reaches his eardrums almost imperceptibly.

And turning, he sees a dark-haired girl, with a tanned face and mahogany eyes, who is watching him without blinking. In her hands, she carries a well-worn ragdoll with floppy arms and tousled hair.

"Nothing."

"You look bored."

Jacob shrugs. The child squints into the sun's glare, which makes her face wrinkle as if she were an old lady.

"What about you?"

"I don't get bored. I play with my doll."

Jacob regards her almost disdainfully. "It's funner to play with horses." And, since there is no reply from the girl: "I have one you know."

"A real one or a fake one?"

"A real one, but it's made of wood."

"Then it's fake."

Jacob decides that the girl is pretty dumb.

"If it's made of wood, then it can't be real," she persists.

"Well, for your information, my horse can fly."

The child's curiosity turns to astonishment.

"If you don't believe me, you can ask my uncle." And pointing off to the right, he says, "he lives over there, near the lighthouse."

"I don't see any house."

"That's because the mountain is blocking it. But it's there on the beach at Can Boig."

Still squinting, the girl raises a hand to her forehead like a visor.

"Didn't you ever hear of Eduardo Santillana?"

The girl says no, she has not. This is the first time she has spent the summer in the village. "I don't know anybody," she confesses.

"Well, he's a famous painter. Everybody knows who he is. And I live with him."

The girl gazes at Jacob admiringly, hastening to add that, if he say so, it must be true. And to prove she is sincere, she sits down beside him on the wall.

"So where do you live?"

The girl points to a side street. "Over there. You have to go up that street and then turn right."

"What is your name?"

"Conchita."

"Mine's Jacob. How old are you?"

"Seven. What about you?"

Jacob hesitates a moment. "I'm seven too," he lies.

After all, he is taller than she is and he can lie without any risk of getting caught.

"If I had a flying horse like yours, I would never be apart from it," says Conchita.

Frowning, Jacob stares down at the water. It is dense and boggy, its surface coated with algae. "The thing is, I ran away from home and I couldn't bring him with me."

Conchita's eyes brim with a mixture of confusion and admiration. "I wanted to run away once," she says, gaining confidence. "But when it got dark, I was scared and I decided to go home."

"Did your parents get mad at you?"

Conchita scrunches up her face and responds with a firm no. "They didn't even find out. Anyway, they're not even my parents. Well, he is. She isn't."

"Why did you want to run away?"

Frowning, Conchita ponders the question, her gaze fixed on the edge of the seawall. "I'm not really sure. I was tired of all the grown-ups. They're always going around whispering stuff, and I don't want them treating me like I'm dumb. What about you? Why did you run away?"

Jacob straightens his shoulders and reaches deep inside himself, searching for a logical explanation. The truth is, he had not been planning to run away when Quasimodo brought him into the village this morning. The idea had come to him later, when he remembered that the *Poseidon* was still anchored off his uncle's beach. But it is difficult to explain all of that to Conchita. It is not easy to talk to a girl—especially if you are a boy—hard to explain the ultimatums and suspicions and frustrations—and the emptiness.

They are all abstract feelings even Jacob cannot explain: bursts of nostalgic sentiments that trigger an amorphous sense of rebellion in him and are occasionally linked to certain incidents, furtive glances, or awkward gestures. All of which is condensed into a single hate and a single desire: to protest. To make it known that there are people around who exist, and suffer, and wait . . .

And he suddenly knows the answer. It is as plain as day. "When I grow up, I'm never going to do anything mean to a child," he states firmly.

"Have they ever hit you?" she asks.

Jacob does not answer immediately. Something deep inside him is saying yes, the grown-ups *have* hit him. They have hit him with their looks, and their scolding, and their mockery . . . The evidence is real. Just like Clavileño's flights and Ruan's status as an extraterrestrial. But at the same time, he knows if he says yes, he will be telling a lie. And that is why he is experiencing a growing uncertainty inside him, and also why he is stalling. Sometimes it is difficult to coordinate so many ideas at once.

"Tell me, Jacob. Has your uncle ever hit you?"

Jacob finally comes to a decision: "Not my uncle, but she has."

"Who is she?"

"The witch."

Conchita's eyes open wide in distress. "You're not going to tell me there's a witch living in your house."

Jacob can no longer contain himself. It all comes flooding out. "She came to Can Boig in a yacht . . . Her name is Teresa . . . First she grabbed me by the neck . . . She wanted to strangle me . . . Then, when I couldn't breathe any more, she started to slap my face . . . And that's when I decided to run away."

There. He has said it. And it is not a lie. It is not a lie. He can almost feel Teresa's slaps on his face and the bruises on his skin, and his hot, flushed cheeks . . .

"What about your uncle? What did he do?"

"Nothing. He let her."

He says it convincingly, his eyes glassy, as if they might be welling up with tears. And to reinforce them, Jacob tells her his whole story. At least the one he wishes were his. The one that could truly justify his escape. He is not telling lies, but rather his own exclusive truths. Truths carried deep inside him and they shove all reason aside, similar to what happens to a pathological liar who is seeking attention, understanding and help. In reality, it is as if he were not lying at all, or as if his lies were real: a true reflection of his life, only explained with different words. An authentic description deformed, perhaps, by a magnifying glass containing made-up colors.

"What are you going to do now?"

"I'm going to wait until that woman goes away. And when she does, I'll go back."

Conchita's admiration is growing by the moment. Perhaps she is thinking she should do the same thing.

"Do you think she'll end up leaving?"

"Sure. The yacht can't just sit there forever."

Conchita nods doubtfully, looks at her doll and says, "But in the meantime you could die of starvation."

"I have a friend here and I know she'll feed me."

"Maybe she'll tell your uncle. Grown-ups always stick together."

"She won't. She's different. And besides, my uncle had a fight with her."

"What is her name?"

"Lori."

"Where does she live?"

"At the end of this road, near the islet."

Jacob stands up. He figures it is getting late and he should not lose any more time. "I should go see her."

"Can I come with you?"

"Okay."

And so they begin their journey towards Lori's house in silence, stirring up dust with their feet, kicking at the stones they encounter in their path, and letting their imaginations turn them into heroes: the exclusive protagonists of an impassioned story.

"Lori could be a fairy," remarks Jacob after a while. "A good fairy."

And he looks towards the sun, which is about to set, as if Lori's true nature could be discerned there.

"She can talk to dead people, did you know that? She has a three-legged table she uses to communicate with them."

"Have you ever talked to dead people?"

"Lots of times."

"And what do they say to you?"

"I don't know. Things . . ."

"What kinds of things?"

"They talk about their life away from earth. And they give advice to the living. They tell us what we have to do to be happy."

"Can I watch when you talk to them?"

"I'll ask Lori if it's okay. I'm sure she'll say yes."

And he returns to the subject of Teresa. He tells her that Lori is nothing like Teresa. She has never been beautiful and so she could never be a witch.

"That's why my uncle doesn't love her. Because Teresa has cast a spell on him and now he only loves her."

And to buttress this contention, Jacob continues his story, relishing it in the way of someone who has been unable to speak his mind for a very long time. He returns to the subject of Teresa, her negative influences, her desire to control everything. "She was not satisfied with just hitting me. She also stole my uncle Eduardo, and she broke my paper saber, and she put poison in my glass of milk, and she turned the dog into a rat."

"Some luck you have. I've never seen a dog turned into a rat before."

"It's very common among witches."

"So now you don't even have a dog."

"When she got tired of looking at him turned into a rat, she turned him back. She didn't want my uncle to find out about what she was up to. She just did it to annoy me, because I always play with him. That's Teresa. She's always tries to be annoying."

"And what about the poison? Did you drink it?"

"Of course. And I got really sick. I had diarrhea and I threw up and I got a fever."

"That's horrible!"

Hearing her words, Jacob feels vindicated, understood, supported.

"You were right to run away." And she reinforces it by saying that grown-ups are impossible and cruel. "Did your uncle know what was going on?"

Jacob says no: ever since *she* arrived, his uncle never tries to find out about anything that is going on and lives only to please her.

"You should tell him," Conchita advises him.

"It won't work. He'll never believe me."

But Conchita believes him. She believes him because she too is a child and she can understand what Jacob is going through.

"Maybe he'll wake up from the spell soon."

"That won't happen until Teresa leaves."

"What are you going to do?"

"I'm not sure yet. Wait I guess. Maybe Lori can tell me."

22

Lori lives in a little chalet ringed by pine saplings. A low fence surrounds the garden. It is so low, in fact, it seems to have been put there to announce the house, rather than protect it. Above them, the balcony overlooking the sea is groaning indecisively, as if to provoke the still-dark lighthouse. Lori can probably see Can Boig and the *Poseidon* from that balcony. If she had some binoculars, she could probably even see Teresa.

"Let's jump the fence," Jacob proposes to Conchita. "I'm sure Lori is back from the beach by now."

The front door is closed, but the adjacent window is wide open. The children do not wait for Lori to let them in, since it is just as easy for them to climb in the window. It is not the first time Jacob has used this system when visiting Lori. When his uncle used to be a normal person—before Teresa came to Can Boig—they would often sneak into the house that way to surprise her.

The living room is spacious, adorned with all the crafty objects typically found in the homes of foreign residents. A motley collection of Spanish products fills the room: straw burros, pottery jars, vases from Ávila, filigree from Toledo, knives and daggers from Albecete, ceramics from Manises, clay whistles from Majorca, bull's heads from La Mancha and baskets woven in Ronda. I want to have a complete collection of Spanish crafts, Lori always said. It was the collection that Jacob stood to inherit when Lori died. But when Jacob had asked her to hurry up and die, she had responded, laughing, that she was planning to live for a good long time.

Then his uncle had given her an affectionate pinch and warned her that, if she continued abusing her artificial paradises, he wouldn't bet on her lasting another year. "You're killing yourself, Lori dear. You're almost as far gone as your friend Coco."

But she just laughed it off whenever his uncle said things like that. Until one day, she had promised him she would not drink, or smoke, or sleep with the first poor cuckold that showed up on her doorstep: "Except for you. Are you happy now?" Furious, his uncle had forbidden her to use the word cuckold with reference to him ever again, because cuckolds were people who had run out of juices and he still had plenty in him to give and enough left over to sell. She had only to look around her for proof of that.

The proof, it seemed, were the paintings Lori had hung all over her house. His uncle had painted almost all of them and they usually featured Lori, posed among crags, crystalline waters and sea shells.

"Lori, are you there?"

There is no answer. But from upstairs, they can hear the unmistakable crunching sound of esparto grass rugs beneath bare feet.

"Can you hear me, Lori? It's me, Jacob."

He rushes up the stairs and opens the door to her bedroom. Lori is indeed there, lying face down on the bed, her head hidden in the pillow, her hair in a mess and the robe covering her body twisted to one side.

"Lori . . ."

Cautious and a little frightened, Jacob approaches the bed. Lori appears to be sleeping, but it is not a peaceful sleep. It is as if she were releasing flows of dead energy and abyssal silences were bursting from her lips.

Her physical appearance is not very comforting either. From close up, he can see that her face is bruised and swollen and there are scrapes on her shoulder, as if someone had beaten her up.

"What's wrong, Lori?"

There is no response. She just opens her mouth as if she would like to say something, but cannot. The skin on her face has become sallow and everything about her is corpselike.

Jacob suddenly recalls what his uncle had said: *if you keep on like that, you won't last a year . . .*

"Listen, Lori," Jacob whispers into her ear, "I just want to know if you're dead."

Her lips open again, slowly, very slowly, and the sounds she is making are as tenuous as the thread of light glimpsed behind the drawn curtain. A weak, sloppy "yes" slips from between her lips.

Jacob does not completely grasp how it is that Lori can speak if she is not alive. But Lori has never lied to him before. So if she is saying she is dead, then it must be true.

"I'm glad to hear it, Lori," Jacob says. "That way you'll be able to help me."

Lori is barely breathing and her lips, bruised and still swelling, do not close.

"I suppose you've seen Richard."

Lori does not respond. She merely offers brief, low-pitched snorts, as if the death settling over her were tickling her nose.

"Can you hear me, Lori? If you've seen Richard, tell him I want to talk to him." But Lori appears not to hear him, and Jacob is getting a little impatient. "It is very urgent. Richard needs to know what is going on, right away."

Hearing this, Lori makes an effort. She opens one eye, but the swollen eyelid obliges her to close it again immediately. "Rich - ard . . . ," she mumbles.

"That's right. Richard." And he runs over to the door to tell Conchita to come up.

His heart pounding, Jacob grabs the girl by the hand and leads her over to Lori's bed. "She's dead," he declares. "Even though you can hear her talking, she's completely dead. She told me so."

Conchita clutches Jacob's arm in fear. She does not understand what is happening. She especially does not understand how Jacob, knowing that Lori is dead, can be acting so normal.

"What did she die of?" she whispers.

"Of artificial paradises."

"What are they?"

"I don't know, but my uncle always said her artificial paradises would end up killing her."

Astonished, Conchita looks around the room. Everything is topsy turvy: there are clothes strewn all over the floor, overturned chairs, broken clay pots and cracked mirrors.

"Does she smell bad?"

"No."

But Conchita wants to be sure. She moves closer to Lori and begins to sniff her. "She can't be dead. Dead people stink and your friend only smells like wine."

"She must have just died," Jacob explains. "When we got here, I heard her moving around in the bathroom."

"What are we going to do?"

"Just wait. Lori will definitely have something to tell me soon. She promised me she'd just talked to Richard."

"Who is Richard?"

"Another dead person."

And to give Lori time to get used to being dead, Jacob and Conchita go out onto the balcony. From this vantage point, the other end of the bay has a completely different configuration. Even Teresa's yacht looks different. But what really has changed is the size of the black islet. Lying close to Lori's beach, it looks like an ice cream cone left behind by nature.

It's fun to see it up close, arrogant, gigantic, and bald—a hard, stubborn silhouette against the horizon—surrounded by frothy foam as the waves smash against its shores.

In contrast, the sea in between the islet and Lori's beach seems calm and that is why the seagulls crowd around there to escape the cliffs.

Seeing the sun is about to set, Jacob suddenly wonders whether his uncle realizes he has run away. Surely, by now, Quasimodo has told him about his trip to the village.

"If your friend is dead, she won't be able to feed you."

But Jacob is unconcerned. He knows exactly where the refrigerator is. "I'll have plenty to eat," he tells Conchita. To prove it, he takes her straight down to the kitchen so she can see for herself. One look in the refrigerator is enough to see that Jacob will not die of hunger. "See? All of this is for me. And so are the straw burro, and the knives and the whistles from Majorca."

Conchita is hungry too, so they dive into the food right away: cold chicken, fish, cheeses, milk . . .

"May I ask what in the hell you are doing here?"

Turning, they see Fabian in the doorway, frowning, his white tunic slightly stained, his hair ribbon slightly askew.'

"Unbelievable," the sculptor continues. "The entire village is searching for you and here you are, filling your belly."

Jacob does not say a word. It has suddenly occurred to him that something is not quite right. He glances sideways at the open refrigerator then at Conchita's face, and his thoughts seem to channel themselves into strange, unanticipated conduits that can only lead to suspicions, accusations and punishments.

In one leap, he is beside the door, figuring the best solution is to run, to escape the house and Fabian, and his dead friend Lori . . . But the sculptor blocks his way and grasps him by the arms.

"Blast you, child. If you only knew what you've caused with your damned disappearing act."

And he goes on to tell him about Lori, tersely, angrily. He tells Jacob how his uncle paid her a visit. Explains the ensuing battle upstairs in the poor girl's bedroom. "And it's all your fault, you little wretch. It's all your damned fault."

"Quasimodo told him you were with her, and the bastard didn't believe Lori when she denied it. You should have seen them. They were tearing each other apart with their bare hands and feet. If I had not intervened, your uncle would still be up there breaking the poor girl's bones. And meanwhile, you're out sashaying all over town."

It is not nice to realize Fabian is no longer the same old friend from before. The friend who said he looked like Cupid and some day he'd have to lend him his pinky finger so he could sculpt it. He has instead become an implacable judge on the verge of handing down his death sentence.

"I've never seen your uncle as out of sorts as he is today. And it's all your fault. It's about time you realized, little Cupid . . ."

Jacob does not move a muscle. He is frozen with panic, a horrible, gripping fear that will not be allayed. Fabian's accusation is eating him up inside. He does not understand why his uncle and Lori have fought. Jacob has never seen them hit each other. He only remembers Lori diving alongside his uncle on sunny mornings, their smiles wide enough to stop the clouds. That is what Lori was to him: a nice woman. A woman incapable of hitting anybody, much less his uncle. A slight woman who acquired titanic proportions only when she was diving into the sea in search of corals, sea urchins, and other unsuspecting creatures. A siren, innocent of evil enchantments, perched on a rock and combing out her long hair—just like the sirens in Ulysses' day—so his uncle could sketch her.

"When she saw your uncle, little Miss Clueless was sure he wanted to get back together with her. That's how stupid our friend Lori is. She had failed to internalize the fact that your uncle has been struck blind by Teresa, the devil woman." And with that, he shakes the child's shoulders and shoves him back into the room and into a chair.

"But your uncle was looking for you. Get it, you snot-nosed kid? He's been out of his mind searching for you ever since you disappeared." Fabian exhales loudly and, with the back of his hand, wipes away the drops of saliva collecting in the corners of his mouth.

"And there you have Lori. Done in by loathing . . . If only she'd listened to me . . . If only she'd seen that your uncle never saw her as anything but a stand-in."

He gasps, sweats, coughs. His voice is getting more and more hoarse. "Want to know what your uncle did to poor Lori? First he simply tosses her aside like a piece of trash. Then he dares to mistreat her because his lunatic nephew has taken it into his head to run off."

It is very strange to see Fabian acting so aggressive, so expressive and, mostly, so masculine. "As if Lori had anything to do with the insanity of the Santillanas."

Slumped in a chair with his arms on the table, Jacob wants to cry, but the tears will not come. All he is able to do is stare at Fabian, frightened, bewildered, unable to grasp exactly what is going on.

"Would you be so kind as to tell me where the hell you've been, boy? Could you kindly explain what in damnation you've been doing since that imbecile Quasimodo dropped you off here in the village?"

Conchita and Jacob look at each other wordlessly. At this point, words have probably turned into something akin to hieroglyphics for them. Most likely they are not at all certain what they should say and what they should keep quiet about. And the silence grows, elongated and sinuous, devouring phrases before they can be uttered and consuming arguments before they can gel into ideas.

"Come on, boy. Out with it. Don't just sit there like a dumbbell. I would imagine you have something to say."

Jacob swallows hard, glances at his friend once more, and allows a nervous sigh to escape. "Lori died, right?"

But the question only serves to deepen Fabian's exasperation. "Don't try to distract me with stupid questions. You can start by telling me who this girl is."

"Conchita," Jacob replies.

"And what in the hell is Conchita doing here?"

"Eating."

"I can see that. You don't have to spell it out. What I want to know is, what is she doing with you?"

"She's a friend."

"And where did you find her?"

"On the road."

"Great place to make friends."

Conchita is offended. She cannot fathom the sculptor's rage. "Don't get so upset," she tells Fabian. "You know if Jacob left home, he must have had his reasons."

Fabian is taken aback by the girl's nerve. "And what reasons could that little snot-nose have? Maybe you aren't aware of this, Doll, but this little tadpole here was running the show at Can Boig. His uncle couldn't do enough for him."

But Conchita refuses to back down. "That was before," she says firmly. "Now they treat him very badly."

Fabian is mystified. He turns his head, looking back and forth between the boy and the girl.

"Go ahead, Jacob. Tell him what they did to you at Can Boig. Tell him everything," urges Conchita.

And since Jacob remains silent, Conchita takes it upon herself to explain. Stubborn and self-righteous, she is convinced what she has to say will clarify everything. "Come on, Jacob. Don't be afraid. Tell him about the beating and the poison, and how they tried to strangle you."

Fabian blanches, frowns, and opens his hands. "What kind of story is that? You're not going to try to tell me that Jacob has run away from home because they were poisoning him."

"Yes they did, Mister. They poisoned him and they hit him and they even wanted to suffocate him."

Fabian rolls his eyes, inhales deeply and reverts to his effeminate mannerisms. "This is too much. Dear God, what have we come to? So your uncle beat you and wanted to kill you? Is that what you're trying to say? Look, kids: I know Santillana very well: he might be an asshole but he has never so much as hurt a fly, so . . ."

"It wasn't my uncle," interrupts Jacob.

"So who in the hell was it then?"

Silence reigns once again, as the liar is overcome by the panic of lying. Jacob does not utter a word. He is resisting it with all his might.

"I'll tell," exclaims a determined Conchita. "It was her. The woman."

Fabian considers, tries to think. He closes his eyes and lifts an index finger to his forehead. "Teresa? Was it Teresa who tried to kill you?"

Escape, Jacob. Run. And above all don't ever look back. Just like in his dreams when grandmother Katherine is there. Except this time, Jacob is not dreaming and Fabian is pushing him to explain. Demanding that he state once and for all whether all this about Teresa is true or not. And Conchita is looking at him searchingly, as if even she were beginning to have doubts.

"Teresa is evil," Jacob says finally. "Nobody else knows how evil."

And Conchita smiles at him: *Well done, Jacob. Now everything will come out.* And Fabian's expression shifts. It is as if the faces he was making ever since he found Jacob in the kitchen had never existed.

"Please, Jacob. Let's be reasonable. Is it true that Teresa has hit you?"

The question is too straightforward to dodge. He has to pick yes or no. There is no other way out and he needs to get Fabian back on his side. Needs him to be the same friend as before. And he is beginning to see that anything he says under the cover of childish innocence will be accepted at face value.

"It's true," he replies, his head bowed.

Fabian raises his hand once again to his head, removes the bow, sighs. A white line appears in the tanned skin above his eyebrows. "How can that be? How could she have dared . . ."

Jacob shrugs, then he bursts out crying. Finally. Finally, the tears come. The blessed tears that can fix anything. Just as with any other innocent, Jacob's tears can soften most any heart. That is why Fabian immediately changes course.

"Come on, Little Pup. Don't cry."

And at the words "don't cry," the child's sobs deepen, become more forceful, become choked and eminently believable wails.

"Calm down, Little Pup. No one is going to hit you anymore, I can assure you of that. This is Fabian talking. Your Fabian. I'll speak with your uncle. I'll tell him exactly what sort of person Teresa is . . ."

And to comfort him, Fabian hugs him, smoothes back his hair, takes off his glasses, and even gives him a kiss on the cheek.

"I beg you, Little Pup. Don't worry. Everything is going to be all right."

23

Three days have passed since Jacob's return to Can Boig. Three days of tension, silence, and grim expressions, which he navigates as best as he can, mainly by shutting himself inside his room.

A telephone call had been placed and Mr. Raimundo had driven to Lori's house to pick up the child. There was no way of knowing what the two men had discussed. They had shut him in the kitchen with Conchita while they spoke. Then they had instructed him to say goodbye to the girl, put him in the car and driven away.

Mr. Raimundo had asked no questions. He had driven in silence, trying to navigate among the diverse assortment of people they came upon along the way.

His uncle, waiting on the terrace, was equally uncommunicative. He merely said "hello," and ordered Dots to give him a bath.

Dots took a different approach altogether. Her movements were brusque and her voice wobbled just like it did when she had had too much to drink. "Just imagine. All of us on tenterhooks since early this morning . . ."

And if it hadn't been—as a grim and scowling Quasimodo claimed—that the painter had strictly prohibited anyone from discussing the matter with Jacob, she would still be repeating that it would have been better if he had just stayed in France, instead of coming there to cause such a fuss and spread so many falsehoods. "Ungrateful. That's what you are. Ungrateful . . ."

After his bath, uncle Eduardo had come into his room. His mood was severe and remote, his body so stiff it almost kept him from moving properly. His words were stiff too. He had said only that, in view of Jacob's behavior, he was grounded and would not be allowed down to the beach until further notice, adding that he deserved to be taught a lesson after such underhanded dealings and offensive accusations. Then he had left the child alone, at the mercy of his thoughts, numbed by the passing hours and plagued by doubts.

Since then, Jacob had occasionally run into Teresa, but he always tried not to look in her direction, afraid she might ask questions. Teresa's behavior was another punishment. She was acting miserable and dejected, and would turn towards him with a pitiful expression as she passed by, as if she were the injured party.

Nor was it pleasant to put up with the intrusiveness of his uncle's guests: the Italians' cynical little smiles, the tsk-tsking of the marquis, Purita the fat lady's biting remarks. And most of all Mauricio Belarmino's pseudo-scientific commentary, especially when he said that, as a journalist, he would be very interested in documenting the whole Jacob episode for publication—changing all the names of course—. He thought it could be an incredible boon to the Freudians: "If we could only understand what the devil goes on in Ceibo's tortured mind . . ."

His uncle had nothing to say about any of it. He was letting them all tear Jacob to shreds—made no effort to defend him. And whenever he found himself obliged to interact with the child, the tension was palpable. Worse yet, he never spoke to him directly. He would talk in generalities, without looking at him. He would say that even though he knew spoiled children were capable of throwing vicious tantrums, he had never imagined they could be so twisted.

Then Purita the fat lady claimed that most children were like that: a little schizophrenic, a little masochistic and sexually deviant. And she would quote some guy called Marañon, who was responsible for a lot of very strange assertions that Jacob, as usual, did not understand.

Once, he ran into Teresa on the stairs. It was impossible to escape her, and she took advantage of the situation to tell him how terribly sad his uncle was: "He is very hurt because you don't come down to the beach anymore, you know that Ceibo?" Between clenched teeth, he had responded that he was grounded and had to wait until he was forgiven. And then she had said, "Well, as far as I'm concerned, you already are forgiven."

And he was seconds away from telling her that her forgiveness did not matter one bit. The only forgiveness that counted was his uncle's. The truth is, Teresa's forgiveness bothered him. It was fake. It was the kind of forgiveness that stripped him of his rights and somehow got him in its clutches, and it upset him more than any other kind of punishment.

In the solitude of his room, Jacob has found a thousand ways to kill time. He has the treasure he discovered in the Pirates' Cave. He has the wooden horse, he has Ruan's stone and the shoe box . . . And he has all those happy memories, which are gradually retreating into the farthest recesses of his mind. But none of it is the same. Not even Clavileño. Try as he might, he cannot get Clavileño to fly.

If his uncle would only speak to him! If he would even do him the courtesy of scolding him, call him on the carpet for what he did. But his uncle has remained aloof. He watches Jacob, he scrutinizes him from a distance, but he will not speak to him.

His uncle's indifference hurts so badly, he sometimes thinks it would have been better if he had died, like Lori did.

To make matters worse, there is the *Poseidon*, right in front of his bedroom balcony, sleek and graceful, and ready to weigh anchor. They had planned it all the night before. They said the sea was going to be like a "mirror" and it would be a crime not to take advantage of it.

"Jacob . . ."

His bedroom door has been flung open and his uncle is there in the doorway, walking stick in hand. "Come on. Get ready. You're going with us." And he extends the walking stick for Jacob to grab on to, just as he always used to do.

But Jacob refuses to grab hold of it. He does not like his uncle's cavalier attitude.

"I'm grounded," he hisses between his teeth.

"Not any more. Your punishment is over."

"Since when?"

"Since right now. I imagine you're sorry for what you did."

He does not know how to answer that. There are things Jacob is unable to define. His remorse probably transcends the bounds of whatever his uncle might understand as sorry.

"In case you're interested, I should tell you that it was Teresa who asked me to forgive you. I trust you will at least have the courtesy to thank her."

Hearing that, Jacob thinks he would rather stay on land. There is no way in the world he is going to thank that woman.

"What are you waiting for? Go on. Grab the stick."

No. This was not at all how he had imagined his reconciliation with his uncle. He had expected something very different. Something more sincere and affectionate: a mutual coming to terms. A more intimate move towards acceptance.

"Everyone is waiting for you."

Reluctantly, he grabs onto the end of the walking stick and trails the painter out of the room.

Two outboard motor boats are waiting for the assembled group.

"So you finally went and got him," remarks Mauricio Belarmino.

"He doesn't seem very happy about it," Flora observes.

"Well he should be," retorts the Italian. "It is always a privilege to take a trip aboard the *Poseidon*."

It is strange to go down to the beach again, to smell the sea so close by and hear the flapping of the seagulls' wings.

As he passes by Quasimodo, the servant's good eye narrows in anger: "I see they've finally forgiven you . . . Don't even think about bothering me again. I'd have to be out of my mind to say yes next time you ask me to take you somewhere."

Jacob pretends not to hear him, but Quasimodo has a whole host of complaints stuck in his craw and he cannot hold back.

Quasimodo's behavior has also hurt Jacob deeply. Ever since his ignominious return to Can Boig, the servant no longer jokes with him and if he sees the boy out on his balcony while he's cleaning fish, he never says, "Hey, Little Pup. Come see how I scale them." Quasimodo has become guarded and barely says a word. If he does open his mouth when Dots is serving the meal in the kitchen, it is only to say that no one will ever yell at him again the way the painter did and, after all that uproar, he is not about to put up with any further outrages.

His uncle has sat him down right next to Teresa, so he can thank her. Once again, the violet perfume and her fine skin brushing against his arms. "Are you happy now, Ceibo?" Jacob says yes, without looking at her. This whole ploy about the outing smells fishy to him: a very strange proposition. So when his uncle says they are thinking of going all the way to France, Jacob's heart does a somersault inside his chest.

Duke starts to bark at almost the same exact moment. It is a nervous, plaintive howl, as if he were warning them about something.

"That animal is becoming more and more annoying," remarks his uncle.

And Jacob thinks Duke is barking because the *Poseidon* is going to France and perhaps his uncle—who has finally tired of him—is planning to leave him there, just like Hop o' my Thumb's parents left their children in the woods.

"Have a good trip," Quasimodo calls out from the jetty.

His uncle shouts back that they should not wait up, as they expect to be very late.

The morning is so bright, the scenery looks like a blurry photograph. There is still a hint of August in the air: a fickle August, which is on the verge of turning into September, but still tints the day with light and sends rays of heat filtering down from the sky at dusk.

Aboard the *Poseidon*, the sailors are rushing about. Jacob has never seen the spectacle of the crew checking the load line or making sure the fenders prevent any contact between the yacht's hull and the motorboats.

"You're finally going to get to see the coastline from the high seas," his uncle tells him.

But Jacob is still distracted, thinking about the strange significance beneath Duke's barking, while back on the jetty, the dog is desperately trying to find a way to jump into the sea and warn him not to board . . . to turn back . . . Quasimodo is having a hard time subduing the dog.

The first boat quickly reaches the yacht. Purita the fat lady is having a hard time boarding and the others are laughing at her. "One false move and the whole boat will flip over," remarks the marquis.

"Here comes the kid," says uncle Eduardo, raising Jacob high in the air. A sailor sets him down on the deck, next to the galley.

"A splendid day," comments the journalist, heartily.

But Mr. Raimundo remarks with foreboding that the radio forecast was predicting gale-force winds after sunset.

Seen from up close, the hatches seem higher, as does the railing that surrounds the deck.

"Come on, Jacob. Don't just stand there. You're blocking the way." And seeing that the boy is trembling: "What's the matter? Are you cold?"

He is scared. He is petrified they might leave him in France. Sure the whole business is really just a ruse to get rid of him.

"We'll be weighing anchor shortly," announces the captain, leading the child towards the stern. Stay here until the boat turns and the sun reaches the bow."

The *Poseidon* is soon inching its way out slowly, very slowly, to avoid the shoals surrounding Can Boig. From the stern, Jacob contemplates the masthead, topped by a flag. It would be easy to climb that pole. The captain is telling him to stay away from the taffrail. Passengers are not allowed in that quarter, Jacob. When the ship is at sea, climbing up on the transom would be suicidal."

He does not like the way the ship backs up. It seems as if it is devouring its own wake. Churned up clumps of algae head for the beach, as if to elude the bubbles.

"What's wrong with you, Little Pup?"

Jacob removes his glasses and rubs his right eye with one hand. "I don't want you to leave me in France," he sobs.

24

And that was when the real reconciliation happened. His uncle had taken him in his arms, rocking him just like he used to, and said everything had been forgotten. "But you have to promise me you'll never say such ugly things about Teresa any more."

Jacob had promised. "I'll never say she's evil, or she tried to strangle me, or she wanted to turn Duke into a rat ever again . . ."

And his uncle had dried his tears and kissed him and, to seal the armistice, he had taken him on a tour of the ship. It was just like the old days when they would climb up the mountain to watch the sun set. Together they had wandered among the decks, inspected the berths, climbed ladders and reached the fly bridge so Jacob could steer as if he were the captain. See that porthole Jacob? It's called a gualdrin. He also told him that soon, very soon, they would be passing in front of the Pirates' Cave, and Jacob told the captain that a long time ago he and his uncle had discovered a treasure, which had lain hidden there for centuries.

As they approached the islet, Jacob could see Lori's house. From out at sea, it looked tiny, as if it were a toy. The child wondered whether they had already buried Lori. Conchita had told him that dead people had to be buried within three days. But since the cemetery was close by, maybe Lori had been able to just walk over there.

Then they had descended to the living room—where the hatch leading to the foredeck was almost as big as a picture window at Can Boig—and they had explored the lower decks, locating the engine room and the crew's berths. See those hammocks, Little Pup? This is where the crew sleeps."

It was dark and close, situated well below the load line and lacking in direct ventilation. A place where the machines clanged noisily and stank of burning grease and too many human bodies in close quarters.

Jacob was learning so many new things. His uncle has been regaling him with one new piece of information after another. He taught him how to tie different kinds of mooring knots and explained how the rigging worked.

Now, as they approach the mainmast, he is telling him how, when Ulysses' ship was about to pass by the island of the sirens, he had ordered his crew to tie him to a pole such as that one, so he would be able to hear their song without any danger of throwing himself into the water.

But Jacob's happiness is abruptly curtailed, because Mr. Raimundo comes to interrupt them precisely at the most interesting moment. "They're waiting for you above, Maestro."

Apparently, Teresa and her guests have settled themselves on the sun deck. Uncle Eduardo excuses himself and asks Mr. Raimundo to take over for him and show the child around the rest of the yacht. Then he disappears. He climbs nimbly up the ladder, whistling as he goes, obviously in a lighthearted mood. And Jacob is alone again, disconcerted and chock full of resentment against Mr. Raimundo.

"I don't want to stay with you," he says shortly. "Take me where my uncle is."

Don Raimundo swallows, clears his throat and adjusts his glasses. "Look Jacob. Children cannot always be with the grown-ups."

"Why not?"

Mr. Raimundo looks exasperated. He is probably the type to hold a grudge. The kind of people who never forget it if someone has given them a bad time. He can tell by the way the adminis-trator stretches out his neck and bites his lip and by his carefully controlled tone of voice, especially when he says something he does not want to have to say.

"Because that's the way it is. They like to talk about their own things . . ."

"What things?"

Mr. Raimundo is becoming increasingly uncomfortable. There is no doubt about it. His face has turned to clay and he seems to be avoiding Jacob's eyes. "How would I know!" And he abruptly indicates the wake of the ship. "Take a good look at that, Ceibo." A thick trail of frothy bubbles radiates silver strokes on the water's smooth surface.

He is trying to distract the child. Get him out of his damned "take me to my uncle" mode. At that moment, Mr. Raimundo is exactly like grandmother Katherine—except he is a man—with all of his moralizing and his own interests at the forefront.

"The stupid wake is boring."

"A lot of children would give anything to be in your position."

That is exactly what his grandmother would have said. She was always saying things like: "You're constantly finding something to complain about, Jacob. You have the TV. You have your toys. You have your story books . . ."

But the truth was, all he really wanted was his mother, and his mother was with Roger. And that is why they had sent him to his grandmother's house in the first place. To get rid of him.

"Besides, when we get to French waters, there's a cove and you'll be able to take a swim. You'll love it there."

"What's the name of the cove?"

"It doesn't have a name."

"I'd rather stay in Can Boig than spend my whole day with you," Jacob says, sulking.

Mr. Raimundo does not take kindly to the remark. Irritated, he sits down on the bench ringing the bow, leans back and crosses his legs. "If it's any comfort to you, I'm not overjoyed at being left to baby-sit either."

And the child suddenly realizes that is why Mr. Raimundo was invited along on the *Poseidon* in the first place: to watch over him. To keep him occupied and away from the grown-ups.

"I'm going to climb up the masthead."

"What are you talking about? You could fall into the sea." And he launches into a speech about how even monkeys avoid such steep dangerous climbs.

"I can climb better than a monkey."

It is going to be a very long day. Very long. As long as the sea is huge. Rosario was right when she told him that the sea is bigger than the land. He could tell just by looking at it, all smooth and shining, losing itself way off in the distance, where the sky begins.

The shore is a long way off. Apparently, big ships do not go anywhere near it except to anchor.

Uncle Eduardo is playing the guitar up on the sky deck. His voice, low and gruff, floats down to Jacob.

"Is it true that Teresa is immortal?" he asks.

Mr. Raimundo is taken aback. "No one is immortal. Not even Teresa."

"Are you sure?"

"Why do you ask?"

"Her friends said she's like Achilles and she can only die from her heel."

Mr. Raimundo shifts uncomfortably, crosses his hands and, once again, looks exactly like his grandmother Katherine. "Why do you care whether Teresa is immortal or not?"

Jacob scratches his ear, looks up towards the sky and squeezes his eyes shut. "What if she stepped on a stone and it got stuck in her heel. Do you think she'd die?"

"Oh for God's sake. A stone . . ."

"What if she got stabbed in the heel?"

Mr. Raimundo straightens his torso and frowns, pausing to adjust his glasses as he turns to face Jacob. "The first thing they'd do is send her attacker straight to jail."

"But would she die?"

"What kind of question is that? I suppose if the blade were poisoned . . ."

The administrator is sitting there gaping at the child, whose slight frame is reflected in his eyeglasses. He must be thinking what a strange creature this Ceibo is. What a tortured mind he has and what twisted questions he asks, such as how to kill somebody by sticking them in the heel.

"Do you think you would be capable of sticking a knife in Teresa?"

"I can't. I promised my uncle I'd leave her alone."

"So what are you getting at with all these questions?"

Jacob stares at the floor and plays with his toes. At least the ones that poke out from his sandals.

"You have to stop thinking such terrible things, Jacob. Hasn't anyone ever told you that nobody should ever wish someone else dead?"

"Not even their enemies?"

"Not even them."

But Jacob does wish Teresa were dead. Especially after he hears her laughter floating down from above, while his uncle strums the guitar.

"Not even witches?"

"No."

And as he says it, Mr. Raimundo takes him by the shoulders and shakes him gently, sending a warm breath into the child face. "It doesn't seem possible," he says. "Anyone would think Teresa had done something terrible to you! You should be ashamed of yourself, Jacob."

But Jacob turns his face towards the sea and barely hears what Mr. Raimundo is saying. It is a bland sea. A dull, boring sea.

"Why do you hate her so much, child?"

But Jacob's hate is a slippery thing. Something he could never begin to explain. As soon as he thinks he has it in his grasp, it slithers out of his mind, just as an eel might slither out of his hands.

"Just so you know: it was Teresa who asked your uncle to forgive you and bring you along with us . . ."

"So they could leave me with you . . ."

Perhaps that is why he hates her so much right now: because he owes her a favor and it is not even a favor.

"Right. So they can leave you with me, and so you can breathe the fresh air, and look at the sea and act like a happy, grateful, sensible boy."

Every once in a while, a boat crosses the yacht's path and Jacob tracks it with his gaze, just as he used to watch the Kangaroo pass by from his uncle's study. The freighter operated on a schedule and his uncle would say, "Get ready, Little Pup. It's about to come into view."

Maybe now some child is watching from the coast as the *Poseidon* heads towards France and he is telling himself how lucky it would be to sail on such a big, white ship.

"It isn't possible to live with all that hate, Jacob."

Visitarana had said something like that too, about how hate and revenge were worse than a toothache. But Jacob has never had a toothache so he really cannot compare.

"If you would at least stop that frowning."

Frowns do not seem to leave when people like uncle Eduardo go up to sky decks to be with Teresas who are stuck up and only think about sunbathing and slathering themselves all over with perfumed lotions.

"Teresa wishes she could reign over the whole sea."

"And what does that have to do with what I'm trying to tell you."

"The dolphins are the ones who reign over the sea."

"I agree. But whoever told you that Teresa wanted to reign over it?"

Nobody. He had just known it from the moment he saw her there on the beach, the day she arrived. But he would never be able to explain why. The good think about being old is that the right words are always on hand when you have to answer questions. But Jacob is still a child and he still finds it difficult to convey his inner dialects into the world of the living.

"Kilsa also wanted to."

"Who in the hell is Kilsa?"

"The princess who was kidnapped by Malabrun the pirate."

Taken aback, Mr. Raimundo opens his mouth, cocks his head, and for a few brief moments, he even stops looking like grandmother Katherine. "Of course. I had forgotten."

"I bet Kilsa didn't really die," says the child. "I bet the princess Malabrun stole was really Teresa . . ."

25

Lunch is an animated affair, punctuated by voices, clinking glass and silverware scraping plates. Claude is quick on his feet and he makes sure no glass lacks sangria.

Jacob is seated beside his uncle, under the canopy stretched over the foredeck. The *Poseidon* has been anchored before the nameless cove for quite a while now.

No sooner had they had arrived there, than the painter had gone in search of his nephew. "Come on, Little Pup. Put on your flippers and your mask and jump in with me."

They had leapt into the sea through a porthole along the gangway, before the sailors even had a chance to install the ladder. "Do you dare swim all the way to that rock?" It was a solitary mound topped by the silvery silhouette of a gull.

Jacob dared. All the other passengers had remained behind paddling about right next to the ship, or splashing themselves from the last rung of the ladder, because none of them would have been capable of jumping from the porthole.

As they approached the crag, it seemed to grow taller and taller and full of crannies, and the water's thousand hues splayed around it like a fan in a fluid display of shape and form.

As they climbed up the rock, the seagull flew off petrified and the two flung themselves down on their stomachs, panting under the hot sun. From their vantage point, the *Poseidon* looked like another rock, whitish and desolate, surrounded by bodies clad in life jackets splashing idiotically and churning up lots of unnecessary foam. Not even Teresa knew how to swim properly, his uncle had told him. And he'd made fun of her because a sailor up on deck was holding on to a rope attached to her life jacket.

The swim had been unexpected: a dazzling, amazing interval in which his uncle had once again given Jacob his undivided attention. They had both laughed, their hilarity contagious, because when they emerged from the water, Eduardo Santillana's beard looked like a damp sponge and his nephew had teased him, saying "Look at your beard." And he had twisted the strands to squeeze water onto his cheeks.

It was getting late when they heard the ship's horn sound and the captain's voice over the megaphone announcing that lunch was ready. "We are bound to obey, nephew of mine."

They had returned spent, gasping for breath, their smiles irrepressible. Back on deck, they had left two puddles next to the porthole and Teresa, obviously in a bad mood, had ordered the sailors to dry the floor immediately.

Teresa had looked almost ugly in her white tunic, her eyes flashing with irritation. She resembled a spiteful ghost. "She's like that because I didn't swim with her," his uncle had murmured in Jacob's ear. And later, as if to increase her exasperation, he had told Teresa that if she wanted to go swimming with him, she was going to have to learn to swim as well as Jacob did. Then his uncle had insisted Jacob join them at the table. He said that now that he was on board, he should be able to do as everyone else did.

His uncle's happiness was evident. It was more like euphoria—perhaps a little exaggerated even. This kind of happiness seemed to put Teresa out even more because, every so often, she gets very stern and says Eduardo is acting like that because he has been drinking like a Cossack.

But the others have been drinking too and that is why lunch is turning out to be such a boisterous affair, punctuated by voices and grating sounds. The conversation is becoming more and more colorful, difficult, and full of yawning gaps for the child.

"Friendship is a gossip dressed up as affection," remarks Purita the fat lady.

And the marquis confirms that happiness is all about timing because, by the time your heart's desire finally arrives, you have already lost interest.

"Isn't that right, Flora?"

Flora does not reply. Her head has been flopping around for some time now, as if the sun and the sangria had numbed all her senses.

"Bah. There's no worse patient than the one who doesn't want to be a bother," persists Purita the fat lady in a nasal voice.

There is no rhyme or reason to the conversation. It is a mishmash of nonsensical remarks and no one seems to be paying attention anyway. It is as if they are all talking just for the sake of it, without waiting for a reply, just to prove they are dining under a sun-drenched canopy and breathing in the warm salt air.

"A rabid cat . . ." Purita interjects. And she goes on to tell a horrifying story that appears to have left a mark on her psyche.

And the marquis brings up the case of a friend of his who woke up one morning to find all his furniture riddled with bullet holes, even though no one had entered or left the house. "It was a case of telepathy . . ."

It seems even grown-ups like to share their fantasies. The ones today are impregnated with terror, mystery, dead people who appear . . . The strange thing is that grown-ups are also afraid sometimes and they have horrible dreams too, like the ones about the hydrocephalic child or the pillar of salt.

"Spain is full of terrors," says Mr. Raimundo.

And at the sound of his voice, everybody turns to look at him in astonishment, because Mr. Raimundo hardly ever opens his mouth when Uncle Eduardo's guests are around.

But Mr. Raimundo has also been drinking and cannot seem to deny his own alcohol-induced euphoria.

The Italians laugh. They say they feel very happy and Spain has wonderful qualities, and the best part is not exactly its climate but the scenery . . .

"Those orange groves . . ."

"The vineyards . . ."

"The mulberries and those walnut trees . . ."

But uncle Eduardo is paying no attention to any of them. He just keeps on talking about his own subjects, his obsessions, anything that comes into his head. Because ever since they had returned from the swim, uncle Eduardo has been drinking sangria non-stop and his head has turned into a maze of abstract theories.

"We have to make sure nobody gets lost . . ."

The ever unflappable Claude is serving coffee. Teresa is sitting ramrod straight in her chair, clearly annoyed with his uncle's behavior. That is why, every time he opens his mouth, she snaps at him, just as Coco used to do when he would say her dances were affected.

"The most important thing is to defend our rights," uncle Eduardo is saying. And he starts spouting off in favor of nudism, because human beings do not come into the world bundled up in diapers.

Teresa cannot stand his language. She says Eduardo has a tendency to confuse social justice with social pornography.

And the painter gives her a sardonic look, wriggles his finger at her and asks her when she turned into such a puritan.

Teresa's fury increases. She finds it absolutely intolerable when the painter talks to her like that. She says if she had only known it was going to be like this, she would never have proposed the trip and, if he keeps on drinking at that pace, as soon as they disembark at Can Boig, she and her friends will head straight back to France once and for all.

"Come on now, Teresa. Don't get so upset," ventures Purita.

But all dignified and in a huff, she rises from the table and heads towards the lower deck.

Eduardo does not move. He simply serves himself more sangria and says she'll get over it and sometimes women get hysterical for no reason. "According to her, you just need to kill the dragon to put an end to all evil. But real life is something else again . . ."

Then Mauricio Belarmino, more clammy and puffed up than usual, his protruding lower lip almost purple, says the bad thing about our day and age is that there are no more St. Georges left capable of killing dragons.

At that, Jacob is about to say that he saw those dragons when they ran across the road leading to Can Boig the day he arrived, but he thinks better of it, because the only things he actually saw were the dragons' caves.

It is funny to see the guests' noses, which have suddenly become all bright and colorful, and whenever they say something, the words slip and slide around their lips as if they had been greased.

Flora wakes up abruptly, looks around at everybody wide-eyed and announces: "I'm drunk."

His uncle thumps her on the back and tells her, "Don't worry, Flora. We all are."

Jacob suddenly recalls the night his uncle slammed the talking table against the terrace floor: *Don't pay any attention to me, Little Pup. Sometimes I drink too much and I act like an ass . . .* He is behaving badly now too, but with Teresa, instead of with his nephew. So Jacob is almost grateful his uncle has drunk so much sangria. He had gone on to say: *The truth is we humans are pretty stupid. We drink to be happy and end up sad . . .*

But this time he seems inclined to be happy and happiness can never be bad.

The only one who has suddenly become all serious is Mr. Raimundo. Especially when the captain appears to tell them some angry clouds are approaching fast and an inclement weather warning has just been issued.

But his uncle does not listen. He does not want to listen. He just keeps repeating that men of the sea are alarmists and cowards and they're always dreaming up problems like all good doomsayers.

"Whatever you say, Mr. Santillana, but please be warned."

His uncle replies that as long as the sun is out and the sea is calm, they will remain anchored at the nameless cove.

"What's the worst that can happen if the sea is a little rough when we return?"

"Nothing in particular," responds the captain, "but you'll all be as sick as dogs."

"Well, here's to seasickness," says the marquis, raising his glass.

By the time the cloud has drawn near, however, they are all overcome with drowsiness. No one wishes to stay on deck. They all move into the living room and then gradually confess they are so sleepy they can hardly stand.

"Lightweights," says uncle Eduardo. "You're all a bunch of lightweights."

And once again, he assumes the blustering air of the night when Richard tried to speak with him through the table.

Jacob finds it entertaining to watch his uncle so wobbly and flushed. Now he resembles the uncle who once played the castanets in the chamber of useless objects. Every step he takes resembles a dance step, but not like any of Coco's dances. His uncle's moves are slow, like a bear's.

As the engines groan into life, the boat vibrates and the passengers can hardly keep their feet under them. The cloud is fast approaching, a dense mass that seems to loom larger with every passing minute.

One by one, they file towards the berths. No one is paying any attention to Jacob. And the child remains behind the closed window that gives onto the deck, watching the sky grow darker and darker.

26

He soon tumbles onto the sofa because the sea is beginning to crash furiously against the port side and, even though it is moving very slowly, the ship is meeting undulating swells that knock human bodies back and forth and make them lose their balance.

Jacob recalls what the captain said: *You're all going to be sick as dogs.* Maybe that is why they have all taken refuge in the berths, even as the gusting, violent wind the captain had predicted darkens the sky and coats the ship in dampness.

Jacob would also like to sleep. But something is keeping him from dropping off: he feels an ominous sort of threat nearby, like pulsating heat. "Don't try to pretend you're asleep, Ceibo."

Startled, Jacob turns in her direction. It is a white, almost ghostly threat, with a voice, a look, and a particular determination about it. "Where's my uncle?" he asks in alarm.

But Teresa does not answer. Without moving her gaze from his, she walks towards him from the opening where the ladder is, her body taut, her features twisted into an ugly expression: "I know everything, Jacob. Absolutely everything."

Frightened, the child shrinks back into the sofa. "Don't come near me. Don't you touch me."

Teresa pauses. But she continues to speak, and every word is like another step towards him, as if she were wringing his neck without even laying a hand on him. Her voice is different. It is no longer the sugar sweet, childlike voice she always uses in front of his uncle. Now her voice is grating and filled with rage. All at once, she is spitting out reproaches, confusing trains of thought, and aggressive arguments that gravitate towards Jacob and settle inside his chest.

Teresa is not kidding. She does know everything. She knows the hidden reason behind his trip to the village. Knows about his interview with Visitarana, his desire to stick her in the heel to get rid of her, put an end to her once and for all . . . And, as if that were not enough, she knows about his overpowering desire to get her away from his uncle.

"I want to see him. I want to go where he is," insists Jacob.

But Teresa says that will be impossible. His uncle is resting and she is not going to let Ceibo disturb him for anything in the world.

And when Jacob looks up through the hatch he can see that the cloud is no longer a cloud. The *Poseidon* is shrouded in an obscure wasteland of sea, sky, and shuddering air.

"Then I want to go to Mr. Raimundo."

He cannot do that either. Teresa informs him that Mr. Raimundo is also resting. Everyone is asleep in the berths and Teresa is the only one who is still awake. "And it is high time to set things straight, because my patience has a limit, Ceibo. I have no intention of letting you drive me away from your uncle."

A sudden wave crashes into the ship and Jacob must clutch the armrest to keep himself from tumbling off the sofa. But Teresa just stands there, as if the waves were having no effect on her at all.

Bewildered, Jacob cannot quite understand how Teresa could have found out about Visitarana and the part about the Achilles heel. She must have telepathy. He should have taken precautions. He should have known that witches like her know everything.

"Have you given them a potion?"

Teresa lets out a grunt that seems like a forced laugh. Then she launches her tirade: she is sick and tired of his attitude, his backtalk, his demanding behavior. She and his uncle have had their first argument because of Jacob and she is not about to let a sniveling little brat, who is not even three feet tall, come between them and jeopardize their happiness.

It seems like a nightmare. The kind of nightmare that just goes on and on.

Teresa inhales deeply and keeps going. She mentions the nonsense she has to listen to day and night. "I'm tired of your uncle's constant, 'be careful, Teresa, make sure Jacob doesn't find out about this, that, or the other.' I'm tired of hearing about enchanted rocks and hidden treasures and petrified pirates and flights on Clavileño. I'm not going to play those idiotic games anymore. It's over and done with, Ceibo."

And as she speaks, she clenches her fists, driving the nails into her palms. She even clenches her teeth. It is a powerful rage she has managed to keep in check up to now. "I'm a free woman, Ceibo. A woman with a right to be happy with a man who is also free. And I have no intention of letting the fantasies of some snot-nosed kid get in the way of that."

"Are you going to kill me?" the child asks, panicked.

Teresa clears her throat because the whole diatribe has made her voice hoarse. She says she has half a mind to, but the only thing she is going to do is make sure that Jacob is taken firmly in hand, for his own good and everybody else's.

She sounds just like his mother did when she talked about his father. She had said all the same things and had criticized her husband for being a Spaniard in the tradition of Don Quixote.

The ship is lurching. It is not nighttime but the day has turned black and, in the advancing shadows, Teresa's eyes seem to grow wider and wider. She is telling Jacob that his uncle is fed up with him. He is counting the days until the child returns to France: "Your escapade the other day made him absolutely sick. He is not about to let your father hold him accountable for such an irresponsible child."

"You're lying."

Teresa bites her lip and brushes her hair back.

"You're lying because you're bad and you're jealous of me."

But Teresa is not about to take that kind of insolence from Jacob. Going over to the child, she grabs onto his cheeks with both hands and repeats what she has just said. A sour odor assails Jacob's nostrils. Her breath is disgusting and makes him feel nauseous. "Come on, Ceibo. Repeat what I just said." Never in his life has Jacob ever seen such an ugly, tense face so close up.

"You're hurting me," he complains.

But Teresa does not release him. She says he has hurt her too and he should just prepare himself, because if he doesn't shape up, she's going to tell his uncle everything.

"I don't care. You're ugly: ugly and evil."

Teresa is panting. She coughs and sputters, and then she starts saying terrible things. Things Jacob does not want to hear. It is as if his ears were being violated, as if someone were forcing them to listen. "It is all a lie, Jacob. Nothing is what you think it is . . . and paper sabers are just that, paper sabers . . . enchanted rocks are just rocks . . . Ruan's stone is just an old piece of brick . . . no goldfinch can fly higher than a kite . . . Peter Pan is just a literary creation for stupid children . . . Clavileño is a ridiculous horse invented to deceive a lunatic . . ."

"You're lying. Shut up. You're lying."

But Teresa will not shut up. She has been set off. She tells him Ruan is Quasimodo and only the stupidest child would ever really believe in extraterrestrials like him. "Bottom line, Ceibo? It was all a show to make fun of you."

"I hate you. I hate you . . ."

She says she hates him too and when you really come down to it, so does his beloved uncle. "All that lovey-dovey stuff is enough to make you sick. Look at what he's accomplished with all of his spoiling and coddling." And she says his uncle is fed up with him. And to make matters worse, he's a little intimidated by him too . . .

And as she speaks, something paralyzing is taking over the living room: something well beyond the wind, and the sea and the ship itself. It is as if a filthy, slimy morass had engulfed them both and was keeping them from breathing.

"I don't believe you. I don't want to believe you."

But Teresa tightens the noose, throwing in his face that he will believe her soon enough. As soon as his uncle wakes up, he can just ask him. And Jacob is finally convinced she is not lying.

"Why do you think we brought you along today? Don't even think we enjoy your company. We were simply afraid you'd run off again. That's the only reason we brought you aboard, Ceibo. To keep you from running away . . ."

"Leave me alone!"

Teresa will not leave him alone. To the contrary, she is pinching his face even harder and her nails are digging into his cheeks. Her face very close to his, she continues, "I'll leave you alone just as soon as I've said everything I have to say . . ."

His father had yelled in his face too: *Idiot. You just drank somebody else's saliva: spit it out, spit, spit . . .* And the whole place had started to spin around, because a stranger's saliva can cause all kinds of contagious diseases. The worst ones. All those unknown illnesses that constantly plague careless children like him. And his mother was laughing. *What was going on in your head?* And the stunned faces of all the other people were blending into theirs. Just as they had the day he thought he'd swallowed a match head. It was all designed to make Jacob's anxiety grow and become intolerable. *You have to wait until the waiter comes, Jacob. Everybody knows you have to wait instead of drinking out of a used glass . . .*

It was a bottleneck of mistakes that cut off his breathing and took away his desire to live. That is why it hurt him so much when his father made him do his fat face and his skinny face for company, because he knew that, next, they were going to tell the whole episode of the café-au-lait and start laughing at him. *When it comes to kids, you just never know* . . .

You had to get rid of those contagious diseases. You had to spit them out: there was nothing else for it.

It seemed as if his father couldn't stop saying it: *You have to spit, Jacob. You have to get rid of all those microbes. You have to spit them out.*

And the *Poseidon* has taken up the chorus. Every pitch, every splash is mimicking his father's voice: *Spit, Jacob* . . .

So in order to keep from getting infected by the disease Teresa is puffing into his face, Jacob decides to fight back with the only weapon available to him. His only possible defense. The one his father recommended to him that day, long ago, in the café in Paris.

27

Teresa screams out the words: "Oh, that's disgusting. You spit on me. How *dare* you spit on me . . ." But Jacob is no longer there to hear her. In a flash, he has opened the hatch and is running headlong towards the ship's stern.

Whirlwinds of air rise to meet him, cutting off his breath. But anything is better than putting up with that half-witch, half-ghost woman.

The *Poseidon* appears to be deserted. The wind and the rough seas have swallowed up the crew. It is as if a solitary ship were adrift in the maelstrom of an ominous, intractable and infuriated northerly.

Teresa's voice occasionally reaches him, carried on the wind: "Jacob . . . Where are you hiding, Jacob?" And Jacob tells himself he has no other choice but to flee that voice. He has to get away from her forever. But the voice is insistent, it calls out to him and he runs . . .

The gunwale might serve as a refuge. Even though the railing is flimsy and the handholds hardly protrude at all, he knows his only salvation is to climb the masthead, up to the flag, where he knows Teresa can never reach him. "Jacob . . ."

He suddenly spies her near the hatch, her tunic disheveled and stuck to her body, her hair plastered on her face, her hands reaching towards him. "Jacob! What are you doing?"

He is up on the platform in one leap and pauses there, squatting, trying his best to keep his balance as the ship sways.

"Are you crazy? Come down from there at once." And her voice is like the sirens' when they sang their toxic melodies to drive the sailors crazy.

"I don't want to," he screams. "I won't come down."

She is coming closer to him, arms outstretched and a look of terror on her face. "Don't you realize you could fall overboard?"

But Jacob is certain that the sea is safer than Teresa, less dangerous by far, in fact. It does not matter that the waves are cresting furiously, their frothing wake spattering the flag and turning it into a tattered rag. What does matter are those outstretched arms, and the disheveled tunic, and the hateful voice trying to trap him.

"Don't touch me," he yells again. "Don't come near me."

But Teresa has long arms and her hand has almost reached the child's body. She pauses. "Please, Jacob. Don't move. Don't move," she screams in desperation and, for a moment, it looks as if she might leave him there. She probably wants to run for help. But she does not dare. "I can't leave you, Jacob . . ." Then she starts crying out for help, a pitiful cry that is carried away by the wind. A cry for help that seems to travel back down her throat rather than come out of it. Meanwhile, Jacob's small frame is being tossed about and splashed. "I'm begging you, Little Pup, please . . ."

But Teresa calling him "Little Pup" is something Jacob absolutely cannot tolerate.

"Shut up," he yells. "I'm not your Little Pup."

And before Teresa can stop him, he slithers like a snake until he reaches the mast. It is futile for her to keep calling for help. Nobody can hear her. The guests are asleep below in the berths, and the crew is huddled on the other side, where the ship's hull serves to break the wind. "You're right, Jacob. I've been bad. Very bad. But please, I'm begging you to come down from there. Come back . . ."

Jacob does not listen to her. He does not want to hear her voice. He is sure that if he listens to her before he climbs the mast, he will be lost forever, just like the sailors who threw themselves into the sea. "Forgive me, Jacob. Please, forgive me . . ."

Jacob does not forgive her. He cannot forgive her. That is why, when he reaches the mast, he scrambles right up and clings to the top of it letting the flag wrap around him. "God help us all, Jacob. Come down from there. I'll help you."

"I won't come down," the child repeats. "I won't come down until you go away."

Teresa has not given up. "Wait," she says distraught. "I'm going to try to save you. Don't let go, Jacob, you hear me? Hold on tight."

And navigating as best she can between the ship's lurches, she climbs up the back of the bench cushion to the top. She is probably dizzy, because when she reaches the platform, she stretches out flat to keep from losing her balance before she can reach the mast and grab onto him. It would be rash to try to stand. The waves are too violent and one misstep could plunge her into the sea. But her strength fails her. She is overcome with terror and the mast is farther away than she thought.

Her mouth drops open and unintelligible words are coming out. It is as if she were screaming out silences or swallowing a roar.

Jacob does not move a muscle. The battering of the waves is becoming stronger by the minute, while the strength seems to be ebbing from Teresa's body. And the sea is an immense break for the swirling wind that is causing the vessel to shudder without rhyme or reason. "We're both going to die," she exclaims in despair.

And all at once, her body begins to slip to one side. Then there is a harsh, prolonged, animal-like wail. Jacob does not see her fall, but when he looks back towards the wake, he can see an outstretched arm, the hand rigid, bobbing above the swirling water as it recedes into the distance.

Jacob had had a hard time dragging himself back towards the canopy pole, but as soon as he managed to grasp hold of it, he had jumped onto the cushion and run back down to the living room. At first he had had the feeling Teresa was following him. Perhaps it was not true that the sea had taken her away. More than once, he had heard her voice screaming for them to save her, and he had even thought he glimpsed her mounted on a dolphin chasing behind the yacht.

Back in the living room, he had looked at himself in the mirror: his glasses were fogged up and all he could see was the outline of a skinny little boy, his hair a wet rag, just like the tattered flag.

He had been about to wake up his uncle and tell him everything, but had decided against it, because he was afraid his uncle would punish him for climbing up the mast. And to him, the most important thing was to see his uncle happy and anxious to go swimming with him again, just as they had earlier in the nameless cove.

The *Poseidon*'s living room was chilly and the child's clothes were soaked through and beginning to bother him, so he had burrowed into the large sofa cushions and fallen asleep. When he had awakened, it was nighttime and the *Poseidon* was still rocking wildly, although the engines were only sputtering, as if they had lost their impetus. He could tell his clothes had dried and that he must have been sleeping for quite a while.

All at once, he had heard voices and footsteps and murmurs near his ear and when he opened his eyes and looked around, he had seen a ring of concerned expressions and heard a million questions at once. "When did you last see Teresa." "What did she say?" "Where could she have gone after she left you in the living room . . . ?"

And as usual, Jacob had no answers. Flora had said, "Don't be cruel. You're confusing the poor child. What in the hell could he have to tell you?" That is when he had realized that Teresa had not come back. She had remained behind somewhere in the sea.

The worst part was he could not see his uncle. No matter how much he had insisted, nobody would take him to where he was. They had all offered vague responses. "Your uncle is beside himself." "They've had to give him a tranquilizer."

His eyes opened wide in fear, Jacob had clung to the armrest of the sofa because the rocking of the sea and his drowsiness made it hard for him to keep his balance.

He had asked where they were and they told him the ship had drifted far from the shore, but they were following the current in search of Teresa. Above him on deck, sailors were setting off Bengal lights, which reminded him of the fireworks on his birthday. But all you could see in the illuminated water were choppy waves.

Somebody had suggested that Teresa had probably had too much to drink and when she went to throw up, the waves had caused her to lose her balance. Then they had told him that they would be sending him back to Can Boig just as soon as the rescue boats arrived.

After that, a sailor had taken him below deck, where it stank. There were the crew's hammocks swinging wildly, sending out wafts of foul air that reeked of human sweat and greasy machines. "Come on, little one," they had told him. "The boats will be here soon and you'll be able to go home." That was when he had burst out crying and said he did not want to go anywhere without his uncle.

The hours had passed by slowly, while the leaden night closed in upon the sea. Minds were empty, hopes were pinned to an illusion, and the salt air pervaded everything.

Jacob's refrain had not even been audible. It was white noise, like the ship's groaning and the sailors' voices. A refrain abandoned to its own devices: "I want my uncle. I want my uncle . . ."

Until finally, wrapped in a towel, they had carried him to the porthole for the transfer. Aboard the rescue boat was a technician with a knowing expression. "So this is the child . . ." By then, Jacob was no longer saying, "I want my uncle." He was just whimpering the cadence of the phrase, because he no longer had the strength to repeat it.

A slew of boats had surrounded the *Poseidon*. And there were voices too, countless voices tripping over each other over the megaphones. And searchlights. Immense beams that cast shadows on the waves and turned the foam to silver.

They had returned against the wind, amid giant waves, hoping in vain that the night would have brought at least one single star, a semblance of natural light to drill through the mist.

A long time passed before they had glimpsed the lighthouse at Can Boig. The technician had assured the boy that he had not seen such a dense fog in the district for years. And Jacob had repeated, one last time, that he wanted his uncle.

Dots and Quasimodo met them at the jetty. Duke was not there. They had barely greeted the people milling about them. They had spoken only with the technician, riddling him with questions. The technician had insisted that the wine was to blame for the whole business: "The blessed sangria, the heat . . ." And he had added that people should always avoid alcohol when they are out at sea.

Dots, like a soul in torment, had said you can never be certain about those things.

After that, they had removed Jacob's wet clothing, rubbed his body with cologne and given him a pill dissolved in a mug of warm milk. Then Dots had lain down next to him and allowed the night to run its course as it always did: slowly, painfully and frustratingly, just like every other night in the world.

28

He had waited for days and days, but nothing was like before. Not even the *Poseidon* seemed like the same ship. They said that it was still anchored at Can Boig only because the investigation had not been closed, and the best thing for Eduardo Santillana would be to get out of there before he went crazy for good.

When his uncle had returned, Jacob had seen that his beard had grown and his body was a jumble of bones caked with fuzz and grime. The sun had been in his eyes, and his uncle had covered his eyelids with his hands because they burned.

He had walked straight past the child without even noticing him. He was so distracted he had not even turned to look his way. So Dots had taken him by the hand and suggested he not try to talk to him. "He's destroyed. He hasn't slept for days."

The others were also just shadows of their former selves: marionettes flitting about the house like aimless ghosts. Even Mauricio Belarmino had lost his grandiloquence and his booming voice was rarely heard. Purita was the only one who remained unchanged because she said the more something affected her, the fatter she got.

The house had been filled with new people. Serious people from the Police, the Coast Guard, and the courthouse. They had asked a lot of questions, but could not seem to achieve any clarity. One had suggested that perhaps the child might know something, but when they had drawn near, Jacob had burst into tears and said he wanted his uncle.

Dots cried too. She had spent the whole first day asking where poor Teresa might have ended up. She just sat by the magnolia, staring at the sea as if she might be able to glimpse Teresa's body floating out there.

Little by little, Teresa's guests had begun to depart Can Boig: the Italian couple, the marquis, Flora, Purita the fat lady, Mauricio Belarmino . . . And his uncle had said goodbye, without comment or protest. Some of them had seemed hurt or angry at his coldness and indifference, but Mr. Raimundo had insisted they should not take it personally: "The maestro is not himself . . ."

Once, when Jacob was alone with his uncle, he had grabbed onto his pants leg and pleaded with him to say something. But his uncle, almost without looking at him, had only patted his head absently and said he could not talk like before, because Teresa had taken his capacity for self-expression with her when she went away.

Then Jacob, seeing him so forlorn, had suggested that he could stay with his uncle forever, but his uncle had sat him on his lap and said that was impossible. The best thing for Jacob to do was to return to France as soon as possible, because he would never be happy at Can Boig.

After that conversation, everything seemed to lose meaning. Even the shoebox. It was as if Jacob suddenly had shed his status as a child. As if he really was a ceibo.

"Are you ready, Jacob?"

He says he is. And Dots, also listless, directs Quasimodo to fetch the child's suitcase.

"Where is your shoebox, Little Pup? I haven't been able to find it anywhere."

Jacob wrinkles his nose, because the glare from the terrace is hurting his eyes, and reflecting off his glasses. "I don't have it anymore," he says calmly. "I threw it into the sea this morning."

"And the horse? Where's the horse?"

Jacob does not reply and Dots is getting angry. "I can't believe it. Such a lovely horse . . ."

He had tossed it all out of the studio window. The stone, the treasure chest, the shoe box and the wooden horse. They had fallen, bouncing among prickly pears, pebbles and rocks. Later he had spied the horse floating along in pieces at the foot of the cliff. Until a wave had come along, swirling into an eddy, and it had disappeared from view.

"You're incorrigible, Jacob."

Dots' opinion means nothing to him. Ever since Jacob discovered that all grown-ups do is lie, he does not care one whit about what they think of him. His disillusionment had reached its limit when he saw Lori back at the house again. "You weren't dead, Lori?" And shaking her head, she had told him very seriously that, if she were dead, she would not be able to speak, or walk, or anything.

"Mr. Raimundo is waiting for you, Jacob."

They are on the terrace, contemplating the lighthouse, the beach, and the sea, and he thinks that something very much like a fire has burned everything down . . .

"Quasimodo has already put your suitcase in the car."

. . . and even the terrace is nothing but ashes.

"Hurry up, Jacob. You're uncle is waiting to say goodbye to you."

Dots does not realize that Jacob is still holding out one last hope. Dots cannot know that the child is waiting for his uncle to say, *It would be better if you didn't go, Little Pup. What would I do without you?*

"Okay. Let's go."

But he stops, because his uncle is standing in the door frame, blocking his way. It strikes him to see his uncle wearing blue, just as he was that first day, with his walking stick in hand and his shirt unbuttoned to the waste.

"So you're leaving now . . ." And the painter is looking at him with his new, indifferent gaze, as if Jacob were just any child.

"I'm sorry I can't go with you, Jacob, but I'm tired. Very tired."

They exchange looks. His uncle's is not really a look at all, just a set of motions he uses in order to see.

"Did you brush your teeth?"

Dots answers for him. She says yes and he's washed his face too.

"You should probably get going. Mr. Raimundo is in a hurry."

He extends the walking stick to him. Jacob looks at it and then shakes his head.

"No," he says very seriously. "I don't need the stick anymore."

Duke is chasing along behind him, tail wagging and ears cocked. There is something very nervous about the way the dog is licking his hands. As if he were only just arriving, instead of leaving.

"Give us a kiss, Jacob," says Dots, offering her cheek.

Jacob is slightly repulsed at the thought of kissing her cheek, which is sticky with tears and sweat.

"Don't forget me, Little Pup."

Then Quasimodo approaches. He too looks sad and he also wants to kiss him.

"If you ever come back here, we'll clean the fish on the rock . . ."

Jacob settles himself into the back seat of the car, because in Spain, children are not allowed to ride up front.

"Goodbye, young man."

Uncle Eduardo does not even offer his hand, nor does he bend down as the others have for Jacob to give him a kiss.

"Come on, Jacob. Answer him. Don't be stubborn," interjects Mr. Raimundo.

226

" 'Bye," he says, without looking up.

And the car pulls away from Can Boig, leaving a trail of dust in its wake that, depending on how you look at it, calls to mind the wake trailing the *Poseidon* when Teresa fell into the sea.

They quickly reach the village and the horseshoe shaped bay, and the foam that rises up as the waves crash into the rocks. And the church, lofty and soaring, with its tourists and the God Jacob does not know . . . And the ruins on the hillock, and the cemetery covered with cypress trees, and the esplanade with its tamarinds full of second-rate goldfinches that cannot even fly to Venus. And the Garota Bar, empty because the summer crowd is still asleep at this hour. And the boats anchored at the jetty or tied up in dry dock. And the flocks of seagulls flying overhead or perched on the islet . . .

It is all being left behind. All slipping away, just like the happiness at Can Boig and the August heat.

They soon turn onto the winding road that leads to the highway. This road, too, has changed. The holes in the hillsides are no longer dragons' caves, the tile roofs in the village are not flying carpets and the scarecrows in the vineyards are not warlocks placed there to defend the grapes.

"Are you sleepy?" asks Mr. Raimundo.

And Jacob has no choice but to say yes. He'll probably stretch out on the back seat because, when it comes right down to it, he no longer cares whether or not they think he is just a baby who still takes a nap.

A huge yawn briefly closes his eyes.

"And when I get to France, what then?" he says, staring up at the roof of the car.

Barcelona, 1975–1977

www.ingramcontent.com/pod-product-compliance
Lightning Source LLC
Chambersburg PA
CBHW030413020726
47493CB00003B/1049